love will
keep us together

love will keep us together

a miracle girls novel

Anne Dayton and May Vanderbilt

NEW YORK BOSTON NASHVILLE

Unless otherwise indicated, Scriptures are taken from the HOLY BIBLE: NEW INTERNATIONAL VERSION®. Copyright © 1973, 1978, 1984 by International Bible Society. Used by permission of Zondervan Publishing House. All rights reserved.

FaithWords
Hachette Book Group
237 Park Avenue
New York, NY 10017

www.faithwords.com

Printed in the United States of America

First Edition: April 2010
10 9 8 7 6 5 4 3 2 1

FaithWords is a division of Hachette Book Group, Inc.
The FaithWords name and logo are trademarks of Hachette Book Group, Inc.

Library of Congress Cataloging-in-Publication Data

Dayton, Anne.
   Love will keep us together / Anne Dayton and May Vanderbilt.—1st ed.
      p. cm.
   Summary : As Riley McGee faces an extremely difficult and confusing senior year of high school, the Miracle Girls help her to hold herself together even as they seek a way for the four of them to stay together after graduation.
   ISBN 978-0-446-40758-8
   [1. Friendship—Fiction. 2. High schools—Fiction. 3. Schools—Fiction.
4. Family problems—Fiction. 5. Christian life—Fiction.] I. Vanderbilt, May.
II. Title.
   PZ7.D33847Lov 2010
   [Fic]—dc22

                                                              2009032802

Anne

For May, who taught me everything I know about writing and most of what I know about friendship.

May

For Anne, I can safely say I never would have done any of this without you. You make me a better writer, a better person, and you helped me keep the faith. In short, my life was forever changed the day I met you.

acknowledgments

Is it really over?! It's such a testament to the whole FaithWords team how quickly these few years have flown by. Thanks to Anne Horch, our faithful editor; Miriam Parker for cheering on the books day and night; Katie Schaber; Whitney Luken; Shanon Stowe; and April Frazier. Thanks also to our supportive friends Serenity Bohon, Katie Noah Gibson, Erin Etheridge, Robin Erickson, and Deborah Khuanghlawn. And last, but most certainly not least, thanks immensely to Claudia Cross, who took a chance on us so many years ago and is a true friend.

Anne: Thanks to Wayne.

May: Well, I made it and I couldn't have done it without the help of not one, but two, families. It takes a village to support a writer on a deadline. I love you guys and will never forget how you rallied around me during this project. And, of course, to Nathan. You're my anchor. Let the seas kick up and the world crash down—I've got you.

love will
keep us together

The whole world has gone maroon. The bricks are maroon, the dress code is maroon, and even our peppy tour guide's hair is dyed a deep maroon.

"Hi, I'm Kiki, and I'm a *real student* here." She grins from ear to ear as she walks backward across the giant lawn. "Welcome to the home of the Harvard Crimson."

Pardon me. The whole world has gone *crimson*. The parents and prospective students around me press forward, following after our tour guide, but I slowly edge toward the back, hoping the rest of my family doesn't notice.

The Great McGee Family College Tour is finally winding down, and not a moment too soon. We started off last week at Duke, then drove up to see Johns Hopkins, Penn, Princeton, Columbia, and Yale. This morning we got up early to do MIT, and if I can survive a little longer, we'll check Harvard off the list and only have Cornell to go. Dad and I talked Mom out of Dartmouth. Way too much snow.

I thought it would be fun to tour colleges, but I didn't realize everybody was going to ask me the same question again and again: "What do you want to do with your life, Riley?" Or sometimes they stick to, "What's your passion, Riley?" And I haven't figured out how to answer them. Somehow, "I have no earthly idea" doesn't seem to be what they're looking for.

"We are now entering the famous Harvard Yard." The group falls silent, almost reverent, and Kiki stops on the other side of the crimson-bricked archway and waits while we file through. As she recaps the history of the university, which involves a bunch of dead white guys—just like every other school, Mom spies me slouching low at the back of the crowd.

"Isn't this beautiful?" She takes a deep breath and closes her eyes. "I could really see you being happy here, Riley." I nod because it's easier than trying to explain. "Did you know the Latin word *veritas* on the seal"—she holds out a brochure for me—"means truth?" She flips the brochure open and starts paging through photos of students sitting under autumn trees.

I put my pointer finger over my lips, then point at Kiki. Mom nods and jogs back to my brother, Michael, who has Asperger's syndrome, or high-functioning autism. Mom and Dad have done a ton of work to help him with his social skills, but he's still prone to legendary meltdowns. After the scene he caused at MIT this morning, she's been watching him like a hawk.

"This really seems like a good one." Dad comes up behind me in a sneak attack. I glance across the group and see Michael pulling on Mom's hand, trying to get over to a statue of a seated man. "These kids seem like your kind of people."

Dad and I look around the yard at the students hauling mattresses and carrying plastic crates stuffed with junk. A group lounges on the steps of one of the historic buildings, drinking from eco-friendly metal thermoses.

I shrug and pull my short hair into a pathetic ponytail. Not my best look, but it's sweltering today.

"Do you like it better than Princeton?"

I try to avoid his stare, but he follows my eyes until I give in and focus on him. In the weak afternoon sunlight, I notice that the gray patches at his temples are spreading through his warm brown hair, like two silver streaks down his head.

"I don't know. Princeton was fine." Princeton is Ana's thing, her dream. All I could think about the entire time I was there was, *How did she choose this school? How did she know it was for her? Is there a feeling you get? Is it like how I knew about Tom?*

Kiki climbs a few steps up to an old brick building and claps excitedly. "Massachusetts Hall is *special* for two reasons." She beams at our group and holds up one finger. "First, it's the oldest building on campus, dating back to 1720." Everyone in our group oohs, and Mom whispers something to another mother. "And"—Kiki makes eye contact with the prospective students in her pack—"it's a freshman dorm! Let's go take a look, shall we?"

We walk in a tight-knit pack up the stairs and down the third-floor hallway. Loud music pours from the rooms, the beats clashing. Finally we stop at a dorm room with two neatly made beds and two tidy desks with crimson folders emblazoned with the Harvard seal. I realize there's nothing real about this room or this choreographed moment, like almost every moment of every college tour we've taken. How am I supposed to get a feel for the campus with these phony experiences?

As Kiki begins explaining dorm security, I slip out of the room and try to collect my thoughts. This is merely a minor case of butterflies, nothing more. I'm sure everybody gets them when touring colleges. I'll call Ana, and she'll talk me through this.

I rummage through my purse, searching under all the brochures and school spirit junk until my fingers find my phone's
smooth edges.

Wait, I can't call Ana. She loved every second of her college tour. When she came back from the East Coast a few
weeks ago, she couldn't stop talking about Princeton's amazing science labs. Plus, she already knows beyond a shadow of
a doubt she wants to be a neonatal surgeon. She had open-
heart surgery as a baby and has always felt called to follow the
path of the doctors who saved her life.

Zoe would totally get it. I scroll through my contacts, all
the way down to Z.

But maybe it isn't fair to call Zo. Her parents are doing a little
better, but money is still tight. She didn't get to go on a college
tour this summer, and I'm not really sure there's any money put
aside for her education. I'd be a jerk to call and complain.

I scroll back up to Christine. She's headed to New York
next year to become a painter. All she's ever wanted is to get
out of Half Moon Bay. We've always understood each other
in that way.

But as I'm pressing the button for her name, I remember
that today is Tyler's birthday and she was going to surprise
him with a scavenger hunt through town.

That leaves one person. I find his name and quickly punch
the button. "Pick up, pick up," I chant quietly. A voice in my
head reminds me I shouldn't be calling my ex-boyfriend, the
only guy I ever loved, the one who went off to college and left
me behind, but I try to quiet it. All these months I've been
strong and not e-mailed him, not called him, but I don't have
anyone else right now.

"Hey there." Tom's deep voice is a little scratchy, like he just woke up, and it sends a shiver down my spine. The guys at Marina Vista still sound like chipmunks. "How…What's up?" he asks.

Technically the breakup a few months ago was mutual—technically. I want to talk to him, but it's just as friends. He's already gone through the whole college application process, so he'll help me get my head on straight.

"I hate Harvard." A woman glares at me as she passes down the hall. I lower my voice. "Well, I don't hate Harvard—that's not it. My parents love it, and the teachers all love it. Actually, everybody loves it except me."

"What are you talking about?" He yawns loudly.

"I'm on my college tour, standing in the hallowed halls of Harvard right now. Well, a dorm hallway anyway." Two girls pass me, talking loudly. "They want me to go here, but it doesn't feel right."

"So don't apply. You're not like everybody else."

I bite my lip. It's such a Tom thing to say and exactly what I need to hear. After months of not talking, he still knows how to make me feel better. Tom always put the Miracle Girls on edge, but they never got to see this side of him, the big heart hidden inside his chiseled chest.

The noisy tour group pours out of the dorm room, and Kiki ushers them toward the exit at the end of the hall, pointing at some posters on the wall. Mom spots me on the phone and motions for me to rejoin the group.

"It's funny that you called," Tom says. "I actually wanted to tell you something."

The tour group files into the stairwell. Dad lingers for a moment, frowning, and then goes with them.

"I'm transferring to UCSF and moving back to San Francisco."

"What?" I press my finger to my ear, trying to block out the noise in the hall. That can't be right. I've just gotten used to him being in Santa Barbara, which isn't that far, but far enough for him to feel really and truly gone from my life.

"Santa Barbara wasn't working out, and now I can live at home and save some cash."

My heart begins to pound.

"I miss my old friends, you know—crazy blond girls who call me out of the blue and stuff. I miss...talking."

My pulse drums loudly in my ears.

Mom peeks her head back in the door and widens her eyes at me. "You're missing everything!"

"I—" I wave at Mom. "I've got to run, but I'll call you later." I snap the phone shut before he can respond and chuck it back into my purse. He's coming back? I lean my head against the wall to keep it from spinning.

"Riley!" Mom plants her hands on her hips.

"Coming." I jog over to her lingering in the stairwell. I file in at the back of the group and wind down the few flights of stairs with Mom hot on my heels. I can't think about Tom now. I'll deal with that later, once I'm back home and I've had time to wrap my mind around the fact that he isn't gone, that his voice almost sounded like it used to before we drifted apart.

We re-enter the Harvard Yard, the sun stinging my eyes, and Kiki yammers on and on about the different types of architecture, pointing out stuff like Doric columns and neoclassical facades.

It's not that Harvard isn't beautiful. The campus is historic and hallowed and dripping in ivy, and there's no question that it's one of the best colleges in the country. If I went here, I'd get a great education, have opportunities I'd never get anywhere else, and meet all kinds of new, fascinating friends....

My mind flashes to Half Moon Bay, the faces of the Miracle Girls.

I can't believe that in a year this is going to be my life. This could be *my* freshman dorm, but looking out over this crowded lawn, I can't picture it. I try to imagine myself lounging in the courtyard, heading to fascinating lectures, eating in the dining hall, but my brain refuses. The only life I can imagine is at Marina Vista, hanging out with the girls, being close when Michael needs me.

Mom grins at me as Kiki explains how the meal plans work.

They think I want to go to Harvard, but I don't. They think I'm excited about this, but I'm scared out of my mind. They think they know the real Riley McGee, but even I haven't met her. They think I have it all figured out, but I'm totally lost.

So much for *veritas*.

2

"Wait, you guys!" Ana is laughing so hard she can barely run. The four of us are sprinting to catch the last bit of the sunset. It feels good to run, to feel my legs stretch and pound across the sand, to feel the grains give way softly under my feet. "Slow down!"

Zoe slows her pace, but I keep on going, pulling far ahead of the others. My legs kick up golden flecks behind me as I run, and it feels nice, just for a moment, to do something I'm good at. I gulp, inhaling deep lungfuls of salty air.

The shore is dotted with bonfires, their orange glow bright against the darkening sky. Zoe wanted to celebrate her birthday on this familiar stretch of sand, down the beach from the cliff where I fell freshman year. She didn't say so, but I know she chose this spot on purpose. This was where the Miracle Girls really became a *we*.

Zoe, Ana, and Christine catch up, and we plop down on the blanket together, laughing and trying to catch our breath. I prop myself up on my elbows. The blanket is some weird woven thing Zoe's parents got in Mexico a long time ago, and it feels rough under my arms.

"It's amazing, isn't it?" Zoe stares out past the gently sloping shore toward the waves, where the sky blazes a glorious bright orange, staining the high, narrow clouds. We watch in silence as the sun slides lower and lower.

"It's a huge ball of fire. What do you expect?" Christine smirks but won't tear her eyes away from the horizon.

"I meant this." Zoe stretches out her arm and gestures toward all of us. "Us. All of it. Who would have thought we'd be closer than ever three years later? That we'd survive high school at all?" She lies back on the blanket and puts her hands behind her head, her auburn hair cascading across the blanket.

"Do you realize that when we step into that building tomorrow, Ms. Moore is going to be there again?" Ana shakes her head. At the end of sophomore year, our favorite teacher was mysteriously fired, and last year we fought hard to clear her name. Getting Ms. Moore hired again at Marina Vista is the biggest thing we've ever accomplished, but after everything she did for us, we couldn't have done anything less. "How did we even survive junior year without her?"

Ms. Moore is the reason I met sweet, shy Zoe, bold and brash Christine, and Ana, our fearless leader. She threw us together in detention one day freshman year, and that's how the four of us learned we share a secret: we've all cheated death. Three years later, we're still trying to figure out why God spared us, but in the meantime, we're going through this world together, arm in arm, as the Miracle Girls.

"I really can't believe we're seniors." I stretch and watch the last few fingers of light disappear. "All those years I couldn't wait to grow up, and now it feels like it went by too fast. Don't you wish we could start over and do it all again?"

"Hardly." Christine's voice goes a little hard, and I cringe.

A few years ago, she was in a car accident with her mom, and while Christine emerged without a scratch, her mom didn't make it. Shortly afterward, Christine's dad remarried, and Christine acquired a stepmom and stepsister in one fell swoop. She's had a hard time and probably wouldn't relive these years for anything.

"I don't know about that either." Zoe digs her toes into the sand. "There are a lot of things I would never want to repeat."

I press my lips together. Maybe I've been blessed, but am I really the only one who's not looking forward to the great big, bright future?

"Riley?" Ana's voice is loud and self-assured. "There's nothing to worry about, okay? I know your college tours were kind of a bust, but you're amazing at everything. It's going to be fine."

"Thanks." I stare out at the rolling ocean and try to steady my breathing. "I'm sure I'll figure it out. Tom said he went through the same panic when he applied to college." I'm lost in my thoughts for a moment, thinking about helping Tom move back into his parents' place in San Francisco last weekend, when slowly the silence grows loud in my ears.

"So you guys are really talking again?" Zoe tries to smile, but anxiety is written all over her face.

"We've talked a few times." I dig my toes into the warm top layer of sand, wriggling down to the cool layer beneath. "I don't know if we're *talking*."

The silence persists, and I have the nearly uncontrollable urge to scream at the top of my lungs. I started dating Tom my sophomore year, and it nearly tore the girls apart. They've never really trusted him because he is older and he's not a

Christian, but they never seem to acknowledge the good things about him, like how he helped out when my brother was floundering.

"Guys, can you trust me here? I haven't forgotten that he went away to college and stopped calling." The stars start to twinkle at me from above. "He's just helping me figure some things out."

"But we can help you figure out where you're headed too. Who knows you better than us?" Ana's face shows a twinge of desperation.

"That's what we're here for," Zoe says, giving my shoulder a squeeze.

"Thanks, guys." I sit up and brush my palms together to rub the sand off. I know the bond that holds us together is strong, special, but this may be the one battle they can't help me fight. They're not in college yet, and they already know what they want to do with their lives. "Let's just focus on making right now count," I say quietly. "And making this our best year together yet."

Something about that word *together* makes us go silent again. The only noise is the steady crash and retreat of the mighty Pacific Ocean. The warm, woody smell of bonfires reminds me of camping when I was a kid, when life was simple.

"I hate to say it, but I gotta get going," Ana says at last. I nod. Tomorrow's a big day. The first day of senior year. The beginning of our last year together.

Zoe sits up and begins to dust the sand off her back. "We'll walk you home," she says quietly. Ana's house is in Ocean Colony, right on the beach, so we're not too far. Ana pushes herself up and holds out her hand. We stand and stretch, and Christine shakes out the blanket and tucks it under her arm. The four of us link arms and take a few steps.

"Wait!" Zoe screams and drops out of line. She grabs a stick from the clump of debris at the water's edge, then runs over to the flat, dry space where the beach becomes the sea. She bends over and starts to scratch out a message. When we figure out what she's writing, the rest of us cheer her on. Finally she finishes: *The Miracle Girls Forever.*

She runs back to join us, and we slowly begin to weave our way up the beach toward Ana's house. The others laugh and joke about senior year as we walk down the silvery stretch of the shore lit by the brilliant moon, but I stay quiet. Waves lap at the hard-packed sand, and with each step, I fight the urge to turn around. I can't bear to see if our little mark on the world has been washed away already.

3

ye, Riley!" Emma chirps but doesn't dare break rank as I dash for the door. This summer Christine's stepsister tried out for cheerleading and made the freshman squad easily.

"Next time plan to stay later, okay?" Ashley calls after me in a firm voice, adjusting a sophomore's spot in the dance formation. Ashley is captain of the varsity squad, so she's our cheer overlord this year, and she intends to make us the best squad this school has ever seen. Naturally, this means practice ran late again. Hopefully Michael hasn't been waiting too long.

I jog to the parking lot, my bag slamming against my back. Mom usually picks him up right after school, but this year his Boy Scout troop, which meets in one of the classrooms at Marina Vista, gets done right at the same time as cheer practice is supposed to end.

I scan the parking lot. There's Michael, standing in front of the gym in his scout uniform, surrounded by a few other guys. I breathe a sigh of relief. I don't think any of us has recovered from the time a few years ago when he got on a bus to go visit Grandma Philips without telling anyone.

"Varsity!" The word cuts through the air, and I quicken my step. That doesn't sound like one of Michael's friends. It sounds like...

I squint. Why is Paul Pera hanging around my brother? The wind whistles in my ear as I run toward him. Michael is in the middle of a group of basketball players who are laughing their heads off. Jordan Fletcher is hunched over, clutching his side. My feet pound on the pavement, and I reach the crowd quickly.

"Michael." I call out to him, but my voice is lost in the confusion.

"Hey man, maybe we should recruit this guy for varsity basketball." Paul knocks against Michael's backpack. Michael's thin legs look so pale sticking out of his uniform shorts, and he's flapping his arms like he does when he's happy or upset—anytime his emotions are running high.

It doesn't take me long to figure out what's going on. The high-school level of Boy Scouts is called Varsity Scouts. These guys are making fun of Michael's uniform, which looks like a letterman jacket.

A dark-haired guy steps into the center of the circle, a skateboard tucked under his arm. He's thin and kind of geeky, and it dawns on me that I know him. It's Ben Nayar from my youth group. His family moved to Half Moon Bay last year, and I think I knew he went to Marina Vista but we've never really talked.

"Wow, they tell you jocks are stupid, but I always thought it was a stereotype." Ben lifts his chin, but he fidgets after the words come out of his mouth.

"Shut up, stoner." Paul pushes Ben hard, and he stumbles backward, dropping his board with a loud thwack. The other idiots begin to ooohhh at the commotion, and the skaters and burnouts start to gather around. Suddenly the air around us changes, and I realize there's going to be a fight.

"Stop it!" My voice is shrill and high. The guys all stop and turn to me, as if surprised to see me standing there.

"Oh, hey, Riley." Paul doesn't look the least bit ashamed.

I push past him and reach for my brother, but the crowd is blocking me. "Come on, Michael." I put my hand on his arm and pull him toward me, but Michael doesn't budge.

"Don't be like that. Riley's a cheerleader." Jordan slips his arm around Michael's shoulder, and Michael shirks it off sharply and balls his fists. I say a quick prayer that Michael won't snap and hit somebody. "All the varsity guys date cheerleaders."

What in the...I spin on my heel and get right up in Jordan's face.

"He's—my—brother!" I hiss. Jordan rears his head back and blinks, and I knock him out of the way and grab Michael's arm. "Come *on*." This time he follows, a step behind me.

"Whoa. Riley's brother?" Paul is almost whispering, but I still hear him. I flip back around and give him a hard stare.

"What is your problem," I say, making it an accusation, not a question; then I clamp my mouth shut. All I really want to do is scream at him that Michael can't help it, that he's doing really well in a regular high school, that he's made so much progress, that even if he wasn't my brother, it would still be horrible to make fun of him. But I stomp silently back toward the car, chasing after Michael, because I learned long ago that losing my temper at people who don't understand my brother only makes me feel worse.

"Riley!" Jordan yells. I can hear him chasing after us. "I . . . I didn't know."

I refuse to turn around and give any of them the satisfaction of apologizing to me. Let them feel horrible. What they did is despicable, and how could they not know? Michael is a male version of me—tall, blond, bony.

"I'm sorry I was late," I say quietly, but Michael doesn't respond.

I love him a lot, but it's not exactly like we hang out much at school. I hardly ever see him, actually. He's got his own classes and a few friends, and I've got cheerleading, and the clubs, and the girls, and . . .

"I'm so sorry, Michael. Those guys . . . Well, no one likes those guys, so you don't have to worry about that."

Michael's eyes are watering so I keep going, but I'm not sure what I'm apologizing for. For leaving him stranded. For being a terrible big sister. For not taking better care of him at school. For the twinge of embarrassment I felt when I saw him standing there.

"I'm sorry for not calling Mom to come get you when I knew I was going to be late." I wasn't that late, but I have to keep talking to keep myself from breaking down. Those guys have it so easy, and they're making fun of my brother, who's had to fight for everything he has in this life.

I unlock the van's doors, and we both pile in quickly. I try to pray as I strap myself in, but between my barely restrained anger and Michael's watery sighs in the passenger seat, I don't exactly feel like talking to God right now.

4

still don't understand why you want to take extra classes."
I pull the visor down and check the mirror to see if I have
anything in my teeth. "Your applications already look
incredible."

"It's enrichment." Ana pulls into the parking lot, shuts off
the engine, and steps out onto the pavement, swinging her
purse strap onto her shoulder. "Colleges like students who
show initiative, and community college classes are a good way
to get their attention."

Something about her voice is wrong. Did her mother put
her up to this? We were supposed to study calculus at her
house tonight, but she dragged me along to this with her
instead. I'll pretty much take any excuse not to think about
derivatives for an evening, but now that we're here I'm a little
suspicious.

I follow her toward the open lawn in the middle of a cluster
of buildings. Tonight City College of San Francisco is host-
ing an enrollment fair, and each department has set up tables
around the lawn to showcase different fall classes.

"It's your free time, I guess." I follow after her, and my flip-
flops stop their slapping as we step onto the lawn.

The soft grass tickles my toes. Early fall is often the warm-
est time of year around here, but we won't have too many

more mild nights. It's weird to think this will be my last September in the Bay Area.

"Oh! Biochem—that sounds fun!"

I plant my feet in the grass, and Ana jerks backward.

"Ana, you're a terrible liar. What's this really about?" She starts to open her mouth, but she has a plastic smile on her face, so I interrupt her. "And, no, I don't buy that even you think biochem is fun."

"Okay, busted." She hangs her head, her hair cascading down around her shoulders. This summer she started growing it out and stopped straightening it. It's long and wavy now and helps soften her hard edges. She seems more natural somehow, more laid-back. "But it was for a good cause. I wanted to help you figure out what you want to do with your life." She gestures around the sunny lawn. "I realized Marina Vista doesn't challenge you—our classes are just stupid core requirements. But they have all kinds of choices here. What if there's a future anthropologist inside of you waiting to get out or something?"

"I'm not into bugs."

She refuses to laugh at my joke and beams back her hopeful smile.

We're standing in the middle of the square, surrounded by colorful booths. The English department has a huge bust of Shakespeare on their table. I suppose I could read the classics and get a jump on college that way. I turn to my left and see the physics table. Dry computations bore me to death, but understanding the logic of the physical world has always intrigued me. Beyond that, the art department has drawn a crowd, thanks to a potter and his spinning wheel. I imagine the feel of the clay under my fingers. I used to love art projects. Or, in the other direction, there's math, or history, or economics, or—

I stop turning and press my fingers to my eyes. "This only makes my head hurt more." There are too many choices and not enough time to try them all. How can you rule things out if you like them all about the same? "Maybe I'll hold off on college classes until next year."

"C'mon, Riley." Ana's face is pleading. "Choose something—anything. If you love it, great. Then you'll know what you want to do with your life." She points at the biochem table and shrugs. "If you hate it, fine. You've eliminated a path, and you can hold me personally responsible for wasting your time."

"Wait. What's this really about?" I study her face for a moment. Ana's determination is bordering on desperation. "I'm touched you want to help, but why are you so adamant?"

She sighs, and her shoulders slump. "No reason."

I raise an eyebrow at her. She can't think that after three years together I'm this clueless. "Ana?"

"Nothing." She digs into the soft earth with her toe and lowers her voice. "I'm a little worried about you. Maybe it was that thing you said the other night about Tom."

"There's nothing between us. I promise."

"I'm only saying, be careful. The last thing either of us needs is a new boyfriend—or in your case, a recycled boyfriend." She puts a hand over her heart. "After that fiasco with Dave last year, I've promised myself I'm going to stay unattached this year. I don't want to be making decisions about my future because of some high school boyfriend."

"You're totally right," I say. She perks up, almost in surprise.

"No recycling. Good for the environment, bad for exes. Tom's helping me wrap my head around the whole college thing and the applications process, stuff like that, but we're not getting back together."

Maybe I'll stop answering his calls, and he'll slowly fade away again. Life is complicated enough without him.

Ana frowns and stares past me at a group of people huddling around the philosophy booth. "And you know you can talk to us, right?" She tilts her head, her face showing something like confusion. "About whatever's going on?"

I stare at my sure-footed friend, thinking of how to put into words something I don't fully understand myself. I take a few steps and Ana follows me, slipping her arm through mine. We weave slowly through the crowd.

"How did you know you wanted to study medicine?" The sky is turning a soft orange in the fading light as we aimlessly wander over to the English booth. There are hundreds of colorful pamphlets spread out on it.

"I don't know. I felt called, I guess." Ana takes a flyer off the English table and flips through it. "It's what I've always wanted. Being a doctor has been my dream since I was a kid."

"Called," I mumble to myself. Is that what I'm missing? "All my life people have promised me that if I work hard, I can do anything in the world, but no one has ever told me how to figure out what that is. If God has a plan for my life, he could be a little clearer about it."

She bites her lip. "I'm sure it will become clearer, but maybe not on your schedule. God's timing doesn't always make sense to us."

"I hope you're right." The student manning the English booth steps toward us. "But until then, I don't know what to do except watch reruns and eat Cheetos and pray for things to start making sense." The bust of the bard stares at me with a piercing glare. I put my hands over his eyes. "Stop it, Willy."

"You can't do *nothing* in the meantime. I don't think that's what God wants either." Ana thumbs through the pamphlet in her hands and stops on one of the pages. "You could try a creative writing class. That could be fun, and maybe it will help you sort through some of this."

I take the brochure out of her hands, and my eyes scan the syllabus: two fifteen-page stories and one thirty-page story.

"Well…" I never really thought about writing. I've always been pretty good at composing essays, but I haven't tried to craft a story. And yet for some reason, I think Ana's kind of right. Trying something—anything—sounds more appealing than standing here floundering. Who knows? Maybe this is what I'm supposed to do with my life. Maybe all along I was called to be a writer, and I never realized it. "Do you think I could? This is a massive syllabus."

"You'd be great at it. First of all, you're good at everything. Second of all, I've seen your writing and it's excellent." Ana grabs a clipboard off the table with a pen clipped under the clasp. "Come on. Sign up for it, and I'll take it with you."

"Really?"

Ana nods, her face determined. "I'll even drive us. Tuesday nights are perfect for me. But we have to do it together." This is exactly why she's such a good leader: saying no to her is almost impossible. And it is sweet that she wants to spend time with me—or, knowing Ana, keep tabs on me.

"Okay," I say, feeling a small bit of hope take root.

"Awesome." Ana doesn't wait for me to answer and immediately begins to fill out the registration form. "You're going to love it."

"Sure." I grab another form from the table. "Who knows? Maybe I'm the next Steinbeck." I begin to scratch out my name and fill in bubbles and boxes, signing away my Tuesdays for a semester. This is crazy, and it feels like grasping at straws, but straws are all I have at the moment.

5

et's open with a quick prayer, shall we?" Assistant Pastor Jandel peers through his outdated wire-rimmed glasses at the people in the church pews. Right now he looks more like a used-car salesman than a preacher. "Dear God, today we ask you to bless our church's finances and reward our hard work in your name tenfold so that we might bring greater glory to your kingdom—"

I see my window of opportunity and take it. If my family wants to attend yet another insanely boring meeting about the state-of-the-art new wing of the church, that's their business. I already sat through Sunday school and church on an incredibly gorgeous day.

"Please lay it on the hearts of our brothers and sisters to give generously to the causes of your temple—"

I move down the row, careful not to nudge Michael, who is sound asleep and sprawled out in the pew. I pad quietly down the right-side aisle and slip behind the giant fund-raising barometer to reach the door.

"Amen." Pastor Jandel steps up to the podium with a slick smile. "I'd like to officially call this meeting to order. Today's first topic is growing the church's budget to provide for the new Trinity Center."

I peer over at my parents. They are so busy checking on

Michael they haven't noticed I'm gone. Pastor Jandel seems to glimpse me at the back. I roll my eyes, wondering how well he can see me, then shut the door quietly, not sure where I'm going exactly. Just...away.

I wander out of the foyer, and my feet choose a meandering path through the building, seeking a quiet place where I can be alone and think. I check the bridal parlor, but it's full of scurrying people.

I try the nursery, but when I peek in the window I don't see Mrs. Martinez inside. Did she stop working the nursery? Ohmigosh. Did she finally pass away? She changed my diapers every Sunday, and then Michael's....She's like everybody's second mom. There's a young woman in a rocking chair, but I don't know her so I don't feel comfortable asking if I can hold one of the babies.

I fork left, dragging my hand down the wall, wondering when everything changed. Was it when they hired Assistant Pastor Jandel? No, maybe it started before that, when we got the new sanctuary.

I arrive at the gym and peer in the window. "Thank God," I mumble to no one and push through the old metal door. A few slices of light decorate the floor, but otherwise the gym is deserted. In the corner, there's a basketball that someone forgot to put away. I take off my high heels and slide over to the ball in my tights, slipping on the dusty floor. The outside of the orange ball has been worn thin with age, and when I drop it, it halfheartedly bounces into the air once and then rolls across the floor.

I pick it up, walk over to the basket, and savor the sound of it hitting the rim, the loud, empty echoing. I need more still spaces in my life.

The side door scrapes open, and I sigh but don't turn. Maybe whoever it is will go away if I don't acknowledge him. But as I take another shot, making it this time, the sound of dress shoes on the old wooden floor grows louder.

"Hey," I say, startled. That Ben guy. I shouldn't be that surprised since he technically attends youth group with me, but his appearance here reminds me that I haven't seen him since that day in the parking lot. Where's he been? "Skipping the fascinating fund-raising meeting too?"

He scratches his nose and shrugs. "Did you hear they want it wired for videoconferencing?"

I roll my eyes. "I liked this place better when everything was simple. I remember when the annual trip to the campgrounds was the highlight of the year. It was kind of lame, but we made it fun somehow. The campfire, the marshmallows, the singing..."

Suddenly I wonder why on earth I'm bearing my frustrations to the likes of Ben Nayar. An uncomfortable pause hangs in the air.

"Up for a game of H-O-R-S-E?" I toss him the ball to break the silence. *Anything's better than being in that stupid meeting*, I remind myself.

"If you don't mind losing," he mumbles, and I have to laugh. The guy's got nerve, that's for sure. He walks over to the three-point line and sinks a basket, bouncing it off the backboard.

"No sweat." I take over the spot, squint my eyes at the

rim, and try to picture the ball swishing through the net. It bounces off the backboard with a lazy thud and hits the ground.

"H." Ben walks over to get the ball.

"I didn't know you were like a young…" I like sports, but basketball is not my area of expertise. "Does Michael Jordan still play basketball?"

"No, he retired a long time ago." He grins from ear to ear. "I'm only good at shooting though. My dad and I used to play all the time."

"Really?" I try to picture Ben's dad playing basketball. I've seen him waiting for Ben and his sister after youth group a few times. He's Indian, and like Ben he's tall with dark hair, and he always seems to wear button-down shirts with dress pants. Ben's mom is a Midwesterner, blond with frosted highlights. "Your parents seem so fancy."

"Believe it or not." Ben walks around to the side of the hoop and jumps off one foot, completing a perfect hook shot. The ball swishes as it goes in. "They were pretty cool when I was younger. It's only…recently…that they've gotten so uptight."

There's a sadness in his face I hadn't noticed before. How have we been going to the same church for more than a year and never even scratched the surface with each other? Somehow in a group he fades into the background. I always thought he was shy, but maybe there's something more behind it. He takes a difficult shot and finally misses, making it my turn.

"Hey, so you know everybody at school." He picks up the ball and walks it back to me. "What do you think about Dan Rice?"

I scrunch up my nose. "He's really into dirt bikes." I take the ball from his hands. "Not really my kind of guy. Why?" Dan's a senior and probably best known for the huge tires on his truck and the giant space between his ears. "Is he..." I shift the ball from one hand to another. I don't want to insult Ben, but if Dan is picking on him, I could probably make it stop. I could make it known that Ben's a friend and should be left alone.

"I'm going to kill him, that's all." Ben grabs the ball from my hand and launches a sloppy shot at the basket. It bounces off the rim, and he grunts loudly.

I turn away and jog across the floor for the basketball. I pick it up and try dribbling it on my way back, but it's too flat. I hand it to Ben and cock my head to the side. "Is there something I'm missing?"

Ben glances back at the door as if he's worried someone is listening and shakes his head. "I'm sorry. I'm having a horrible day."

I wait. "Pastor Jandel almost threw my brother out of the sanctuary this morning for screaming at the top of his lungs, so you're not going to shock me," I say finally.

Ben bounces the ball once, shuffles a few steps back, and takes another ugly shot. The ball hits the backboard and flies through the air at a weird angle. "Dan Rice got my sister pregnant."

I cover my mouth with my hand, then put it down again quickly. I don't remember his sister's name, but I know who she is. She comes to youth group too, but she's younger. She has Ben's same creamy light brown skin, dark hair, and fine features.

"Asha told us a few days ago, so I'm really not in the head-space for church today." He smiles sarcastically and then looks up at the ceiling with his hands spread wide. "Just being honest."

I stare at the ball across the floor, listening to the quiet of the gym for a second. "I'm really, really sorry." Ben's in my class, but she must be fifteen, maybe sixteen at the very oldest. "Has she told Dan yet?"

Ben rolls his eyes. "Let's just say he's not looking to be Father of the Year."

"Yeah, that doesn't shock me." I scramble over to the bleachers and grab the ball from underneath them. I hurry back with it and put it in his hands.

"I hate myself for it, but I'm really mad at her." He traces the word *Spalding* on the ball with his finger. "She's really smart, and now I don't know what's going to happen." He grabs the ball in both hands and launches it in the vague direction of the basket. It slams into the metal framework, and a ringing hangs in the air. "Your turn. I'm pretty sure I got H-O-R-S-E already."

The ball rolls back in our direction. I grab it and take a dramatic granny shot, goofing around on purpose. It falls short of the basket by several feet, and I catch Ben smiling a little.

"You're terrible at basketball." He raises an eyebrow at me.

"I don't have to take this abuse, you know." I take a few steps away. "I've got the world's most boring meeting to attend if I want to."

"Don't go," he says, his voice suddenly not teasing any-more. "I mean, um." He bows at the waist deeply and then comes up. "I humbly apologize for insulting your abysmal basketball skills."

I laugh, then we both go silent, listening to the overhead lights hum with an electrical buzz. "I should probably be getting back anyway. The meeting will be over soon." I slide over to the door, find my shoes, and loop my fingers through the straps. "But I'll...see you around."

He waves at me almost sadly, but I can't force myself to stay. It got very intimate there for a moment, and I feel strangely self-conscious—like I'm wearing my underwear on the outside of my clothes or something. "It'll work out. Somehow." I cringe. What a stupid, worn-out, half-truth kind of thing to say. It's like what people tell children.

Ben shrugs and takes another shot, sinking it easily. Even though I'm still standing there, hesitating for a moment, he looks lonely, and it gives me the chills.

6

ook what the school spirit blew in." Ms. Moore rushes across the classroom and wraps me in a big hug.

Even though we have a big game Friday, Ashley excused me from cheerleading practice because Ms. Moore wanted me to attend this meeting with my parents. I'm not sure what's on her mind. Did Mom ask her to help me with my applications? Does she want them to do something for Earth First?

"I can't believe you're really here." I can't keep the dopey grin off my face. I saw her around town several times during the summer, and the Miracle Girls helped her assemble some IKEA furniture one afternoon in August, but after everything it took to get Ms. Moore's job back last year, it doesn't seem real somehow.

"The big senior! How does it feel?" She pulls back and sits down behind her desk. Her brown hair is longer, almost shoulder-length, and she looks tan and rested.

I try to make my voice sound light and airy. "Really awesome." I lift my bag off my shoulder and lower it to the ground, then take a seat at a desk in the front row. "Great." I trace my fingers over the fake wood grain of the desk.

"Riley." I don't have to look at her to know that she doesn't believe me. Her voice says it all. She crosses her arms over her chest. "Your parents will be here soon"—she glances at the big clock on the wall—"but we have a few minutes. Talk."

"No, don't worry. It's fine." I tap my fingers against the smooth plastic. "It's just…"

Ms. Moore has a different classroom now, in the B-wing. The desks are arranged in a funny pattern, and the posters on the walls look fresh, like she made them last night. There's a new blue carpet, and her desk is clean and tidy, not piled high with papers and books like it used to be.

"I don't know."

She watches me for a few moments. "Did you enjoy your college tour?" She props her head in her hand.

"Yeah." I glance at her, but something in her eye makes me look away. "I—" I should tell her. I know I should. Of all the adults in my life, Ms. Moore is the most likely to listen, to not judge, to understand. Plus she can already tell something's wrong, and she'll drag it out of me one way or another. It's that kind of determination that makes her such a good friend.

But this classroom smells funny, like new carpet and paint fumes, not the damp smell of old books that used to permeate her room. She's wearing pressed black pants and a V-neck sweater instead of the funky T-shirts that were her signature. "It was weird. I don't know what I—"

The door whooshes open, and voices from the quad fill the room. My parents walk into the classroom, and they look so out of place here in my world. Mom's helmet hair is freshly "frosted," and she's wearing her best suit. She must have come from a closing.

"Natalie." Dad holds out his hand, and Ms. Moore shakes

it. He's come straight from work and is wearing his dot-com dad uniform: Dockers and a knit shirt. "Good to see you again."

"Thanks for coming." Ms. Moore pulls my mother in for a quick hug, then rushes to arrange a few desks in a circle around me. My parents sit down. Dad folds and unfolds his hands several times, then rubs them down his khakis.

"I wanted to talk to you." She clears her throat. "All of you." Ms. Moore glances at me, and I give her a weak smile. "Because what I'm going to say involves the whole family, and it's going to take all of you to make this work." Ms. Moore grabs a folder off her new desk and settles into the fourth chair, across from Dad. "I know Michael's at his scout meeting, so I'll get right to the point. I'm worried about him."

"We're concerned as well, and we appreciate your attention." My mother's voice is too high, and she's speaking slowly, choosing her words too carefully. "What exactly is the issue?"

"I'm not sure that Michael is"—Ms. Moore brushes a lock of hair behind her ear—"having such an easy time."

"He did okay last year." Dad crosses his legs and hits his shoe on the underside of the desk.

"He did *okay*." Ms. Moore shuffles some papers on her desk and pulls her mouth into a downcast pout. "He didn't fall too far behind, and he didn't excel."

"Of course he didn't excel. But how—"

She cuts Mom off. "Michael is, like Riley, a borderline genius. We all know that." Ms. Moore lifts a paper from her pile and leans forward a little. "Which is exactly why we can't sit back and watch him do okay. He's far above grade level in math, but he's already fallen behind in my class."

"We make sure he does his homework every night." Mom brushes her hand against her cheek. "We sit there with him and make sure he gets it done."

"But much of English class is about discussion, and he has a very hard time participating in a seminar. And it's not only my class. Ms. Lovchuck and I are in frequent contact about his progress, and she has confirmed he struggles in other areas too."

My nostrils flare at the mention of Old Lovchuck. Marina Vista's principal is thin and joyless, and up until last year, I thought she hated every living, breathing thing on this planet—but I was wrong. As it turns out, she likes Ms. Moore. After the lawsuit was dropped, she immediately offered Ms. Moore her job back and begged her to return to Marina Vista.

"As you know, kids on the autism spectrum have different struggles. Michael can keep up academically, just barely, but socially I fear we're losing him."

"What do you mean?" Mom wrinkles her forehead and leans forward.

"Recent events have made me wonder if there is a better academic plan for Michael. There have been a couple...well, incidents, I guess you would call them."

"Incidents?" Dad repeats, like he's trying to figure out what the word means.

"Riley, you know how it is around here. It's"—Ms. Moore seems to expect me to offer some gesture of agreement, but I stay still, boring my eyes into the space above her head—"challenging even for the most outgoing students."

I nod my head slowly, trying to wrap my head around

what's happening. She's way off base here. First of all, Michael is doing just fine at Marina Vista, thank you very much. And second, even if he weren't, she could have come and talked to me about it first.

"The other day I caught a couple of students who'd taken his lunch from him. He was having one of his outbursts." She purses her lips. "He kept challenging them to a joust."

Mom pats her hair. "He's in a medieval phase. Lots of knights and quests and things." She eyes Dad's profile and sighs. "That could be a good way to interest him in English literature. Or history, maybe."

Ms. Moore doesn't seem to hear her. "And there's class too. When he does respond to direct questions, some of the other students laugh at him. He pretends he doesn't hear them, but I know he does." Did she hear about the incident with Paul and Jordan? Rumors travel fast at this tiny school. I try to catch her eye to signal for her to stop this, to talk to me about it later, but she's so focused on Mom and Dad that she doesn't look at me. The only sound in the room is my dad tapping his foot against the desk.

"What are you saying?" I almost whisper it, but I still want to take the words back as soon as they're out.

"I love having Michael in class. He thinks differently, and he's so smart, so please believe me when I tell you he is one of the reasons I get out of bed in the morning. But he did so well after the residency program at UCSF two summers ago. According to his records, it gave him such a leg up for high school . . . and I know he didn't go this past summer. I thought it might be helpful to address the situation."

"The *situation*?" Dad cocks an eyebrow.

"I believe he might be better off in a special program." Ms. Moore is calm, but my heart is lurching around in my chest. We all stare back at her blankly, as if none of her words makes any sense. "I guess what I'm saying is, I'm very worried about Michael. I don't think Marina Vista is meeting his needs, academically or socially. He may need to be enrolled in a special program, and we don't have anything like that at Marina Vista."

Michael needs help, sure, but who doesn't? He didn't go to the residency program in San Francisco this past summer because it was hard on the whole family when he went last time. How can Ms. Moore even suggest that he leave again—and not just for a summer but permanently? I reach for the strap of my bag.

"I don't want to upset you," Ms. Moore says quietly. "But I thought you should know." She closes the folder silently, and no one says anything. I feel my stomach clenching, and my fists slowly start to curl.

Michael has always struggled, but he's always made it. He will get through this rough patch too because we're here for him.

Ms. Moore wants to help, I know, but she wasn't here for his whole freshman year. How can she know what he's capable of? That file can't tell her everything.

My hair falls over my eyes, and I stare out through the space between the strands. Dad is tapping his fingers on the surface of the desk, and Mom looks like she's about to cry. Ms. Moore tries to catch my eye, but I turn away.

When my parents and I step out into the courtyard, I walk away from the classroom door as quickly as possible.

"How's Michael doing at school, really?" Mom asks once we're safely out of earshot of Ms. Moore. Dad leans in to hear my answer. This is the most interested in me they've been in months—well, not in me exactly, but whatever.

"I want your honest opinion. Is he...fitting in? Is there some truth to Ms. Moore's assessment?"

I swallow a lump in my throat. I really can't believe Ms. Moore didn't come to me first. Whatever Michael is going through, I can handle it. She didn't have to make my parents panic like this.

"Um..." Our shadows are long on the smooth cement of the courtyard. "I guess. I mean, as much as anyone, I suppose."

Dad takes in a slow breath and lets it out. "We should have sent him to the residency program this summer." We walk past the front office, and Mom glares at him. For the first time I wonder whose decision that really was.

"Have you noticed the kids being..." She brushes her hair back as we walk down the breezeway. "Treating him differently?"

"He's..." I think back to that day in the parking lot. Were they picking on Michael because he's autistic? Or because that's what jocks do to geeky underclassmen? "I'm looking out for him. It's going to be okay."

My parents are doing the best they can, but I'm there every day. It's up to me to fix this. I'll take better care of him.

Dad smiles at me as we edge around the fence that encircles the pool. "You're so strong, Rye. I thank the good Lord every day Michael has a sister like you." He gives my shoulder a squeeze as we head toward the gym, where we're going to meet Michael. Mom gazes at me, her eyes getting misty, and suddenly I want to be everything they think I can be—for them, for Michael, for our family.

"It's going to be fine. I can keep better tabs on Michael—introduce him around and stuff. Ms. Moore is totally overreacting. That's how she is, you know. A little too involved." I hear the words coming out of my mouth and I know they're mine, but for some reason I feel detached from them. Have I always felt this way about Ms. Moore? Maybe somewhere in the back of my mind? "Michael is going to be fine. I promise."

The tension in the air relaxes, but as Michael comes into view, I can't figure out why I don't feel any better.

7

There, that's our ferry." Tom points at a big white boat coming into dock behind the Ferry Building in San Francisco.

I should have said no when he showed up tonight. I was going to try to get started on my college applications, but Tom said he'd planned a surprise to take my mind off things, and like a fool, I went along with it. Maybe I didn't want to say no.

"Here we go." We walk over to the loading dock, hand our tickets to the attendant, and climb aboard. Tom heads straight up to the top deck, and I follow him.

I point at the different landmasses across the bay from us. "Which island is Tiburon?" One of those is Oakland. I know that much.

Tom joins me at the railing. "Tiburon's not technically an island. You can drive there, but I thought a ferry would be so much more"—he smiles at me and my stupid stomach warms—"fun."

The air is cool, and the wind blowing through my hair feels incredible, liberating. Behind us, San Francisco is lit up like a Christmas tree, twinkling against the clear, black night, and all the noise of high school fades away: the application deadlines, Michael's problems, Mom and Dad. I grab the railing and look up at the couple of stars shining through the lights of the city.

"How's Michael doing?" Tom asks.

I tense up but quickly remember he's not plotting with Ms. Moore or anything. Tom's asking because he genuinely cared about Michael when we were together and did more to help him than the rest of us put together. Tom's mom is a doctor at UCSF who specializes in autism, and she's the one who got Michael into the program two summers ago. She's moved on to a more administrative role on the hospital board now, but Tom's whole family still keeps tabs on Michael.

"He's okay." I sigh and stuff my hands into my coat. "We're worried he's regressing some."

"I'm sorry," he says quietly, and I know he means it. No lecture, no prescription, just honest empathy. "I'm sure it's hard to consider leaving him next year. Do you think that's part of the reason you're having trouble choosing a college?"

I pull my jacket tighter around me and stare at the tall shipping cranes across the bay. "No." They almost look like stilted monsters from this angle. "Yes? I don't know." I steal a peek at him and notice he's hanging on my every word. My heart expands. "I've always felt that Half Moon Bay was too small to hold me for long. And I spent my entire childhood dreaming of that magical day when Lovchuck would hand me that rolled up piece of paper, my one-way ticket out of there."

In the distance a foghorn blares, and we both turn in its direction to listen to its moody timbre. I lose myself in it for a minute, and Tom patiently waits for me to go on, giving me all the time in the world.

"But now that it's time to go, my feet won't budge. I stare

at my applications and have no idea how to answer the questions." A smaller boat zips alongside the ferry, threatening to overtake our slow, steady progress. "The questions are like, 'Why is Yale the right school for you?' Well, how should I know? You're the ones that run the place."

We both stare out at the long stretch of the bay, rolling up and down over the big waves. The small boat pulls ahead and eventually disappears into the night.

"Don't even get me started on the ones that ask what I plan to do *after* college." I give Tom a sly grin. "For those I write, 'Not applicable. Do not have degree yet.'"

Tom laughs from deep inside, and after a few seconds, his chuckling sets me off too. "At least you've still got your humor. Just try to remember you don't have to settle everything today. You could easily apply to a bunch of schools and let fate decide where you go." He nudges me playfully. "You're cool and all, but you won't get into every single college you apply to."

I punch him softly on the shoulder, and he fakes like he's mortally wounded. "You're no help." But I think even he knows this is the biggest lie I've ever told. He's a much bigger help than I want to admit to anyone, even to myself. I know the Miracle Girls are trying to be there for me, but for some reason it's so much easier to open up to Tom. We've shared so much, and he doesn't think I'm...perfect. He doesn't believe in the legend of Riley McGee.

"Have you thought about sticking around here?" Tom wanders back to a long bench, takes a seat, and pats the spot next to him. I sit down too but curl my right leg up to put some space between us. "You could probably get into Stanford or Berkeley."

This is not a date, Riley McGee. You are just friends with Tom Garrison.

"Then you could stick close to the area and be near the ones you love."

He means Michael. But when I look into Tom's face, his eyes sparkling against the dark night, suddenly I'm not sure how much is really there and how much just seems to be there because I want it to be.

"Why are you doing this?" I gesture around at the scenery, the boat ride, everything. "What is this about?"

"Rye." He slides over, and I drop my leg down so he can sit closer. "I wanted to see you. Is there any reason we can't hang out from time to time?"

"No." Our official breakup happened on the phone with a dorm party blaring in the background on his end. I kept my tone light and casual long enough to get through it and then hung up and cried myself to sleep. The overwhelming grief of it took me by surprise. All those guys, all those years—I never cared about any of them. Tom was something different, something I couldn't explain even to myself.

"Are you okay?" He puts a hand on my arm.

"You don't have to do this or anything. I mean, I'm really thankful for your advice about college and stuff, but I get it, you know?" I blow into my hands nervously, then realize they aren't cold. "It doesn't mean we're dating or anything." On the right we pass a big, hilly island covered in green trees.

He takes a huge breath and bites the right side of his lip, something he used to do when we were officially a *we*. "I've made a lot of mistakes in my life," Tom says, sliding his hand up my arm and around my shoulder. I don't shrug it off. "But the biggest was letting you walk away."

I stare out at the choppy water, trying to figure out how much to believe.

"I know I didn't do well with the long-distance thing, and I guess, tonight, I wanted to say that I'm sorry." He runs a hand through his hair, and I notice it's longer than it used to be. It's still short, cropped close to the head, but the new style looks good on him. "I know I'll never be able to win you back, but if we could just be friends," he leans in so his face is only a few inches from mine, "that would be awesome." I can smell his sweet, woody aftershave. "I miss having you in my life."

I turn away to hide my smile. Maybe he doesn't know how much the breakup hurt me, how long it took—well, is taking me—to recover.

8

Cecily Vandekamp and her gang of juniors are swaying to the rhythm of the music together. I elbow Christine, who pretends to gag.

"I could sing of your love forever.... I could sing of your love forever...."

What is this? The third time through? I keep my lips moving, but my eyes can't help finding the wall clock. It's already twenty minutes past eight o' clock, which is when youth group is supposed to let out. I peek around the room. Asha Nayar is swaying too, but for some reason it doesn't look fake when she does it. I spot Ben in the back, sitting with some of the other senior guys. We lock eyes, and I give him a small wave. He nods back, and for some reason I have to force myself to turn away.

Dave Brecht—Ana's ex-boyfriend—and Tommy Chu lead worship on their own now that Tyler has graduated, and they seem to be really into this song. Suddenly Cecily raises her hands in the air, and Maddie immediately follows her lead.

"I could sing of your love forever.... I could sing of your love forever...."

I love praise and worship time as much as the next guy, but my short story for Tuesday's writing class still needs so much work. Plus...I hate to admit it, but in the back of my mind is Tom. I told him I'd call tonight, but he has an early class in the morning, and if I don't get out of here soon, I'll never catch him in time.

"We've been singing this song forever...." I turn at the sound of Christine's reworked lyrics, and she gives me a smirk. "We've been singing this song forever...."

The song finally winds down, and Dave strums the final note instead of continuing. Christine silently mouths, "Thank you, Jesus."

The lights come up, and Tommy Chu thumps the bass drum with the pedal a few times. A loud Christian rock song starts blaring over the speakers, and I turn back and check on Michael. He's bent over the soundboard, sliding buttons up and down, biting his lip. Working the sound is probably the only reason he actually comes to youth group.

People begin to mill around, and Zoe immediately launches into a long, involved story about her boyfriend, Dean, and the ninja movie he's writing and directing for his application to USC's film school. And though it's kind of awful of me, I can't help but wonder how long I have to linger before I can slip out without making them suspicious. From somewhere far off I hear my name.

"I think he wants Riley to be the star," Zoe says. "Would you do it?"

"Um, sure." I stand up slowly and grab my purse off the floor, pretending I'm looking for something in it.

"Where's he going to film it?" Ana asks, and my heart sinks, but I try to ignore it.

Better attitude. Please, Lord, give me a better attitude and help me focus on being a good friend... even if Tom and I haven't talked in two days and our nondate last weekend was kind of awesome.

Zoe tells us he wants to film down at some docks or something. I shift from one foot to the other and can almost taste my freedom.

"Ditching us for Tom again?" Playful tone or not, there's an edge to Christine's voice.

My stupid face breaks into a smile against my will. "I want to call him before he goes to sleep...."

"You guys sure hang out a lot for two people who aren't dating." Christine doesn't even bother to pretend she's joking. Instead, her face shows serious concern. "How does he explain how he totally forgot you existed when he went away to college?"

"That's not fair." I turn to the other girls for support, but Ana has an eyebrow raised and Zoe's face is pinched. "Remember *I* broke up with *him*. And he admits he didn't handle the long-distance thing well."

Zoe puts a hand on my arm and tilts her head to the side. "Just be careful, okay?"

"Tom's kind of like your Kryptonite, Riley. Somehow you lose all your magic powers around him," Ana says.

My nostrils flare. "Guys, I don't have magic powers. And this time things are going to be different." I take a few steps toward the soundboard to get Michael.

Christine crosses her arms over her chest and seems resolved to say no more.

I slowly begin to walk away, avoiding their piercing looks.

"I really do have to go, so..." Christine shakes her head as I walk toward the sound table at the back of the room. "Michael, I'm leaving."

He nods but keeps his attention focused on the complicated series of knobs in front of him.

"I'm serious. Come now," I call as I walk toward the door. He bobs his head but doesn't move. He has an Aspie ritual he goes through every time he turns the sound equipment off, but hopefully he'll hurry today. "I'll be in the car."

I let out a big breath and thread my way across the parking lot. Ugh. Maddie and Cecily are sitting on the bumper of Maddie's Beemer, which is parked next to my van. I give them a fake smile, which they both return, and hop into the front seat of the RealMobile. I shut the door and slump down in the seat to wait.

Through the thick glass, their voices pierce the silence inside the car. I turn the key a little, click on the radio, and search for music to block them out. Michael has exactly one song to get out here before I go back inside and drag him out.

"There she goes," Cecily says, nodding at a figure across the parking lot. "How long do you think it's gonna be before Asha starts showing?"

I freeze. How could they know about that? I turn quickly and see Asha and Ben ducking into a car on the other side of the lot. I peer at the girls next to me out of the corner of my eye, but their backs are to me. Can they honestly believe no one can hear them?

"She's so gross. I always said so." Maddie's tone seems to seek approval from Cecily. "Can you imagine getting down and dirty with Dan Rice?" She shudders. "Anyone gross enough to do that seriously deserves to get knocked up. It's, like, God's punishment for being slutty."

My nostrils flare, and my heart begins to pound. Punishment? I mean, sure, getting pregnant was a mistake, but God's not punishing the poor girl. That isn't how it works, right? A moment later, Ben backs his car out of the parking space and drives away.

"I almost died when my mom showed me the e-mail from Pastor Jandel. He seemed really angry."

I feel my fingers curl around the car's door handle.

"'Dear Prayer Warriors, I'm afraid I have been informed of a horrible situation. We have an unwed mother in the youth group. As we are trying to figure out how to deal with the girl, I hope the prayer circle will pray for our church,'" Cecily says, doing her best imitation of our assistant pastor's voice.

Did Mom get that e-mail? She's probably too busy to notice even if she did. And what did he mean *deal with the girl*? He didn't have to call it a horrible situation to everyone.

Maddie snorts and pulls her hair up into a high ponytail, slipping an elastic band around it. I should go out there and shut them up, remind them that everyone in earshot can hear them making fun of poor Asha.

"My mom totally freaked out. She was like, 'Do you know who he's talking about?' And I was like, 'Duh. Dan Rice told everyone.' Asha Nayar. Mom e-mailed everyone in the church to, you know, 'pray' about it." Cecily laughs.

Okay, that's it. I open my door, and both girls startle and shut their traps.

"Riley." Cecily smiles conspiratorially at me. "Did you hear what's going on?"

Just then Michael darts across the parking lot, and Cecily and Maddie fall silent. I hold my head up high and ignore them. I've never been so glad to see my brother.

9

T his is my favorite one." I point to an amazing oil
painting of Tyler at the mic, his eyes pinched tight in
concentration, belting out a song with all his might.
"You've always been amazing at art, but this stuff is different
somehow. It's really great."

Before this summer, I never realized there was a kitchen in
the painting studio in Christine's backyard, but after her baby
brother, Ellis, arrived, Christine moved her stuff out here to
get some space. Sharing a bedroom with her stepsister was
one thing; sharing a house with a screaming baby was another.
We've spent a lot of time in the studio in the past few months.
It's across the lawn from the main house and far enough away
to not hear any of the family noise. It feels very grown-up, like
Christine has her own apartment or something.

"Which"—Zoe turns around and waves the University of
Southern California brochure in the air—"is yet another reason why this school is so perfect for us. USC's got a great art
school."

Zoe's on one of her missions. She showed up this after-
noon with a ton of colorful brochures and pamphlets for
USC. It looks gorgeous in photos, just like any other school.
Ivy-covered halls? Check. State-of-the-art facilities? Check.

Preppy, wholesome-looking students? Check. Blazing fall foliage? Well, they've got palm trees in LA, but it's the same idea.

The popcorn is starting to pop in the microwave, filling the tiny studio with a rich, buttery smell.

Christine's back is toward me. She's focusing on boiling noodles for mac and cheese. I'm feeling lazy, so I'm sprawled out on the lumpy flowered couch Christine loves so much and flipping through a brochure.

"The most important thing is that we all stay together, right?" Zoe calls over her shoulder. I'd be happy to make it through senior year, but I nod anyway. Ana leans down in front of the cabinet under the sink and digs around inside. She pulls out a few paper napkins as the timer on the microwave dings.

"We're all really different, so that's going to be kind of hard." Zoe opens the microwave door and lifts the bag out gingerly. "But that's okay because USC has something for everyone. They have a great art department"—she looks at Christine, who perks up as she lifts the pot of pasta off the narrow stove—"but they also have awesome science labs." She glances at Ana, who nods and drops the napkins on the coffee table in front of me. "It's not cheap, but it's not crazy expensive either. Since I'm in-state, I could probably get financial aid and stuff. And, Riley, you could…Well, you could do whatever you want. It would be perfect, because at USC you don't have to decide on a major till sophomore year." She shrugs. "And you'd be pretty close to home so you wouldn't have to miss Michael too much."

Christine sniffs the air. "Do you guys smell that?" She lifts her nose slightly. "Does it smell like a girl chasing her boyfriend off to college?"

Zoe fakes like she's going to throw a handful of popcorn at Christine, who is dying laughing.

"Fine. Dean does want to go to film school there. But that doesn't mean this plan isn't amazing." Zoe pours the popcorn into a bowl while Christine sprinkles cheesy powder over the noodles. "Look, they have all these majors."

Zoe sets the bag of popcorn on the low coffee table and plops down on the couch beside me. She gestures for me to flip to the back of the brochure. The serious set of Zoe's face scares me. Does she really think after all these years Ana's going to give up Princeton for us? That Christine will give up New York?

"I don't know, Zo," I say, but she doesn't seem to hear me.

"I can totally picture it. We could live together, just the four of us, in an apartment like real adults. It'd be exactly like this, actually, and we could come back to visit on weekends and stuff."

"I'm in." Christine walks toward us with four spoons sticking out of the pot of macaroni and cheese. She puts it down on the table, and I reach for a spoon and shovel in a mouthful.

"You are?" Ana lifts an eyebrow as she flops down on the other side of me. The cushions bounce up and down for a second as she finds a comfortable position.

"Sure." Christine grabs a handful of popcorn, then settles down on the bed.

"But what about New York?" I gesture at all the paintings of Tyler. "What about art school?"

"There are art schools on this coast too. I've been thinking about sticking closer to home. It's not a big deal." She grabs a brochure from Zoe and flips to a random page. "USC is a good school, and we could all stay together, so why not?"

Zoe claps her hands and bounces.

"But why?" I drop my spoon, and it clatters against the pot. "What happened?" I feel my heart start to beat faster. The flippant way she tosses aside her long-held dream scares me. I don't have any inkling of what I'm going to do with my life or what my natural calling is, but I do know one thing: Christine is a born artist.

"I don't know." Christine tucks her legs up under her and runs her hand over the gray silk comforter. "No one has ever been there for me like you guys. What we have together is really, really rare. I'm not going to move halfway across the world from you. That doesn't make any sense."

"It'll be perfect." Zoe leans back and gives me a quick hug. "All of us together, like I always dreamed." She locks her eyes on me, and her face is full of hope. "What do you think, Riley?"

I try to buy myself time. "I want to be near you guys, of course."

"I'll apply if you'll apply." Ana slowly breaks into a nervous grin.

"But you always dreamed of going to Princeton," I sputter. Christine giving up New York is one thing, but this? Ana practically bleeds orange and black.

"I don't know. It's just…I mean, what if we could pull it off? I never really thought there was a way to stay together." Zoe hugs Ana frantically. She's obviously about ready to pee her pants.

I try to keep my feelings from my face. My best friends in the world, the ones who taught me what it really means to be there for someone, the girls who'd do anything for me, want

to go to college together, and for some reason, the idea completely stresses me out.

I trace a floral pattern on the couch with my finger and
try to ignore the way they're hanging on my every syllable.
Maybe this is why I can't talk to the girls.

I clear my throat. "Let me think about it, okay?"

"I knew it! I knew you'd never let us down." Zoe launches
herself across the couch at me and crushes me under the
weight of her hug.

10

Did you want to take a spin around the restaurant and make sure he isn't already here?" The dyed blond hostess gives me a saccharine smile.

"You're sure there was no reservation under Tom or Garrison?" I glance at the clock over her head.

"Nope. I have nothing under either of those names." She smacks her gum and marks through something on her seating chart with a wax pencil.

"I'll call him again. Traffic, I'm sure." I nod at her and exit the dark seafood restaurant. My call goes straight to voice mail again, and I don't bother to leave another message. I slump down on a long wooden bench in front of the restaurant to wait, squinting into the fading evening sunlight.

I arrived five minutes late to avoid this, but now it's fifteen minutes after seven. I don't want to be anal about it, but Mom didn't want me going out tonight, and coming home late is only going to make her more frustrated. Tom was busy all weekend, so this was the only time we could get together.

The door to the restaurant opens, and I'm startled when I realize it's Ben, his eyes bloodshot. He doesn't see me and strolls down the sidewalk in the other direction, pressing his phone to his ear. Maybe it's because I feel so alone or because he seems alone too, but suddenly I want to say hi to him.

I wander after him and wait until he closes his phone. "Fancy meeting you here."

He turns and drags the back of his hand roughly over his eyes. "Riley." He shakes his head and seems to be trying to pull himself together.

"Are you all right?"

"No." He laughs bitterly, then gestures at the restaurant. "Another dinner with the Nayars. In this very special episode, America's favorite family faces the tough issue of teen pregnancy."

"I'm sorry. I know what it's like to have dinners like that." My face blushes at such a stupid thing to say. "Well, not exactly like *that*." Cars rush past on the street behind the restaurant, but none of them look like Tom's car.

Ben grabs at the worn-out sports watch on his arm and rotates it slowly around his wrist.

"Do you"—I try to meet his eye, but he's staring at the sidewalk—"want to vent or something?"

He lifts his head slowly and shrugs. "Do you know that lady, Mrs. Vandekamp?"

I nod. She was on all those church committees with Mom— the ones Mom used to attend before things with Michael got too overwhelming.

"She took my mom to tea and convinced her that Asha should give the baby up for adoption." He undoes the Velcro strap of his watch and smoothes it down again. "And now my mom's got my dad all convinced too."

"What does Asha want to do?" I wander over to the long wooden bench and sit down. I motion with my head and Ben joins me, extending his feet in front of him, leaning back.

"She's not sure yet, and I'm stuck in the middle, trying to keep everyone from killing each other."

"Wow. I'm sorry," I say, and Ben shrugs.

A comfortable silence spreads between us, and my thoughts drift. It's funny how much we have in common. It's kind of weird to admit it, but I find his story a relief. I'm surrounded by people whose lives are swimming right along, no problems to mention whatsoever. It's kind of nice to know that at least one other student at Marina Vista is having the year from hell.

"What do you think of Pastor Jandel?" He loops his fingers behind his head and glances over at me.

"Huh?" I stare at his beat-up Vans with frayed shoelaces and caked-on dirt. Does Ben know about the awful e-mail Pastor Jandel sent around about Asha? "I don't know. He's only been with the church for a few years. Why?" I cross my legs under me and play with the small hole in the knee of my jeans, making it bigger.

"Just curious." Ben stares vacantly at the parking lot. I wait a minute, but he doesn't continue.

"Okay, truthfully, he kind of bugs me. He talks to my brother like this." I conjure up a canned booming voice. "OH, HELLO THERE, MICHAEL. ARE YOU ENJOYING HIGH SCHOOL? YOU ARE? WELL, ISN'T THAT WONDERFUL."

Ben plugs his ears and cracks up. "You sound just like him."

"It's totally insulting. Michael's not deaf or slow." I turn around and glance at the road, but there's still no sign of Tom's car. "His brain works at lightning speed. He could run intellectual circles around that guy." I squint at Ben in the dying evening light.

He nods slowly and drops his eyes into his lap. "He's taken this weird sudden interest in Asha."

Should I tell him about the e-mail, or will that only make things worse?

"And he's always over at the house, calling me *son*. Like, 'Son, can you bring me a glass of water?'"

"Did you..." I steel my courage. "Did you see the e-mail he sent about Asha?"

Ben snaps his head at me, his face clouding. "The e-mail?"

"Yeah." I say a quick prayer that this is the right thing to do. The Nayars have a right to know what was said about them, even if it casts our assistant pastor in a bad light. "He sent out this e-mail saying there was an unwed mother in the youth group and that he was going to *deal* with the *problem*."

Ben leans forward, his jaw clenching. "He did what?"

"Well, he—"

"First of all, he does not even have the right to share that." Ben begins to pace back and forth, his hands balled into fists. "Not with the church. Not with anybody. My parents went to him for counseling in confidence."

I pinch my lips together. "It didn't say Asha's name."

"It didn't?" He stops short and glares in my direction.

I shake my head, almost afraid to speak. That's what the e-mail said, right? I flash back to that night at youth group and the conversation I overheard between Cecily and Maddie. I was stressed. I remember that. The Miracle Girls were panicking over Tom, I was rushing home to try to talk to him, and Michael was refusing to leave.

Ben keeps muttering under his breath, a vein popping out in his neck. "'Deal with the problem'? What's that supposed to mean exactly?" He shoves his longish hair out of his face. "This is so messed up. Maybe I should pay him a quick little visit right now. We can talk about it, just the two of us. I'm not afraid of him."

"Ben, you've got to calm down. No one is going anywhere right now. You need to sit and talk with me. We'll figure it out."

He turns and points at me. "No, I'm glad you told me this. At least *you're* being honest with me."

What did Cecily say? Deal with the situation? I didn't actually read the e-mail.

"Forget it. I'm just going to tell my parents." Ben shakes his head. "It's time they see this wolf in sheep's clothing who's been prowling around our house."

"Wait." I spring from my seat and put a hand on his arm. His face is flushed red, and his eyes are wild. I haven't known Ben for long, but he doesn't seem like the kind of guy to lose it like this.

He snatches his arm away from me and takes a few steps forward. "No, it's fine. I'm going to let them deal with it."

What if I'm wrong and his parents get involved? It will only make everything worse. My heart begins to beat wildly in my chest.

"Look, Jandel's kind of a jerk and all that, but maybe he didn't mean it like it came out." I hear my words, but I'm not sure if even I believe them. Was it an innocent mistake? Or was there malice behind his e-mail? "You said he's been over at your house trying to help, right?" Ben stops pacing and loosens his hands, letting them dangle by his sides. "And the people at church, all those ladies in the prayer circle, most of them are saints. You know, eighty-year-old grannies who knit caps for orphans and stuff. They wouldn't have any idea who it was about—and even if they did, they would never judge Asha." There, that was true at least. I can't vouch for Jandel, but most of the people at church are awesome.

Ben's shoulders relax.

"Never in a million years." I push out of my brain the image of Mrs. Vandekamp and Cecily and Maddie. There are bad apples in every bunch.

"Maybe you're right." He gives his head a good shake.

We fall silent for a minute or two, and I can't help but steal a glance at my phone. Tom is now a full thirty minutes late. I am officially being stood up, and I'm going to have to explain to Ben why I'm hanging around Captain Mac's Seafood Restaurant on a Thursday night by myself.

"I should probably get back in there," Ben says sheepishly and motions at the wall behind us with his head.

"Of course." Maybe he's so distracted he won't think to ask about it.

"Another good chat." He holds out a fist, and I bump mine against his. A slow smile creeps up on his face. "You're not how I thought you'd be, Riley McGee."

I cross my arms over my chest. "What's that supposed to mean?"

"You seemed a little too...perfect, I guess." He lets his hair fall in front of his face and peeks through it. "I don't know. You're always running around school smiling and stuff. I guess I thought you might be Supergirl." Ben gives me a sly smile.

"Supergirl?"

"You know, Kara Zor-El, blond-haired, blue-eyed crime fighter? DC Comics? Superman's cousin? Cape?"

I stare at him blankly.

"It would explain why you're always in costume."

"It's a cheerleading uniform."

"Right, sorry." Ben smiles, and I notice a small dimple on his right cheek.

"My life is a lot messier than most people realize." I stand up and grab my purse. I might as well start heading home. "But maybe everyone's is."

"I hope not, for their sakes." A noisy family passes us and enters the restaurant, their voices echoing in the silence between us. "Are you waiting for someone?"

"Yeah." I dig in my purse for my phone. Does Tom even deserve a call to let him know I'm going home? "A friend."

"A friend." Ben watches me carefully, so I shrug and try to act nonchalant.

Just then Tom's reliable black Honda pulls into the parking lot, and he honks a few times at me and waves. I look away and don't wave back, but it's too late.

"Ah, I see." Ben takes a few steps toward the door. "See you around, Riley McGee." He pulls the handle and disappears into the dark restaurant. Before I can even process our conversation, Tom dashes across the parking lot to me.

"Hey there." He reaches out to wrap his arms around me.

I reach my arm back and sock him hard in the shoulder. "You're so dead. I can't believe you showed up thirty minutes late."

He holds his hands up in the air and laughs. "Wait, wait."

He motions at the parking lot. "My car overheated on the way down here."

I glance at his Honda. When I first met him he had an old white truck, and if he still drove that, I might believe him.

"Do you think I'd miss hanging out with my favorite girl?"

He wraps his arms around me, and I feel a little better, almost good enough to forget the other question I have: Why was his phone off?

||

Nice job, Riley." Aiden, our cool college professor who bears a striking resemblance to Patrick Dempsey, makes a note at the top of his printout. I sit up straighter. For our third week of writing class, we were supposed to write a short story that really "dug deep," and today we're workshopping everyone's stories. I wrote a story about a kid with Asperger's. Telling Michael's story was, well, it almost felt good in a way. It was nice to sort out the jumble of emotions I feel, let them air out on the page.

"I love the way the main character felt guilt about Matty's condition. You've got a really great start here," Aiden says. My heart sinks. *Start*? I slaved over this story. "Keep hammering away at it, and I think you could really make this into a story."

"Make this into a story"? I stare down at my paper. Isn't that what this is? It has a beginning, a middle, and an end, and I even put in themes like Ms. Moore is always going on and on about.

A few people make comments about my story, but for the most part the room is quiet. There's a moment of awkward silence, then Aiden turns to Ana.

"Let's move on then. Ana?" Aiden turns to the right to face

Ana. A few people rustle papers and search for Ana's story in their piles.

"Okay. I didn't really know what to write about, so I—"

"Hey, no apologies." Aiden cuts her off. "You cannot be embarrassed about your work and still call yourself a writer. As a rule, writers have *huge* egos. Better to start cultivating that now." He gives her a goofy grin, and she laughs. "Besides, what you have here is great. Really, really good." Aiden flips to the last page of her story, where even from here I can see the exclamation points and underlines he's drawn all over the paper.

Ana wrote about her old housekeeper Maria's *quinceañera* all those years ago in Mexico. She fictionalized it some and made it sound like a story, but what really comes through is how much she cares about Maria. Maria was like a second mom to her, but she moved back to Mexico at the end of Ana's freshman year because her health was failing.

"Did anyone else notice how she used the diamond as a symbol?" Aiden asks. "She points out the crystalline stars here on page one"—Aiden flips back to the first stapled page of her story—"and there's the twinkling of the grandmother's eye, and the jewels in the tiara Maria's wearing in the last scene." He flips to the last page of the story and rips the paper a bit in his excitement. "It's a great use of repeated imagery to build meaning. Nice work, Ana."

A few more people talk about how awesome the story is, and with each comment I slide farther and farther into my chair. I tune them out and start to draw waves on the edge of my paper. I don't get it. It's obvious they like her story better, but why? What makes hers more interesting? And isn't it all relative anyway?

Ana is taking furious notes, and I'm glad for her, I really am, but she already knows she wants to study medicine. We took this class so I could figure out what I want to do. She doesn't need this like I do. If this isn't it, where does that leave me?

12

"R ye." I turn at the sound of Ashley's voice. "Hold up." I stop and wait as she jogs across the courtyard, her strawberry-blond hair streaming behind her. She's wearing some funky boots and carrying a bag I swear I saw in *Vogue* last month. She always was more stylish than anyone else around here. "I wanted to tell you something." Ashley stops in front of me and gasps to catch her breath.

I'm already running late for the Earth First meeting, and Ms. Moore likes us to start on time, but I can read her face well enough to know this is important. Ashley and I were best friends all through elementary school. We hit a rough patch a few years ago, but last year she helped the Miracle Girls get Ms. Moore reinstated at Marina Vista, and we've been hanging out some since then.

"You know how Michael's in my trig class?" Ashley plays with the zipper of her cheerleading jacket. "Have I ever told you how humiliating it is to be in a class with your baby brother, by the way?"

"Math is kind of his specialty." The thing is, Ashley's not dumb. She always got good grades in middle school, but once we hit high school she adopted this ditzy cheer-girl persona and sort of stopped trying.

"So, anyway, today Mr. Ragonisi was finished with, like,

the most boring lecture known to man." Ashley rolls her eyes. "Seriously. I mean, cosine curves? What in the world?" She shakes her head.

I try to wait patiently. She must have a point. She'll get there eventually. "Anyway, we had a little time left before the bell rang, and so a few of us were talking about our weekends, and out of nowhere Michael jumps in with how he chopped off a bunch of people's heads."

I suck in a breath.

Ashley nods, her face grim. "He was going on about shields and how the heads went flying across the grass and how everyone cheered when he rode past them. And I remembered how he used to sometimes mix up what he saw on TV and what's real, and I thought—"

"We were watching *Braveheart* this weekend...."

"I mean, I changed the subject right away, and I tried to talk to the guys afterward to explain, but I..." Words seem to fail her. "I just...wanted to let you know."

"Yeah." I swallow and try to string my thoughts together. "Thanks for telling me."

"No biggie." Someone calls to her across the quad, and she turns her head. "I've got to run, but I knew you'd know what to do about it."

"Thanks."

She smiles, and for a second I see her in pigtails again, missing her two front teeth, just like second grade.

"I'm glad you told me. It means a lot."

"See you at practice tomorrow?" she calls as she turns toward the quad. I nod, and she runs off to join a group of football players.

I press my shoulders down to release the tension.

Michael *knows* he didn't actually behead anyone this weekend, but when he gets excited about things and tries to talk about them, sometimes they come out wrong. But the other kids don't know that, they'll think he's...

And what if they tell people what he said? What if the whole school knows?

I turn and head for my meeting, but my heart sinks when I think about who'll be there. Ms. Moore couldn't have heard about this, could she? But what if she did? What if she tells my parents?

I shake my head and take off down the breezeway. I'll have to make sure she doesn't find out.

"Last order of business." Ana is so professional at the podium—it's no wonder the freshmen are all huddled together in the corner. She's been president of Earth First four years running, ever since Ms. Moore started the club when we were freshmen. Well, technically, the club didn't meet last year because our advisor had been suspended by the school board, but Ana was still in charge.

"The Half Moon Bay Arts and Pumpkin Festival. We'll be selling organic pumpkin bars this year, in addition to the face painting booth Christine will run." The club has grown now that everything green is all the rage, and there are a couple juniors in addition to the cluster of freshmen. "She's crunching on a deadline today and couldn't be here, but if you want to help her with the painting, please put your name on the sign-up sheet. And find Zoe after the meeting if you want to help bake. Any questions?"

We don't dare open our mouths. Ms. Moore sits at her desk at the front of the room and pretends to grade papers, but she keeps sneaking glances at us, so I know she's paying attention. I try to ignore her.

"In that case, I move we call this meeting to end. Does anyone second that motion?"

"I—" Zoe opens her mouth, and one of the freshmen begins to pack up her stuff, but I cut her off.

"Wait!" As much as I want to escape, there's something I need to do.

Everyone freezes.

"Riley, you're supposed to bring up any new business before I motion to close." Ana puts her hands on her hips.

"I didn't realize you were going to move so fast." Things have been tense with the girls lately. I have this creeping feeling that...Well, obviously they've never been Tom's biggest fans, but I'd never sell them out for a guy. They have to know that. "I have something to say. Actually, to vote on. We need to nominate a member to the homecoming court, and I want to nominate Ana Dominguez."

Ana's eyes widen. I didn't check with the other girls, but obviously Ana should be our Earth First representative. Marcus Farcus, Zoe's ex-boyfriend, nominated Zoe for the band, and Christine easily clinched the Art Club nomination.

"I second that," Zoe says, grinning. Ana's cheeks turn red, but a smile traces her lips.

"All in favor?" I twist around in my seat and smile at the freshmen in the corner. I'll probably get nominated by the cheerleaders because Ashley already accepted the nod from

Student Council. Well, I hope I will anyway. The Miracle Girls should do homecoming together.

"Aye," they say in unison, and others scattered around the room echo the sentiment. I turn back, and out of the corner of my eye I see Ms. Moore watching me, but I pretend I don't.

"All opposed?" No one answers.

"Good then. Ana will be our homecoming representative. I think we're ready to close the meeting for real, Prez."

Ana stares at me for a minute, her mouth open, but she's beaming. At least I did one thing right today. Ana runs through the formalities of closing the meeting one more time, and as soon as it's over, I hike my bag over my shoulder and head toward the door.

"Gotta run," I say quietly, and Zoe nods. She'll pass on the message to Ana, who's still gathering her papers at the front of the room. I can feel Ms. Moore following me with her eyes. I've almost made it all the way to the door when she calls out to me.

"Riley! Hold on for a second."

I pause, my hand on the doorknob.

She walks quickly across the classroom and puts a hand on my back, nudging me into the hallway.

"I'm so sorry. I'm running really behind for something." I point toward the end of the hallway.

Ms. Moore nods quickly. "I'll be quick. Your mom and I were chatting, and she said that Harvard is your top choice."

"She did?" Is that what Mom thinks? That I'm Harvard-bound and it's all settled? It was my parents who fell in love with Harvard, or rather the prestige of Harvard.

"I think she only told me because she knew I could help." Ms. Moore studies me, concern etched all over her face. "My friend is a professor there and is in good with the Dean of Admissions. Are you doing the Common Application or the Universal College Application? I can have her take a look at your Harvard Supplement and make sure you've done everything you can."

I clear my throat. "Thank you. That would be great." I slide away from her slowly. A few more steps and I'll be free. "I'll... let you know if I could use the help."

"Riley—" Ms. Moore drops her head to the side and looks up at me. When did I grow taller than her? "How are the applications going, really?"

"*Really* well."

Her eyes pierce into me, like she knows that I'm lying through my teeth.

"Ha ha. Just some application humor for you."

She doesn't stop with the piercing look.

"The truth is that they're going. That's all I can hope for at this point, right?" There, that was at least kind of true. I have filled out a few information blanks on the Johns Hopkins Supplement.

"I'd be happy to write recommendation letters for you. I have a lot to say that I think your prospective colleges would love to hear."

I cringe. How did I forget about those stupid letters? You have to get your teachers to say nice things about you so the colleges will want you. It's so—

"For whatever school *you* want."

"I..." The last thing I need right now is Ms. Moore telling

Harvard what she really thinks of me. "Thanks. I've got it under control."

"Oh." She takes a small step back. "That's good then." She presses her lips together. "Still, if there's anything I can—"

"Gotta run." She keeps talking as I scramble away. I smile and nod like I don't hear her.

13

keep moving until I reach the relative safety of the courtyard. I've been able to convince Mom and Dad I've got
things under control, but Ms. Moore isn't going to buy it
much longer.

I dig my phone out of my purse and punch the button for
Tom's name. He's always so good at calming me down. But
after four rings it goes to his voice mail. I'm sure he's out looking for a job. He's hoping to get an apartment in the city and
move out of his parents' place.

The early October air is brisk, and a quick breeze whips
through the courtyard and howls in my ear. It sounds like a
woman screaming, and chill bumps rise on my arms.

I grab my phone and try Tom again, but it goes to voice
mail again. "Hey, it's me. Please call me the moment you get
this. I need you." I shut the phone and fight the urge to throw
it across the courtyard with all my might. I pinch my eyes
tight and focus on getting my breathing under control.

Christine, my brain offers, and a smile spreads across my
face. Even if she is on board with Zoe's USC plan, she won't
judge me for having doubts. She's been through some hard
stuff over the years, and she's really close to Ms. Moore. I'm
sure she finds Ms. Moore's relentless prying a little annoy-
ing too.

I push off from the courtyard wall and pick a roundabout way to Mr. Dumas's art classroom. I wonder if Christine even has an art deadline today. Maybe she can only handle Ms. Moore in small doses and made up an excuse to miss the Earth First meeting.

I reach the J-wing quickly and knock on Mr. Dumas's open door. "Is Christine around?" There are a couple of other students at easels and scattered around the long tables, but I don't see her long black hair.

"You just missed her," Mr. Dumas mumbles, looking up from an oversized, colorful art book.

My shoulders slump. Mom picked up Michael from school today. Maybe I can catch Christine at home if I go right now.

"Miss me already?" A familiar voice makes me turn. Ben smiles and walks over to the doorway.

"Oh, hey," I say, but edge closer to the door.

"You know, I'm beginning to think you're stalking me, Supergirl." He raises an eyebrow.

"I was looking for Christine." I toss Dumas a wave and head out the door, Ben following on my heels. "I'm having an insane day, and I..." Should I open up to Ben? He's been a pretty good listener in the past and he's, well, he's at least here. That counts for something.

"Come on." He starts walking down the hall. "I've got some shots I'm developing in the darkroom, and I could use your help."

I guess I knew you could take photography at Marina Vista, but somehow it never really interested me. "I should go. I'm going to try to catch Christine at home."

Ben stops halfway down the hall and shakes his head. "Just

come. Why not? You're having a rough day, and everyone knows when a cheerleader cries, a unicorn dies."

"You're kind of a weird guy. You know that, right?" He doesn't answer, and I give in to my curiosity and follow him down the hall. When we stop, I'm greeted by an empty, utterly normal classroom—well, normal except for one detail.

"Right this way." Ben motions to a big black tube on the right. He slides the door open, slips inside, and waits. I join him in the booth, and he slides the door until we can see nothing but utter blackness. Finally the tube opens up behind us, and a weird red glow stings my eyes.

Ben grabs my arm, carefully avoiding my hand, and pulls me farther into the small room. "It takes a second for your eyes to adjust."

"Wow." I follow him through another door. Inside the inner room, there's a warm reddish light hanging from the ceiling and a chemical smell that burns my nose. My eyes adjust after the pitch-black darkness, and I stumble forward to look at pictures hanging on a line on the far side of the room. "Did you do all of these?"

He motions at a picture of two wrestlers locked in a knot in the middle of the ring. "Not all of them. Everyone in the class uses the photo lab." Ben walks farther down the line and motions at a few pictures. "These are mine."

The shots are of the Nayar family doing ordinary things—his dad watering a flower bed with a hose, his mom frowning at a spreadsheet with her glasses on her nose, Asha lying upside down on the couch, watching TV. And yet something about the photos is gripping.

"Things have been…a little weird at home lately, and I guess I wondered if I could capture that on film."

Ben pulls a piece of shiny paper out of a thick black bag and slides it under a lens. He adjusts the height of the lens, presses a button, and suddenly an image of a face appears on the paper. I make out that it's Asha before Ben snaps the light off and the image goes away. Ben grasps the paper with a pair of tongs and sets it in a shallow tub of liquid.

"What's this?" I edge closer, and I feel the heat from his arm through my thin sweater. I can hear Ben breathe.

"This is the best part." He moves the paper around in the little tub. "I'm developing a batch of negatives from my cousin's wedding."

I lean in closer, and in the soft red light, I can see the first hints of something start to develop on the paper. At first it's just shadows of light and dark, but Ben continues to jiggle the paper around, and slowly different shades start to emerge and some gray areas begin to develop. As the image comes into focus, the soft outlines of his sister's face begin to form.

"She looks beautiful." She's wearing a traditional sari, and her arms are painted in ornate henna patterns. She's wearing what looks like hundreds of bangles on her arms and throwing her head back in laughter. But something about the way Ben has shot the picture—maybe it's the angle or the lighting—gives it a melancholy feel.

"Look," he whispers, and his voice catches. He points at something in the photo, and I notice a slight bulge in her belly in the gap between the pieces of her sari.

Ben lifts the paper out of the tray and dunks it into another tray right next to it. He swishes it around for a bit, then dunks it into the final tray. He takes a deep breath. "It's almost done." I lean in a little closer, and he lifts the photo up gently, holding it with the tongs, letting the liquid drip off the edge and back into the tray below.

"That's amazing." I sound like an idiot, but I don't care. His photo developed from a blank piece of paper into something beautiful before my eyes. I start to grasp what it is that drives Christine to spend hours and hours painting and drawing. Ben has turned an idea into a tangible expression. He's taken a shot of his sister and somehow used it to communicate his own complicated feelings in a way words never could. I turn to him, his body is inches away from mine, and I swallow.

We lock eyes, and my breath catches. His face makes me want to tell him every secret I have, to pour out all my worries about Michael and my doubts about the future. He reaches out and traces a finger down my cheek. I shut my eyes for a moment and allow myself to enjoy the careful way he touches me, as if I might disappear before his eyes.

"I should go." I force my eyes open and shake my head. Stepping back and zipping up my sweater, I take a few steps toward the tube. I'll swing by Christine's house. It's what I should have done all along.

14

W hat kind of cracked school makes you take PE all four years?" I squint into the sun and fit my arrow again.

"*This* is what tipped you off that Marina Vista is insane?" Dean raises an eyebrow at me, and I laugh. The only good thing about PE is that Dean and Zoe are in my class, and they're as bored by the whole thing as I am.

"How is this preparing us for college, I ask you." I let an arrow fly toward the target, and the tip sinks deep into the blue ring.

"Come on. Archery is going to come in really handy in our future careers." Zoe takes a shot, and her arrow sticks into the wet earth a few feet shy of the target. She hasn't hit the haystack all morning.

"Seriously." Dean trains his eye on the target, staring down the shaft of his arrow. "After I wrap the ninja movie, I'm going to work on an historical adventure film." His arrow lands squarely in the middle of the red circle. "This could be the most useful class I take all day."

"Ooh." Zoe claps her hands and walks over to Dean's spot, frowning at his target. "It could be about a mythical medieval city. You could call it Zoeville." She launches another arrow through the air, and we watch it wobble before falling short.

"Maybe I will." Dean walks over and puts his arms around Zoe to show her what she's doing wrong. I turn away and search for Michael's class across the blacktop, but I can't pick him out. I've been keeping a closer eye on him lately, and things seemed to have quieted down. He was just having trouble adjusting to the new school year, his new schedule and teachers. That's all.

"Speaking of, have you taken a look at the USC application yet, Riley? Ana said it was the easiest one she'd seen." Zoe lets go of the bow's string, and Dean steps back. Her arrow sinks into the white outer rim. "Yes!"

"Wait, you're applying to USC?" Dean whips around to me and misses Zoe's small victory.

I open my mouth to set the record straight, but Zoe cuts me off.

"Isn't that great? We're all applying now."

Did I tell Zoe I would apply to USC? I don't think I actually said that.

"The idea of sticking together was too good to pass up." She walks over to Dean and wraps her arms around him. "Now I can go to college with all my favorite people."

"Oh." Dean's arms hang uselessly at his side, pinned by Zoe's embrace. He drops his bow to his feet. "But I thought we said it might not be possible for you..." She lets him go and picks up his bow. His face is painted in a smile, but there's something funny in his eyes, a strained look. "Because of the stable and all."

"Nick said the money stuff would all work out fine." Zoe

shrugs and pulls another arrow out of our communal quiver. "I'm not worried about that anymore. Ms. Moore's going to help me with the financial aid forms."

I study Zoe's face. It's so full of hope for our futures together, for all her dreams coming true. Then I look at Dean's and see something she's clearly missing, but I'm not quite sure what it is myself. Fear that she can't afford USC? Fear that she won't get in? Fear that she will?

I turn away, fit the nock against the string, and squint at the target.

"Hey, is that Michael?" Dean drops his arrow and points across the blacktop to the soccer field.

I snap my head around. There's a crowd of guys gathered around a blond head. A few of them are whooping and cheering, and then, as soon as Mr. Fuentes turns toward them, they scatter. And in that instant, my heart stops.

Michael's maroon PE shorts are around his ankles, his tighty-whities too bright against the foggy sky. It's only a split second before he has his shorts pulled up again, but in that brief moment I can see his shoulders tense up, and I can read my brother so well that even from here I can see what's about to happen. I take off at a sprint, but Michael is already running headlong toward the cluster of guys, his shrieks piercing the air.

"Riley!" Zoe calls after me, but I don't turn around. I couldn't make my legs stop moving if I wanted to. In some otherworldly, primal way, all that matters is getting to my brother, getting to him in time to stop what's about to happen.

The thing about Michael is, he's scrawny, but when he's upset, it's like he gets this superhuman strength and he can't control his own body. Two years ago, he went into a fit at Safeway, knocking rows of pickles off the shelf, and when Dad tried to hold him down, Michael broke his nose.

I feel a burst of adrenaline, and I pump my legs, closing the ground between us with each long stride, but Michael is already swinging his arms, and before I know what's happening, one of the guys drops to the ground.

"STOP!" I yell, but I'm not sure who I'm yelling at—Michael or Mr. Fuentes, who's jogging across the field, his baggy sweatpants billowing out behind him. Michael is screaming, and he's swinging his arms, aiming for the other guys. I vaguely register whistles from the other teachers on different sides of the field, and I try to speed up, but my lungs are starting to burn, and Mr. Fuentes makes it to Michael before I do. Even from fifty yards away, I can see that Michael doesn't mean to do it, that he doesn't know what he's doing, but as soon as Mr. Fuentes gets too close, Michael's fist connects. Mr. Fuentes's head rears back, and he collapses on the ground. Michael is still throwing his arms around, screaming, but everyone backs away.

I can't draw breath into my lungs, and I slow my steps. Michael doesn't see me. He's trapped inside his head by his rage.

I stop in the middle of the field and gasp for breath because I know it's too late anyway. It doesn't matter how much I want to help him now. I can't argue his way out of this one. Michael hit a teacher. They're never going to let him stay at Marina Vista now.

15

And now, as promised, we have a guest speaker tonight." Fritz, our youth pastor, hesitates, then picks up a blue paperback Bible from the edge of the stage. "Pastor Jandel is going to talk about the importance of Scripture. Here at Seaview, we want you all to rely on the truth of God's Word." He holds up the Bible in his hand. "But to get there, you have to know what the Bible says, and then you can figure out what the words will mean to your life and how they will guide you." He wipes his hand across his forehead. "So let's all put our hands together and show Pastor Jandel how excited we are to have him here tonight!"

Christine nudges me, and I shrug. At Sunday school this morning, Fritz told us Jandel would be speaking tonight, which helps explain why the room is half-empty, but honestly, it's part of the reason I came. I have about a million other things to be doing, but I wanted to hear what this guy has to say. What I've heard and seen on Sunday mornings make me wary, but I'm here to decide for myself.

Fritz claps, and some of the freshmen in the front row join him, but most of us just wait as Pastor Jandel walks up to the stage. His face is kind of red, and he's walking too fast, like he's nervous. He steps onto the plywood stage and rests his Bible and his notes on the music stand at the front edge.

He fiddles with the rickety stand, adjusting it so he can read his notes, and then steeples his fingers, clears his throat, and smiles.

"Thank you, Fritz." Pastor Jandel takes the microphone out of the stand and turns to us. "And would you look at how beautiful you are. God's precious children." At the last word, an uncomfortable feeling settles on the youth room. Someone in the back coughs loudly. "I'm so thankful to be here with you tonight." He opens the leather-bound Bible with gilt edges. "And Brother Barker is absolutely right." I shake my head, then remember that's Fritz's last name. "The beauty of the Word of our Lord is its *certainty*, its truth that has been passed down through the ages."

Out of the corner of my eye, I see Zoe nod. Well, I guess that's fair. I do believe the Bible is true.

"But I'm getting ahead of myself. Let's start with our reading for tonight. I'd like you all to turn in your Bibles to Matthew seven, verses thirteen and fourteen." A few kids pull out their Bibles and rustle the tissue-thin pages, but most of us just stare back at him. I didn't bring my Bible. Fritz always projects the Bible verses on the screen behind the stage. "Got it?" He looks out at us, smiling too widely. "Who'd like to read it out loud?"

No one raises their hand.

"Ana, how about you? Would you read the Scripture for us?" he asks, smiling at her so we all know it's not a question. That's what Ana gets for having involved parents. Jandel hasn't worked with the youth group much, and he doesn't know most of our names.

Ana's eyes widen, but then she turns back to the open Bible

in her lap. "'Enter through the narrow gate. For wide is the gate and broad is the road that leads to destruction, and many enter through it,'" Ana says, her voice halting. She lowers the Bible into her lap and raises an eyebrow at Pastor Jandel, and he gestures for her to keep reading. "'But small is the gate and narrow the road that leads to life, and only a few find it,'" she finishes slowly.

"Thank you, Ana," he says, swiping his hand across his forehead. "Isn't that a neat passage? It's such a great image of how hard it is to stay on the right path, isn't it?"

I try to find a more comfortable way to sit in my folding chair and it squeaks loudly. It's clearly going to be a long night.

"With all the temptations around you guys today, on the Internet, on TV, and in the school yard, it's harder than ever to keep your eyes focused on Jesus and not the hunk from the football team." He gives us a toothy grin, like he thinks he's said something clever.

Oh wow. Okay. That was kind of direct. I take a deep breath and pretend like I'm stretching and glance around the room. Good. She's not here. I know he didn't mean it to attack anyone, but some people might take that last bit to be a criticism of . . . Well, anyway, I'm glad Asha missed youth group tonight.

"What I want to talk about today is keeping your eyes focused on the Word in the midst of temptation." He laughs, but when no one responds, he smooths down the pages of the Bible on the music stand in front of him. "The good thing is, you're not alone. Even when you're facing the worst temptation, Jesus is right there with you, helping you every step of the way."

I tap my fingers against the edge of my chair. Freshman year, I really bought into the whole "the J-man is my buddy" routine, but I don't know. These days I need something more than that. Not a pal or a friend—something deeper, something bigger and more inspiring.

"Isn't that wonderful news?"

He stares at us and a few people nod.

"We'll go into that more in a minute. The other good news is that if you don't know what to do, all you have to do is look in this book." He raises his Bible up in the air. "God's rules are spelled out for you in black and white; all you have to do is follow the path he's marked out."

I cross my legs. I don't know. I'm pretty sure there's nothing in there about what college to pick or how to know if you're doing enough to help someone you love. Are there rules I missed? Because the ones I've found in there are all about what kind of animal to slaughter for what sin and how long women are supposed to stay away from civilization every month.

I raise my hand tentatively.

"Question!" Pastor Jandel points to me, obviously delighted. "Yes..."

"Riley." I clear my throat and scoot forward to the edge of my chair. Christine's eyes widen. "Um, yeah. I was just wondering, I don't know, if there were times when you thought the Bible wasn't totally clear on certain things." I glance at Fritz; he's smiling at me.

"Excellent question," Pastor Jandel says, and I scoot back in the chair. "Now, I know when you're young, a lot of things about life don't seem to make sense. 'Who am I? Where am I

going? Why would God tell me to act one way when my feelings are telling me to act another way?' That kind of thing." He
smiles at me, like he's trying to be encouraging. "But as you
get older, it becomes more clear. The truth of Scripture comes
into sharper focus, and I'm here to assure you that God's
Word is bigger than any of the questions you may have."

"But—" I shuffle my feet. Did he just say I'm too young to
understand instead of actually answering my question? "All
kinds of horrible people have used the Bible to justify bad
stuff, like wars and slavery and stuff. How can you be so sure
you've got the right interpretation?" Behind me, someone
whispers something.

"Riley, I understand exactly where you're coming from."
Jandel gives me a saccharine smile. "I had the same questions when I was young. I know when you're young, you
hear bits and pieces of Scripture but you never get a sense of
the whole beautiful truth that's contained in here, so here's
what I'm going to suggest. I want you to commit to reading
the Bible—the entire thing from start to finish." I open my
mouth to argue, but he cuts me off. "I know, I know, you have
homework and activities and all kinds of things going on, but
you should make reading God's Word a priority, and here's
why—"

"I've read the whole Bible, start to finish." I say it loudly so
he can't talk over me. "I've read it several times, in fact."

Jandel stops dead still and then recovers, pasting a smile
on his face.

"Well, that's just great. And so you know—"

"That it doesn't have answers to all of my questions," I say.
The room is silent. Ana and Zoe gape at me. "It doesn't tell

me where to go to school or who to go out with or what to do with my life or how to help my brother. I want to know how to make the right choices, and I would love it if there were rules that spelled it all out, but there aren't, and I want to know what to do about that."

Pastor Jandel clears his throat and smoothes the pages of his Bible again. "Why don't you come up and talk to me afterward?" he finally says. "We have a lot of ground to cover tonight, and I don't want us to get derailed. But I would love to help answer your questions, Riley." He smiles, a little too wide, and I can see that he actually has no answer for me. Typical.

I nod as he turns back to his Bible, even though I already know I'm not going to take him up on it.

16

My phone beeps to say I've got a text message, and I smile when I see it's from Tom.

Come outside.

Outside? Is he... I open my bedroom door quietly and peer up and down the hall. Mom and Dad's door is shut and so is Michael's. It's been a tense night around here. I tiptoe down the hall, pulling my old sweatshirt around me to stay warm.

I open the front door slowly, being careful not to let it creak on its hinges, and leave the porch light off.

"Hey," I say softly and step onto the cold stone of the front entryway. Instantly my toes begin to sting in the cool November air.

Tom leans down and brushes his lips across mine. "Hey," he whispers into my hair. His warm breath feels good on my skin. "How's it going in there?"

I pull the hood of my sweatshirt up and yank on the cords to draw it around my face. "It's like a death march through hell on a bitter cold day."

He rubs my shoulders to warm me up and laughs. "Yeah, I don't imagine Michelle is taking this too well." This is our little joke, calling my parents by their first names. Somehow it takes away their power and makes us feel older. "Did Aunty Kathy say she'd come down?"

I sigh and blow into my hands. "No, she decided to get all spontaneous on us and go to Hawaii with a friend of hers. So Dad's going to have to stay home with Michael."

After socking his gym teacher, Michael was suspended. It didn't seem like Ms. Lovchuck wanted to do it, but rules are rules, and physical violence against a teacher is an automatic suspension. That means he won't be able to go to the big homecoming game tomorrow. I feel bad for Michael, I really do, but that's the one night I really needed Mom *and* Dad. Oh well. Riley loses again, I guess.

Tom tilts his head to the side. "Rye, I'm so sorry." I try to say something, but he stops me. "I know you say it's no big deal or whatever, but it is a big deal, a huge deal. You're going to be crowned Homecoming Queen."

I feel my cheeks get hot in spite of the cold November air. "We'll see about that." I thread my arms around his waist and pull him in. "At least you'll be there." I tilt my face up, prompting him to kiss me.

He kisses my forehead but seems distracted. "Actually, I—" He takes a step back and digs for something in his back pocket. "That's why I drove down here to surprise you. I'm afraid I'm going to have to wish you luck tonight instead of tomorrow."

"What?" My teeth begin to chatter, and my eyes sting in the cold.

"I got a job, Riley. But they want me to work tomorrow night. They're totally understaffed."

"You got a job!" I brighten up a little in spite of myself. Tom's been interviewing for weeks. Finding a job that fits into his school schedule has been really hard. "That's great."

"It's a really cool place—Velo Rouge Café. And you could get a job there too if you went to UCSF. How cool would that be?" As he talks, he unrolls something long, white, and silky and gently places it over my head.

"What's this?" I look down at the thing he hung around my neck.

"I made you a sash." He beams from ear to ear. "I found this old material in my mom's sewing room. I think it's from some wedding dress or something."

I try to read the letters he wrote with what appears to be Sharpie marker on a strip of shiny white satin. "Most Perfect Girl in the Universe."

"Homecoming Queen doesn't seem to really cover it." He takes my hands and leans back to admire me for a minute.

I turn from one side to the other and do a slow pageant wave. "I want to thank all the little people." I blow a kiss at him, and he wraps me in a hug, pressing my body tightly to his for a kiss.

"So you'll forgive me for missing it?" His face is sad.

I stare down at my toes, and the shiny red polish I put on tonight gleams back at me. I can't be a baby about this. It's not his fault. He's an adult, he found a good job, and they need him to work. That's the real world for you, and I have to take it like a grown-up, not some stupid high school girl who's hung up on fake-diamond tiaras and football games. "It's totally fine." I try to make my voice sound convincing. "I get it."

He leans down and gently, slowly kisses me on the lips. He moves his lips to my cheek and leaves a tiny kiss there, and it dries in the crisp air.

"You're freezing," he whispers, sending another shiver down my body. "Let's go inside."

I bury my face in his shoulder while I think it through. Mom and Dad won't come out of their room until the morning, and they're heavy sleepers. Michael sleepwalks now and then, but he seemed pretty tired tonight.

"I don't want to turn around and drive back to the city without having a chance to be with you." He gently tucks my hair behind my ear and then cups my chin in his hand and kisses me deep and long.

We finally pull apart with my head swimming, drunk on the thrill of him, the way his mouth feels against mine.

"Okay." I nod finally and grab the doorknob without meeting his eye, too afraid of what my face shows. "Just for a little while."

17

I slip my dress over my head and wiggle my hips to get it into place. Someone burns a hole in the ozone layer with a cloud of Aqua Net. The other girls on the homecoming court have been standing around the equipment room at the stadium for a while, but the girls on the squad had to cheer in the first half of the game, so we only have a few minutes to get ready. I pull my hair up into a messy bun, then cast one last glance at my reflection and push the heavy door open.

"You guys ready for this?" I try to make my tone upbeat as I walk toward the Miracle Girls, who are lined up against the entryway to the field.

"How did you do this every year?" Ana is biting her lower lip and staring at her feet. Her long wavy hair is piled on top of her head, and her dress is a deep orange, which looks amazing against her skin.

"You look so pretty! Try not to lock your knees so you don't faint."

Zoe is stunning in a short silver dress that looks like it's from the seventies or something, and Christine shocked no one when she showed up in a short chartreuse tulle number. She designed her gown herself, and it's very rocker-chick-meets-artist.

Ms. Moore claps her hands and yells that we have two

minutes to go, and several of the girls let out a shriek. I press my lips together to try to smooth out my lip gloss. All around me girls are taking deep breaths to calm their nerves, and Christine's sister, Emma, is bouncing around, calling out funny little cheers, but I feel like I'm far away.

The truth is, I'm bummed my dad and Michael couldn't be here, but that's not all. I know it's not Tom's fault that he didn't come, but after everything, after how close we've been lately, how good it felt to kiss him last night until my lips were almost raw, I wish he'd tried harder to make it.

"All right, girls. Showtime!" Ms. Moore calls out. Old Lovchuck deputized her to help with tonight's festivities.

Emma lets out a shriek, and Christine reaches out and pretends to give her sister a noogie. She would never admit it, but I can see in her eyes that she's excited for Emma. Emma runs over to join the other girls for Freshman Princess. Single file, they line up along the entrance to the field, pairing up with the guys nominated for Prince, and head out toward the field. A moment later, the crowd in the stadium starts to roar. Ms. Moore has the sophomores follow the freshmen.

I grin at the girls, but Zoe looks kind of green. "It's not so bad once you're out there." I slide my arm around her shoulder, and she leans into me.

"You ready, girls?" Ms. Moore catches my eye as she ushers the juniors out. I paste a smile on my face. Better to get it ready now.

No one says anything more until Ms. Moore starts calling out the names of the seniors on the homecoming court. "Ashley Anderson."

I give Ashley a thumbs-up as she dashes by. A girl from the

French Club goes next, then Kayleen the bimbo cheerleader, and Ana follows behind her. I pull away from Zoe, and she walks out of the entranceway a moment later, trying to smile. One by one, girls I've gone to school with my whole life walk out onto the field, and I have the strangest urge to call after them that it doesn't really matter, that we'll all be friends no matter what.

"Good luck, Freak," I say instead.

"Cheerleader." Christine holds out her hand, and I bump her fist with mine.

"Christine Lee." Ms. Moore gestures for her to step outside. I'm next alphabetically, so I walk right behind her, but Ms. Moore puts her hand on my arm to hold me back as Christine walks out. I lean away, but if Ms. Moore notices, she doesn't react. She opens her mouth, and for a second I'm afraid she's going to say something horrible, but then she snaps her mouth shut and drops her hand. "You can go now," she says quietly. I nod. The spot on my arm where her hand was feels cold.

I stifle a shiver as I step out into the crisp November air. Jordan Fletcher grabs my arm and gives me a shy grin. I turn away, and neither of us says anything as we walk toward the roar of the stadium. In front of us the football field is startlingly green, too bright against the dark sky.

"I, um, heard about your brother."

I peer off into the distance, hoping the bracing night air will hold back the tears.

"I'm sorry," he mumbles.

I lift my chin and put on my best smile, and the students in the stands clap and cheer as we walk across the spongy rubber track. Jordan and I step onto the football field care-fully. I almost fell over at homecoming freshman year because no one warned me that high heels sink into the grass.

The stadium looked so big back then, and the crowd seemed overwhelming. I don't know if I've changed or if everything else has, or if I've just gotten used to it, but now, as I make my way across the field, this doesn't feel scary anymore. It feels kind of... familiar. I smile at the crowd, picking out the faces of my classmates, and it occurs to me that this is my last homecoming. After four years, this is it. For some reason I don't feel particularly sad about it. I lift my chin and beam as confidently as I can at the crowd. I guess I expected to feel... I don't know. I expected to feel *more*.

I don't listen as Ms. Lovchuck calls out the names of the members of the freshman court, and I only realize that Emma's won because I recognize her patented shrill scream. I come to as she jumps up and down, the soft fabric of her dress fluttering around her. She looks like she might faint with excitement as our principal places the tiny tiara on her head.

I squint at the stands as Lovchuck reads off the names of the sophomore and junior courts. I know Tom isn't here, but I don't see... but then this doesn't really seem like the kind of thing Ben would be into anyway. Too much school spirit.

"And now the moment we've all been waiting for," Ms. Lovchuck says, laughing as if she's said something incred-ibly witty. She reads out the names of the nominees, and the stands erupt in cheers as she announces that Kirk Cattleman, captain of the football team, has been voted Homecoming King. I catch Ashley's eye and smirk. Ashley went out with Kirk for two weeks in seventh grade.

"And now, the Homecoming Queen. Second runner-up..." Ms. Lovchuck opens an envelope that she no doubt sealed herself. "Is..." She squints at the piece of paper in front of her. "Christine Lee!"

Next to me Christine throws her head back and laughs, a loud, belly laugh. Before I know what's happening, Emma has run across the field and thrown her arms around her sister. A second later, Zoe and Ana are there too, wrapping us all in an awkward group hug. Emma's bouncing up and down, and Christine's actually smiling. Actually—I look around quickly—everyone is smiling.

"Congrats!" I squeak.

"Woo!" Zoe yells. "Christine!! You did it!" She looks as shocked as I feel, but she's excited. Ms. Lovchuck waits for a moment, then gestures for us all to get back in line.

"The first runner-up..."

I take a deep breath. I kind of hope it's Zoe. It would mean so much to Zoe. Or Ana. No one deserves it more than Ana. Either way, I'll be really excited for them.

"Is..." Ms. Lovchuck pauses, drawing out the suspense a moment too long. "...Riley McGee!"

For a split second, I know I didn't hear her right, but then she's coming at me with a small tiara and mouthing "Congratulations" like I'm supposed to be excited, when I really feel like someone has punched me in the stomach.

First runner-up.

I stand perfectly still as she digs the sharp plastic combs of the tiara into my scalp, and then blink my eyes as the crowd breaks into a cheer. Christine reaches over and gives me a stiff side hug, and out of the corner of my eye, I see Zoe giving me a thumbs-up. The lights over the stands seem too bright all of a sudden.

"And this year's Homecoming Queen..." Ms. Lovchuck enunciates the last two words, placing too much emphasis on the last few syllables. "Is..." She opens another envelope and squints. "Ashley Anderson!"

Ashley starts screaming, and a few of the other girls on the squad throw their arms around her, jumping up and down. I know I should go over there too. Ashley and I were so close all those years. And then after everything she did to help us last year... But before I can make myself move, Ms. Lovchuck gestures for Ashley to come forward to receive her crown, and suddenly all of Marina Vista is on its feet.

How did this happen? But as Ashley steps forward, I try to remember the last time I ate lunch with the popular crowd or the last time I went to a postgame party. I've been so wrapped up with the Miracle Girls and with Tom. How long has it been since I was really a part of that world?

Ashley ducks as Ms. Lovchuck places the crown on her head. She raises both arms over her head, pumping her fists, and all I can do is pray that I look happy for her.

18

reach under my comforter and feel for my top sheet. I tossed and turned most of the night and then didn't exactly get out of bed a whole lot today, so my blankets are all over the place. I find the edge and yank the sheet up, then pull the comforter over it. There. That looks okay. My stupid homecoming dress is on the floor, so I kick it under the bed. My toe hits the edge of my crown, and I push it under too, as far as it will go.

When Ana called to say she was coming over, I pretended my family was about to sit down to dinner, but she saw through that right away and invited herself over anyway. Then I told her I was working on my application essays and hinted that things weren't great with Michael and now wasn't really the best time, but the girl is pushy. She said she'd be over in a few minutes and didn't leave me any room to argue.

Clean shirt. Clean shirt. That one's clean enough. There's a pair of jeans at the bottom of the closet. Kicking off my pajama bottoms, I slip them on just as the doorbell rings. I take off Tom's old T-shirt and button up the clean blouse, then peer into the mirror. My eyes are still red, and the skin around them is puffy. My hair is totally caked with hairspray from last night, but it's greasy enough that it goes back into a runt of a ponytail. The bell rings a second time.

"Is someone going to get that?" Mom calls from the laundry room.

"Got it!" I call as I run to the door. I can hear Michael playing Wii Bowling in the living room. Through the glass panel in the door, I see Ana biting her lip, but she breaks into a smile when she sees me, then waves.

"Hi." I yank open the door.

She steps in and holds up a paper bag stained with grease. "I brought burritos." She opens the El Bueno Burrito bag, and the smell of ground beef wafts out.

"Oh wow." My stomach turns a little. I haven't really eaten anything today, but for some reason I don't feel hungry. "That's awesome." I take the bag from her hands. "I'm not all that hungry, but if you want one..."

Ana shakes her head. "I brought them for you guys."

"Thanks," I say, leading her to the kitchen. I set the bag down on the counter and notice she brought four burritos—enough for dinner for all of us. "That was really nice. Why don't we leave them in the kitchen for now and I'm sure they'll disappear in no time."

Ana tilts her head and looks like she's about to say something.

"I had a late lunch." I don't want her to feel like I don't appreciate the gesture. She watches me for a moment, then nods. "Come on, let's go to my room." She follows me down the hall.

"So what have you been up to?" I try to make my voice light.

"Riley..."

"How's your story for writing class coming?" I flop down

on the bed. Ana sits in the desk chair. "Thirty pages is a lot, right? I was trying to figure out what to write, and I thought maybe something about surfing. But I'm sure you'll write something awesome, whatever you decide to do."

"I—"

"Have you started your Princeton application? What are you writing about for your essay?" I just have to get her talking. Once she starts talking about something she cares about, she'll forget about whatever it is she came over here for.

"Riley, stop."

"How's Maria doing?" I move a pillow against the wall and lean back to rest against it.

She takes in a deep breath, then lets it out slowly. "I wanted to see how you're holding up after last night." Ana says quietly. "I know it was a big disappointment for you. For all of us, really. We thought you had it locked up."

"Ha ha." I sit up and wave my hand dismissively. "Last night was not a big deal. I mean, of course I wanted to win, who didn't, but I'm over it already." I smile and try not to think about what it felt like to stand there on the field and lose. "But thanks for checking in."

"I noticed Tom wasn't there." Ana narrows her eyes.

"He had to work." I shrug. "He's saving up so he can move out of his parents' place. I totally understood."

Ana doesn't say anything for a moment. "How are the applications coming?" She spins the chair, right to left, with her feet. "Have you figured out which schools you're going to apply to?"

I roll my eyes. "I haven't finalized the list or anything, but I've got time. I'm not worried."

"I know you're not, Riley, but *I* am," Ana says, leaning forward. "You seem kind of . . . I don't know. Different. Unsure."

I thread my fingers together in my lap. "Thanks." I look up and see the concern in her face. "I really do mean that. But it's mostly just stuff with Michael that's stressing me out a bit. Really, I'm fine."

It's mostly true, after all. Maybe I don't have all the other stuff totally figured out yet, but I will soon.

"You can tell us, Riley. We won't think less of you." Ana's eyes are searching, and I look away. "We want to help."

"I'm fine." I know they think they want to help, but I also know what she really means. What they really want is for me to go back to being regular old carefree Riley. "I have everything under control. I promise."

Ana presses her lips together like she doesn't quite believe me but doesn't really know what to say. I think this might be a first.

19

'm sure she'll be done soon." Mrs. Benassi adjusts the glasses on the end of her nose. There are photos of her grandkids covering the entire surface of her desk, and her floral-print blouse is stretched tight across her boobs. She glances at the wall clock again. Mrs. Benassi has been the secretary at Marina Vista since the prehistoric era, and I don't think her wardrobe has been updated in all that time.

I nod, and she turns back to her computer. I wiggle around, trying to get comfortable in the hard plastic chair. Christine has to have her counseling sessions with Ms. Moore after school this year. Down the hall, I hear the soft click of a door opening, then footsteps sound on the worn blue carpet.

"That'll be them," Mrs. Benassi says without taking her eyes off the computer screen.

I stand up, and a second later Christine walks out into the main office. Her eyes widen when she sees me.

"Hey." Christine tilts her head a little, like she's trying to figure out what I'm doing here.

"Ms. Moore," I say. Christine nods and gives me a wave before heading out the office door. "I was wondering if you had a second to talk." I steel myself. Ms. Moore used to be my favorite teacher. There was a time when she would have done anything for me, or for any of us. Maybe she still will.

Ms. Moore smiles, steps back, and gestures for me to follow her into her office. She counsels a bunch of students besides Christine, so the school lets her have a small, dark office down the hall from Ms. Lovchuck. I place my bag on the ground and settle into the chair across from her desk. She stares at me expectantly.

"I know this is kind of...weird." I swallow and twist my fingers together in my lap. "But I wanted to talk to you about Michael." Is this how Christine feels every week, shifting awkwardly in the hot seat?

She nods, and the industrial clock behind her desk ticks loudly.

"I know his grades are suffering because he hasn't been in class...." I wait for her to acknowledge my statement—that he's in danger of failing her class because he got suspended through the end of the year, and class participation is worth fifty percent of his grade—but she just stares at me. "And I was hoping you could give him some kind of extra credit or something to help him catch up."

"Riley..." She lets out a long breath. "You know I can't do that."

"I'd make sure he does the work and everything, and tutor him or whatever he needs to help him catch up a little."

"Riley." She picks up a pen and starts twirling it around in her fingers. "I spell out the rules the first day of class and make sure every student understands them. If you miss class, you lose your participation points."

"You let me make up my work." Freshman year I missed the last two months of school after I slipped off a cliff one night, and Ms. Moore didn't have any problem with that.

"You were in the hospital."

"But once I came home—"

"You were under doctor's orders not to move. Legally I had to let you make up your work."

I cross my arms. "Well, what's Michael's problem if it's not medical?"

Ms. Moore presses her lips together. "It wouldn't be fair to the other students in the class if I bent the rules for him."

I take a deep breath. "I'm asking as a favor." I lean forward and place my hands on her desk. "I know it wouldn't exactly be fair, but it's not really fair that Michael has had to go through life like this either. So I was hoping that maybe, because of knowing our family so well and all, you could cut him a break." I try to keep my voice even and calm, though I want to take the stupid glass paperweight off her desk and chuck it at her.

"Riley, I will never forget what you all did for me last year," she says, leaning back in her dirty desk chair. "I will never forget that you girls fought to get me my job back. But I wouldn't be doing that job if I let this continue. I really do feel like this is the right thing for Michael, so I'm going to have to stick to my guns on this one."

"But it was an accident. He didn't know what he was doing—"

"Exactly." She raises her voice a tiny bit. "That's exactly my point. If Michael's problems are really that bad," she says, "so bad that he can't function in high school without putting other people at risk"—she eyes me—"wouldn't you rather have him be somewhere they can take better care of him?"

I rear my head back.

"I'm not trying to punish him, Riley. I'm trying to help him. And in this case, the best help I can give Michael is to let him go."

I can feel my mouth hanging open. "So just like that, you're going to fail him?"

"I don't fail people. In my class you earn the grade you deserve." She puts the pen down on the desk. "But, yes, I do hope some good will come of this, that failing my class will get him transferred to a school that's better equipped to help him."

I reach down and grab the strap of my bag.

"What might surprise you is that Michael is not the only McGee I'm worried about." She leans forward. "How are *you* doing?"

I stand up and loop my bag over my shoulder.

"You seem distracted this year—distant, fumbling." She reaches across her desk and touches my arm. "What's going on?"

I clench my fists. "I have to go."

"It looks to me like everyone in your life has their own dreams for you, but you have no idea what *you* want."

I push the door open. After all we've done for her... defending her to the other students at this stupid school. I can't believe after all that she would turn on me now.

"I'll never forget the day you first walked into my class-room." I turn back to face her. Her arms are crossed over her chest, and her face is sad. "I'd never seen a student with so much promise. You're the smartest kid in this school."

I think about Ana, and I'm not so sure. She and I have always been in a dead heat for the top spot in our class.

"You're special. You always have been, and you're cut out for more than this"—she gestures around her tiny office—"and it kills me to see you throw it all away."

"What are you talking about?" I step out into the hallway. "I'm not throwing anything away." I stare at Ms. Moore. I used to think she had all the answers, that I could trust her more than anyone in the world. Now I'm beginning to see the truth—she just likes to meddle in people's lives.

She bites her lip. "I want to help. I really do."

I turn on my heels and walk down the hall.

20

Never in the three years I've known Zoe has she asked for help with schoolwork, which is why I knew I had to come. It's two days after Thanksgiving, and we're bent over her kitchen table, math books and papers spread out in front of us, calculating angles.

"That's right." I nod. "You've got it. Twenty degrees. You only have to remember SOH-CAH-TOA. So sine equals?"

"Opposite." Zoe grips her pencil tightly. "Over hypotenuse."

"Exactly." I try to sound excited, but I always thought trigonometry was kind of dull. "Want to try the next one?"

Zoe nods and starts copying the next problem from the book. Her lips move as she writes. I lean back and crane my neck to see out the big sliding glass door to her backyard. Zoe lives in the woods, and from her back patio, you can see miles and miles of leafy green treetops. Somewhere out there there's a stable, but I can't spot it through the trees. Coming to Zoe's house always feels like entering another world, or at least another era, where shag carpet, textured wallpaper, and domed ceilings are considered normal.

"Okay." She points to her paper. "Did I get this one right?"

I scan her work and see that the degrees of her triangle add up to two hundred and thirty.

"Let's take another look at this." I lean over her paper

and try to make out her messy handwriting. Zoe blows out a breath and bends in closer. It doesn't take long to figure out where she's gone wrong, and I watch as she reworks the problem.

"Zo?" I push my chair back and help myself to a glass of water. "What made you suddenly so interested in your math grade?" From the window over the sink, I can see Zoe's older brother, Nick, coming up the path from the stable.

"I don't know." Zoe shrugs, and her pale cheeks turn pink. "I mean, colleges want you to have good grades, right? To get in, and to, like, get financial aid and stuff." She doodles on the edge of her paper, drawing a little heart. "I should have started thinking about this stuff ages ago."

I take a long gulp of the cool, clear water. The water at Zoe's house comes from a well in the woods, and it tastes way better than the stuff that comes through the pipes in town.

"So you're really applying to USC?"

"Yeah." Zoe scratches her nose. "You guys are too, right? And Dean."

I set my glass down on the scarred Formica counter and walk back to the table. The legs of my chair scrape against the floor as I settle back into it. "Let's see what's going on with the next problem."

I make sure Zoe sets up the equation right, then let my eyes focus on a dent in her tabletop. Maybe I would like LA. It's sunny all the time, and you can surf year-round.

"You girls ready for a break?" Zoe's mom, Dreamy, comes down the stairs from the second floor and smiles at us as she steps into the kitchen. "I made some carob chip cookies yesterday."

"Mom, we're trying to work." Zoe rolls her eyes. She's always been embarrassed about her parents' vegan diet, but I think it's pretty cool. I reach for the plate of cookies Dreamy holds out and take one. Carob doesn't taste exactly like chocolate, but it's pretty good. Zoe waves the plate away.

"What are you working on?" Dreamy leans back against the countertop and bites into one of the cookies.

"Trig." Zoe taps her pencil against her paper. "You dug out all the Christmas decorations already?" There's an edge to Zoe's voice, and I look at Dreamy to see if she heard it too. Dreamy meets my eye and shakes her head, like she not only caught it but has heard it before.

"Oh look, here comes Nick," Dreamy says cheerfully. A second later Nick crosses the patio and slides open the smudged-glass door. He waves as he steps onto the braided rug by the door and starts unlacing his work boots.

"Riley, do you know what you're doing next year?" Dreamy asks.

I shove my cookie into my mouth to give myself a few moments before I have to answer. "Maybe USC," I say and pray that will be enough to satisfy her.

"Oh really?" Dreamy's eyebrows shoot up. "So, college then?"

I twist in my chair. Why is she so surprised?

"That's always kind of been the plan." I run my fingers along the rough surface of the table, tracing the grain of the dark wood with my finger. "I mean, you have to go to college, right?"

As soon as the words leave my mouth, I feel my cheeks turn

red. I'm so stupid. She's taking night classes now, but Dreamy never finished college. I put my hand over my mouth.

"Don't worry about it." Dreamy laughs, waving her hand at me. "When I was young, there was a different mind-set on these things. No one had to do anything in the sixties."

I try to imagine what Dreamy was like when she was young, but all I can picture are those hippies you see sitting in the parks in San Francisco.

"But like I keep telling Zoe, there's no reason you have to go to college even now. College isn't for everyone." She pops the last of her cookie into her mouth and crosses her arms over her chest.

"Oh, well, I don't know. . . ." I let my voice trail off.

"Hey." Nick tugs his boots off and steps into the kitchen in his socks. "No fair. You made me go to college." Nick grins at Zoe to show he's kidding, but Zoe glares at her mother.

"And I'm not sure I was right to do that," Dreamy says evenly. "In retrospect, I don't think you were ready to be off on your own."

Nick laughs and steps past her. "Those were the best six years of my life." He bends over and reaches into the fridge.

"Maybe if we'd made you wait a year to mature a bit before you went, you'd have finished on time," Dreamy says. "Would have saved ourselves a lot of money." She grabs a dish towel off the counter and swats at Nick, then turns back to me.

"All I'm saying, Riley, is that if you're not excited about college, maybe it's not right, or right right now, anyway. There's a whole big world out there, and a million different ways for

God to use you wherever you are, whether or not that includes college."

I try to wrap my head around what she's saying, but it's like she's speaking another language. Dreamy has always been a free spirit, but I don't know how to tell her that not going to college is not really an option when your dad is a super Internet geek. They started a college savings account for me the day I was born. I glance at Zoe, and she lowers her head and mumbles something under her breath. Nick opens a bottle of seltzer and pours it into a glass.

"I mean, look at Zoe," Dreamy says. "She loves being outdoors, and she hates school, so I've been trying to tell her to stick around here, take a few classes at a community college, make sure it's really what she wants to do before diving in and moving away. It saves on tuition too when you do a year or two at City College first. Private schools aren't exactly—"

Zoe slams her math book shut and pushes her chair back. "I *want* to go to USC. Why is that so hard for you to understand?" She stands up. "Everyone else is going away for school. The girls are, and Dean is, and the last thing I want to do is stick around here like some loser."

Her voice goes up at the end, and I lean back, away from the family squabble. I don't know if I've ever heard Zoe raise her voice, but I've certainly never seen her talk this way to her parents.

"I *told you* I'd find a way to pay for it," Zoe says.

Dreamy doesn't say anything for a few seconds. She watches Zoe, then, tentatively, reaches out her hand and rests it on Zoe's arm.

"I'm sorry."

Zoe frowns, tears welling up in her eyes, and her shoulders drop. The tension in the room dissipates.

"Don't worry, Zo," Nick says, setting his empty glass in the sink. "If USC is what you really want, we'll figure out how to make it happen."

Dreamy nods her assent, and slowly, tentatively, Zoe sits back down and turns back to her math book.

21

We're all crowded around our favorite picnic table in the courtyard listening to Zoe explain the plot of the ninja movie Dean is making, when something smacks me on the back of the head. I turn, ready to throttle someone, but all I see is a paper airplane resting at an awkward angle on the ground. I grab it off the blacktop and unfold it quickly.

Mavericks is on. Wanna go?

I look around, but don't know who could have...

Ah. There, resting on the grassy hill with a bunch of skaters. Ben. He's leaning back on his elbows on the grass, his legs stuck straight out in front of him. He waves, a dopey grin on his face. How did he get it to fly all the way over here? He must be some kind of paper airplane wizard.

Zoe breaks off her story as I push myself up, but I gesture for her to go on. "Be right back." I grasp the paper and walk over to the group, clustered under a group of pine trees. I stand over them, and Ben lifts his hand to shield his eyes.

"Did you throw this?"

"It's possible." Ben pushes himself up and waits.

"Mavericks is on?" I can't believe I missed that. Mavericks

is a world-famous big-wave surf contest. The waves off Pillar Point Harbor, north of Half Moon Bay, are legendary—as big as a house on average days, close to fifty feet tall at their max—and every winter they host this competition for big-wave surfers. What makes it so cool, though, is they have to wait until the conditions are perfect. Suddenly huge swells begin to form, and they officially call the contest, and then surfers from around the world have forty-eight hours to get there.

"It is indeed." Ben pats the black bag resting on the ground next to him. "And I want to take some pictures. You in?"

"When did they call it?" I was planning to work on my applications after school, but this is Mavericks. Plus, today Mr. Mackey agreed to write me a recommendation, so that counts as progress. The guys sitting around Ben are watching me, hanging on our every word. They don't even pretend they're not listening.

"It started today," Ben says, pulling his knees up. He's wearing dusty black-and-white checkered Vans. "I'm going either way, so..."

I watch him for a second. I went to Mavericks with Tom a couple years ago, and I guess I kind of assumed we'd go again this year, but we haven't exactly discussed it. And it's not like he bothered to let me know it was on, even though he must have known. It's his dream to be out there with the legends someday. He's probably busy with class or something, and I can just give him a call and let him know I'm going with Ben. He won't mind. Maybe he'll even come out and meet us there.

I picture the sight of those monstrous waves. "Sure," I say and kick his shoe gently. "Give me a ride?"

Ben is waiting for me at the edge of the parking lot in front of the gym, as promised. He's clutching his camera bag in one hand and twirling his keys around his finger in the other and whistling as I walk up to him.

"My car's over here," he says, ducking his head. He gestures toward a gray sedan. There's a roof rack on top, but otherwise it's a totally average car—several years old, safe, kind of boring. Ben fumbles with the keys, and I pull open the passenger door and slide into the seat.

Inside it's a whole different story. "Now this is more like it." I reach my hand out and touch one of the glossy decals covering the dashboard. The whole interior of the car, except for the seats and the roof, is covered with stickers. "What are these?"

"Decals." He hesitates for a moment, then hands me a black plastic-covered folder from the backseat. Clear page protectors are clipped inside the binding, each holding a different colorful sticker. They're really cool—a sixties-looking peace sign, a skull and crossbones, and a kind of stylized wave crashing onto a beach. One of them has this weird flower and says, "War Is Not Healthy for Children and Other Living Things." A couple of them look familiar, especially one that has a heart circled in what looks like barbed wire. "I got a new batch in from my printer."

"Did you make these? I think I've seen them on people's boards," I say.

"Yeah, I've got a little business. Decals for boards. Surf and skate." He clears his throat and takes the folder back quickly.

"Wow, you think you know a guy and then..."

"You only know the tip of the iceberg, Riley McGee." Ben cranks the car and pulls out of the parking lot, then clicks on the radio. It's some British lady reading headlines from around the world. Ben taps his fingers on the steering wheel as he turns right onto Highway 1.

I check my phone, but Tom hasn't responded to my message. Maybe he's already there. It's hard to get good reception on the shore.

"Have you ever been to see Mavericks before?" I ask to break the silence. This feels a little weird. Ben and I aren't really close, but it's not usually awkward like this.

"Never miss," Ben says. "The waves are..." He shakes his head. "It's hard to imagine that much power, you know? And I love the audacity of trying to tackle those waves, like shaking your fist at God." He taps his fingers on the steering wheel. "I usually get some amazing shots."

"Yeah." I trace the barbed wire on the sacred heart decal. It's that popular Catholic image that looks vaguely rock and roll.

"So..." I let my voice trail off. He keeps his eyes firmly fastened to the road. "Art?"

"I'm for it."

"How did you get into it, I mean?"

Ben doesn't answer, and for a moment I don't think he heard me. The woman on the radio is talking about a car bomb that went off in Africa. I reach out and snap it off.

"I don't know," he says at last. "Haven't you ever just known you're good at something?"

I turn my head and study his profile, silhouetted against

the late afternoon sun. He's pretty cute, actually. Not Tom's brand of manly gorgeousness, but Ben's got kind of an Adam Brody with better hair thing going on.

"I don't know how to answer that."

"I think you do." Ben weaves past rows of parked cars and finds a tiny space along the side of the road, across from the cliffs. He parallel parks with ease and turns off the engine. The car is silent until I push my door open and step out onto the sandy dirt by the road. We're outside a tiny town, still a ways from the ocean, but there's a one-lane road ahead of us, and judging by the traffic ahead, we're not going to get any closer. We dash across the street and make our way to the cliffs on the other side. There are people standing all over the tops of the cliffs, and we weave our way through the crowd. A head stands out over the crowd, and for an instant my heart stops, but then the guy moves and I can see it's not Tom after all.

Ben grabs my arm in a friendly, easy way as we walk toward the cliff. The beaches around here are not like the typical Southern California beaches you see in those old surf movies. The only way to get to the shore below is to climb down high, rocky cliffs. In some places there's not even sand, just a sheer wall of stone that drops straight into the moody, pounding water below.

Ben proves to be an excellent scout, and soon he's carved out a spot for us near the edge of a rocky point. I squint out at the water. I can't make out who they are, but there are definitely bodies bobbing up and down in the water below. A huge wall of water comes up behind them.

"They've got to be out of their minds." Two guys start

paddling away, and a moment later, they're all swept up in a wave that towers several times higher than them. Another guy gets sucked up into the wave and tossed over the backside. The crowd gasps in unison, and Ben's camera clicks a bunch of times in rapid succession. Everyone stops talking. I close my eyes. It's hard to imagine how a frail human body could survive being tossed around like that; then again, I know from experience that sometimes there's a force more powerful than tides pulling on us.

"They made it, Supergirl," Ben says, elbowing me. My eyes fly open to see two surfers in black wet suits gliding in toward the shore. The guy caught in the wave seems to be struggling, but his head is above water as he bobs up and down, holding onto his board.

I say a quick prayer of thanks. I'm not here to see anybody die. I look up and something clicks at me. Ben squats near me and quickly snaps shots from behind his camera. I turn so he can't see my face. "Do you carry that thing with you everywhere?"

Another wave comes in toward the shore, and a guy pops up on his board.

"No. Just sometimes."

I stick out my tongue and cross my eyes. He snaps a picture.

I bat at the camera playfully while he takes a few more, then plops down next to me again. "I don't want to go in the dark room next week and find a million embarrassing shots of myself."

We both go silent while we watch the horizon, seeing the thunderous waves build and build and build and then explode with the power of ten storms. But somehow, as if the wind has changed, the mood darkens.

I turn to Ben and study his odd, almost angry expression. "Is everything okay?"

He leans into me a little, so slowly I almost don't notice, but then his shoulder brushes against mine. I swallow a lump in my throat. We're from very different circles at Marina Vista. What am I doing here now? Are we both lost and scared and lonely and drawn together out of desperation?

"Asha decided she wants to keep the baby. Keep *him*. We found out it's a boy." He shakes his head angrily.

"Oh wow." I fumble for the right words to say. "Ben, I'm… You're worried about her?"

He rearranges to sit cross-legged, his knee touching mine, his hands resting there, just millimeters from mine. "She's too young to raise a child. She could make sure he was adopted into an amazing family, and then she could go to college, but she won't listen."

"It's not really your decision, I guess." Either way, it's going to be a tough road for her, and I don't know if I'd have the strength to make it in her place. "She has to do what's right for her and her baby."

"Yeah." He moves his hand, and I can feel the heat coming off of it.

"What do your parents think?"

Ben shuts his eyes and just breathes for a few minutes in silence. "They're pretty much in denial about everything right now. They're moping around the house giving her the silent treatment, pretending it's not happening."

"I'm sorry."

"Yeah." He opens his eyes and trains them on the horizon. "It's like they don't want to see what's really going on. It's easier to pretend than to deal with the fact that things have changed, I guess." Ben's fingers brush against my knee. "It's tough when you realize your parents don't always know what's best, you know?"

I nod and stare at the ocean as another wave breaks.

22

They brought in live camels. Where do you get live camels? Sheep, sure. You'd be surprised how many farms are left in the Bay Area, but camels you have to import. The whole lawn smells like poop.

I try to block out the stench and Tom's hand holding mine and focus my eyes on the holy family nestled together around the manger. What was it like for Jesus, stuck right there in the middle of all that? Did he ever wish he'd never come down here to begin with? I step closer to the action. Did he ever feel like the pressure to be perfect was too great?

Just as I am zeroing in on the tiny baby's angelic face, the mother of God bursts into perfectly pitched operatic song, and I lose my concentration. I can see the wireless microphone hidden in her hair, and for a moment I wish that everyone would go away. How is anyone supposed to ponder the real meaning of Christmas when it's all happening in surround sound?

I squint at the crowd and make out Ana on the other side of the manger, illuminated against the dark night by the light from the Star of David. "See you," I say to my parents and drag Tom away before Michael can beg to come with us. Tom wanted to hang out tonight, and he wasn't even put off when

I told him Mom insisted we come to the Living Nativity. He's never come to church with me before, though I asked him a million times, so I know I should be excited that he's here. But for some reason, it's kind of weird to actually be here with him. He's never been interested in this part of my world, and now that he's here, I'm almost not sure what to do.

"Where are we going?" he asks, dodging a bundled-up toddler that stumbles into his path.

"Let's say hi to Ana." I think I see a guy with dark hair across the lawn and try to drop Tom's hand, but he has a tight fix on it. The man turns around, and I realize it's not Ben, thank goodness. He probably wouldn't be here anyway. The Nayars are probably too overwhelmed with everything that's going on.

"There you are!" I finally squeeze my way into the tight spot between Ana and some old guy.

"Happy Three Days before Christmas!" Ana hugs me.

"But who's counting?"

Tom makes space for himself next to me, and Ana moves over. "Oh. Hey, Tom," Ana says. "I didn't know you were coming."

"This thing is insane." He laughs, a huge grin on his face, as the shepherds finally make their way, after much wandering, to the side of the baby Jesus, played by Curtis Watkins, who was born last month. The choir launches into a rousing rendition of "O Come All Ye Faithful."

"Welcome to Seaview. Improving on Jesus' birth since 1989," I say, and Ana stifles a snicker, but the joke seems to sail over Tom's head.

"I think it's cool," Tom says, and the weird thing is, he actually seems to be enjoying this. Maybe if you've never seen it before, it is kind of cool.

"Don't you think it's a little"—I wave my hand toward the scene—"much?" When I was a kid, Seaview's Living Nativity was a couple of volunteers in bathrobes holding a doll. But when Pastor Jandel came along, he saw an opportunity to turn a quaint tradition into an "outreach opportunity," and now it's a fully staged drama in three acts, complete with moving sets, professional actors, a full choir, and an army of volunteers ready to hand out tracts and pray with you by the parking lot. There's even a cherry picker to hoist the Angel of the Lord into the sky. They had to have an intense audition in the 4–6 grade Sunday school class because all the little girls wanted to be the angel.

"Oh, don't be such a Grinch. It's Christmas." Ana laughs, and I try to smile. Tom reaches his hand around my waist and grins down at me. I fidget, pretending to fuss with my coat.

"Do you want me to let you go?" Tom glances at my parents and Michael.

I blush. It feels weird to be out in public with him, and I wonder why. Has it been that long since we hung out with my friends? "Of course not." I don't even convince myself with my unsure tone. I try to recover. "You're an excellent human blanket."

This seems to satisfy him, and he locks his fingers into place.

"Where's Zoe?" I scan the crowd, not really looking for Zo.

"She left for her grandmother's this morning. Christine's got babysitting duty so she's at home." Ana shrugs half-heartedly. I know Christmas has been hard for her ever since Maria moved back to Mexico.

I turn back to the lawn, where the miracle of Christ's birth is being projected onto a movie screen. I guess I can see how it might be a pretty good show if you don't remember back when the choir was half a dozen moms clutching handbells. There was something so beautiful and simple about it all then. Now it just kind of seems like a carnival. Whatever happened to plain old "Silent Night"? How am I supposed to find any sliver of wonder in all this?

And then the worst possible thing happens. Across the lawn, just as the wise men move to present the baby Jesus with huge plates of gold spray-painted rocks, I see him. The whole Nayar family is bundled up in their winter coats and staring intently at the nativity scene.

"Hot chocolate," I say quickly and break free of Tom's hands. I bend over, dig in my purse, and find a wadded up bill. "Can you get me a cup of hot chocolate? I'm freezing." I press it into Tom's hand.

"Sure." He shrugs. "Ana?" She gives him her order while I stare at the ground. Could Ben see us standing there like that all along? Tom walks away, fading into the crowd, and I finally dare to look back at the Nayars. Is Ben's angle better than mine?

"Come on, Riley. Clap for the angel choir," Ana says as a dozen girls in shining gold robes, including Cecily Vandekamp and Maddie Barrow, are raised into the air on a hydraulic lift.

As the choir belts out a mighty chorus, I stare across the crowd, my heart pounding in my chest. Finally Ben turns in my direction, and we lock eyes. I hold my breath, but his face is blank. I raise my hand and give him a small, tentative wave. He rolls his eyes.

23

Go to bed soon or Santa will skip our house." Dad lingers in the doorway, his eyes misting. Down the hall, I hear the sound of water running in the bathroom. Mom is not going to skip her elaborate evening beauty regimen, even on Christmas Eve.

"Dad," I groan as he tousles my hair.

"Yeah, Dad." Michael parrots my tone exactly, and I smile. I'm sure Christine would pummel Emma if she did that, but at our house, it's the sign of a good night. Michael's had a brutal few weeks. As much as he hated attending school, skipping it has been even harder on him because it messed up his routines.

Dad smiles at us again, gives a small wave, and disappears down the long hallway in the direction of the master suite. He shuts off five different lights as he goes.

Michael yawns, and Christmas tree lights bounce off his shiny, über-blond hair. In this light, he looks almost angelic. It reminds me of when we were young. I shake my head and move to go to bed, but then I turn back.

"Want to play tennis?" I raise an eyebrow, but he doesn't notice. He's staring at something across the room.

"We have to play Wii Tennis. It's dark outside."

Never in our entire lives have we played real tennis, and I'm not sure where the closest public court is, but that's not his point. What I said is slightly inaccurate, and he can't tolerate that.

He gets up and walks to the gaming console, not waiting for my response. Michael pulls both Wii remotes off the charging base and goes through his routine to get them ready. Finally, he hands me my remote.

"Are you ready for me to school you at tennis, little brother?"

"Ha *ha*," he laughs loudly, oddly. I almost shush him, worried about waking up Mom and Dad, but can't bring myself to. "I have beaten you forty-five times at tennis. You have beaten me zero times."

The game starts, and Michael volleys a super serve at me, though he knows I can't return them.

"Skunked it!" he says, and I frown. That's one of those stupid expressions Tom taught him.

"Okay, okay. We have to do something to level the playing field." I ready my stance for his next serve, crouching low and holding the wand in front of my body. "No super serves."

"All right." He lifts his arm like he's going to screech the ball down the court again at me.

"Promise?"

"Promise. But I'm still going to serve it pretty fast." He brings the remote down, serving the virtual tennis ball to me on the screen, and somehow I'm able to return it. We even get in a good volley back and forth for a few minutes, but eventually Michael hits the ball inside the line and my Mii can't get there in time.

"Yes!" He pumps his arm in the air again, and I fight the urge to sweep him into a hug. Why don't we do stuff like this more often? It shouldn't take a major religious holiday to slow down and get back to doing a whole lot of nothing together. Time like this is important. I need to enjoy it. I can worry about everything else tomorrow.

"Ready?" Michael turns to me and stares at the space above my head. That's his version of eye contact. His face is calm and beautiful.

Tomorrow I'll really dive into my applications. Once I fill out the Common Application, I just have to do supplements for most schools, but even if I started my applications right now and never once slept or ate, I'd have to eliminate a few of the schools on Mom's list. For some reason, something Ms. Moore said sticks in my head. Yale, MIT, Hopkins—those are all part of my parents' dreams for me. I've never really wanted to go to those schools anyway.

"I'll let you win this one if you want." He rocks back and forth rhythmically, getting faster and faster. The motion starts at his head and moves down the whole length of his body, a bit like Grandma Davis's old bird Baby.

I shake my head, trying to get Ms. Moore's face out of my mind, but something she said in that horrible meeting in her office keeps coming back to me.

"Michael, do you like Marina Vista?" I bite my lip.

"I don't know." He shrugs, serves the ball gently, and I return it.

Well, maybe it's best not to spoil the night anyway. We volley back and forth for a little while, but it's clear that he's distracted. Eventually, I manage to bounce the ball off the net so it rolls onto his side of the court. The avatar crowd hops and cheers for me.

"No," he finally says. "I don't like school. I miss Dr. Matt."

I turn to him, holding the remote in my sweaty hand. "But don't you think your teachers are nice?"

He shakes his head vehemently. "They hate me."

I move toward him, and he takes a few steps away. The only way to comfort him is with words, so I pray for the right thing to say. "Ms. Moore and the other teachers love you as much as Dr. Matt does. And this way you get to live with us. We missed you when you lived in San Francisco."

Michael rocks back and forth, back and forth. "I like it here, but I hate school. I want to stay home, away from those jerks."

I pinch my lips together, my eyes welling up with tears. There has to be a way to get him the help he needs without sending him back to UCSF. I love this kid ferociously.

"Dr. Matt was smart."

I flick a tear off my face and serve the ball to him gently. "We'll figure everything out." He rockets the ball back at me mercilessly and I laugh. This is how I know God is really out there: because I know that it is possible to love someone so much that everything they do is beautiful.

As we settle into a good rhythm again, I pray for Michael to have a smooth return to Marina Vista. I pray that the kids will learn to understand him like I do. I pray for the wisdom and strength to help my brother, and I thank God for these few quiet moments together. Ben, Tom, applications...all the stupid noise of the world. It all fades away when you have a gift as precious as...tennis. Just tennis.

24

stand on Christine's front porch, my hand poised over the doorbell. What if the baby's sleeping? Maybe I should go around back to Christine's studio and see if she's in there first. I lower my hand and start to turn away when the door flies open.

"RILEY!" Emma bounces up and down and claps her hands together. Shhhing comes from the background.

"Come in," Emma says in a slightly quieter voice. "I saw you through the window. What's that? Cookies? I made Santa cookies with my dad last weekend. He's really good at that stuff." I follow her down the hallway, padding across the worn wood floors. "We made the beards out of coconut, and the hats were red sprinkles...." We enter the living room, and Christine smiles at me. "And for the pom-pom at the end of Santa's hat you use a miniature marshmallow. It's sooooo adorable."

"Hi," I say sheepishly. It's almost tradition now that I show up at the Lees over Christmas break unannounced, but I've got a mission today. Of all the girls, Christine is the most likely to understand, so I'm starting with her.

"Couldn't take it anymore?" Christine is sitting on the couch, holding Ellis. He's seven months old now, a full-on toddler who pulls up on everything and scoots across the floor like a turtle, but at the moment he is quiet, his head resting on her shoulder.

"The excitement was too much for Michael." I let the words hang there, not entirely true, but not really false either. Candace bustles around the room, picking up a stack of empty boxes from under the tree, but Christine meets my eye and nods. She can read me better than just about anyone.

"We're gonna head out to the studio," she says, pushing herself up, careful to keep Ellis as still as possible.

"I'll go with you!" Emma runs over to the back door. I wince.

"Emma, I need you in the kitchen," Candace says as she carries the stack of boxes toward the counter.

Emma shakes her head. "You just said we were all done with the cooking." Candace mouths something silently to her, and Emma's eyes goes wide. "Ohhhhh. Right." She winks dramatically across the room. "You need help with that other thing. The one we haven't finished yet. Duh!"

Christine shifts Ellis to her other arm and slides the glass door open.

"Do you want to leave him here?" Candace asks, reaching out her arms for the baby.

"Naw." Christine pokes Ellis in his tummy gently. "After this morning, he'd sleep through the Second Coming."

"Christine, you're totally hogging him again," Emma says as Christine steps outside.

"You get him next. I promise, twerp." Somehow when Christine says 'twerp' it feels more like 'sis,' and Emma beams back at her.

Christine walks slowly across the soft, wet grass, and I

smile at Emma, then follow a few steps behind her. Christine opens the studio door and settles down on the floral couch. I lean against the counter.

"So?"

I don't flinch at her abrupt approach. That's Christine's way.

"I…" I cough and rest my hands on the counter behind me. I remind myself that this is my friend, one of the people who cares most about my happiness. "I don't think I want to go to USC."

"What?" Christine freezes. "What are you talking about?"

"I just…I don't know." I notice a new canvas propped on the easel in the corner, holding a half-finished sketch of Ellis in charcoal. The details are so finely rendered that I have the urge to reach out and pinch his chubby baby legs. "I want to be with you guys and stuff, but when I picture my life next year, I just have a hard time seeing Southern California. And I don't know…." I cross my ankles. "I thought maybe, since you always wanted to go to New York and stuff, you might understand. I mean, is this really what you want?"

"But you have to go to USC." Her eyes are wide, her voice high and a bit panicked. "We're all going there." Christine straightens her brother's legs and settles him against her chest.

"I know, I just—" This was stupid. I thought of all the girls, Christine would at least be a little sympathetic, but all of a sudden I feel like Benedict Arnold. I hang my head, and my eyes focus on the hole in the left knee of my jeans.

"Riley, you have to apply. I'm not going to New York so we can all stay together. You can't back out now."

"I'm not backing out." How do I explain this? How can I

make her understand that I need to figure out what *I* want? "Christine, as long as I've known you, all you've ever wanted was to go to New York. You're really going to give that up?"

"I don't think I can make it without you guys," Christine says quietly. Ellis flutters his eyes a few times and then nuzzles into Christine more. She runs her fingers up and down his back. "We can't split up. You guys are my family."

Christine cradles her brother, and I want to point out that she's holding her family, but I know I can't say that to her. In many ways, I suspect we are closer to Christine than her family. We're a part of her in a way they never can be.

Ellis smacks his lips and sighs. For a minute, we both say nothing and stare at him. If Christine went to New York, she'd be away for months at a time. I wonder how much babies change in a few months. Has she wondered about that too?

"Poor kid. Christmas is pretty exhausting when you have to put everything in your mouth first. Here." She holds him out to me. "Take him."

I slide away. Michael is only two years younger than me, and I was never one for the whole babysitting racket. "I don't think that's such a good idea." I've never even changed a diaper, much less held a baby.

"Go on. He doesn't smell like poop right now." Christine pulls him off her shoulder and begins to hand him to me against my protests. "It's kind of a rare opportunity."

I grab him awkwardly, wondering if I'm supposed to be supporting his head or something, and Christine helps me get him settled in. He barely stirs.

"He's really heavy," I say. I can barely breathe for a moment under his weight.

She shakes her head. "I've tried to tell him to go to the gym, but would he listen? No."

He wiggles, and I worry I'll drop him, but then he cozies up to me in the sweetest way, his little fist balled up around the hem of my T-shirt. My heart soars. "Wow," I whisper.

"He's really pretty rad." Christine beams at me and gently rubs his back. "For a baby, anyway."

I shut my eyes, press my nose to Ellis's head, and inhale the sweetest scent of powder and shampoo and milk. It must be the best smell in the world.

"So you're going to apply, right?" Christine watches me, and I know she won't let this drop until I promise.

"Yes." I run my fingertips over the soft fuzz on his head and try to ignore the twinge in my stomach. "I'll apply."

I wave good-bye to Candace, Christine, and Emma and walk down the driveway to the RealMobile. It's cold and dreary outside, a typical Northern California Christmas Day. While I wait for the heater to warm up in this ancient hunk of junk, I grab my phone out of my purse, scroll down to Ben, and press his name before I lose my nerve. As it rings, I try to figure out what I'm going to say. Do I say I'm sorry? Explain that he misinterpreted things? Do I tell him what's going on with Tom? The truth is, I'm not totally sure what's going on with Tom. I tap my fingers on the steering wheel and wait. The call rings and rings and rings and then dumps into his voice mail. I hang up and drop the phone back into my purse.

I put the van in gear and look over my shoulder, then back out of the driveway slowly. The Christmas lights on Christine's street are starting to flick on in the dying afternoon light. I drive down the street and stop at the corner. There's a plastic light-up nativity set in the front yard just to my right. I smile, then check in the rearview mirror. There's no one behind me. Throwing the car into neutral, I dig my phone back out.

Ben doesn't answer, and this time I'm almost relieved to get his voice mail.

"Hi, Ben, it's me." I clear my throat. Will he know who *me* is? "Riley. I just called to say Merry Christmas, I guess. I'm leaving Christine's house, and she let me hold her baby brother, Ellis. Have you ever actually held a baby before? Their cheeks stick out really far like they have food stuffed inside them, like chipmunks. And their feet don't even look made for walking. They're all round and...This is a stupid message. Whatever. I was just thinking about you and your family. I hope you guys are having a merry Christmas."

25

make my way down the shore, my eyes trained on the water, lugging my heavy surfboard under my arm. And though I'm cold, and the stupid wet suit is kind of pinching my armpits, and the wet, rocky sand stings my bare feet, I feel myself relaxing more and more with each footprint in the sand.

I wade into the ocean and am hit with the cold shock of the water seeping into my suit. Keep moving. If I keep moving, the layer trapped near my skin will warm up. I lie flat on my board and begin to paddle out as fast as I can, keeping my eyes on the horizon. A slow round wave carries me up, and I swim hard to get over it, splashing water up into my hair. Finally, I get out beyond the breaking point, where the water gently rises and swells, and push myself up to a sitting position, letting my legs dangle in the icy water. The pounding of the waves against the sand sounds distant and muffled.

There's a group of surfers up the shore a ways, but on this cold December morning, the water is mostly empty. There's no one near me, and it feels good. I'm not supposed to surf alone, and after the accident I didn't do it for a while, but it's been a couple years since my parents checked up on it. They don't even know about that day I almost drowned. It's not that I tried to keep it from them; if they ever wanted to know about it, I'd tell them, but it's been a long time since they asked what was going on with me.

I look out over the endless gray water. Somewhere out there, across many miles of open water, there's another life for me. There's college, a whole world away from this place. All I have to do is finish those applications, and in a few months I'll be out of here.

A swell moves beneath me, and I hold onto my board, but it passes, drives on through, growing and gaining speed as it races to shore. I gaze toward the sand, listening to the soft splash of water as it bumps against my board.

I should go in. I should go home and get started. I should grow up, stop whining about the attention my little brother gets, and fill out the stupid applications. It will make them happy. I'll be doing the right thing. But for some reason, I can't make myself move.

I whisper a prayer for guidance, for wisdom, for help. I ask God to help me do the right thing, but the only answer is another gentle swell rolling my way.

I'll go in soon. For now, this—just me and God and the waves—is what I need.

26

"Bye, Mom!" I call through the kitchen, then swing open the door to the garage as fast as I can. *Don't look back. Just don't look back.*

"Where are you going?" She comes around the corner at lightning speed, and I freeze.

"I told you. I'm going to San Francisco to see the fireworks with the girls." Zoe has been on one of her missions. It's our last New Year's Eve, so she wanted us to spend it together. We decided on a night in the city, just the four of us.

"You did?" Mom presses her hands to her face and rubs her temples in circles. She's been so stressed out trying to figure out what to do with Michael she wouldn't notice if I told her my hair was on fire. Right now she's thinking of homeschooling him next semester, which is utterly crazy because Mom can barely explain how to turn the DVD player on.

"I did. See you later then." I open the door and nearly have it shut when she puts her foot in the crack.

"Wait, one more thing. What about your applications?" Her lipstick has faded away, and only her lip liner is left.

A familiar tightening grabs my throat, but I force myself to relax and try to breathe normally. "They're not due till the day after tomorrow. I have a few more days on a couple of them." There's no reason to panic. I have actually made some progress on the Common Application, which is accepted at like half the schools on my list.

Mom plants her hands on her hips, and I notice that her manicure is chipped and peeling. "Riley, you were supposed to have them done before you went out tonight. Are they done or not?" Mom holds out her hand like she's going to take my keys.

I glance out the door to the RealMobile. The girls are depending on me to drive tonight. "They're done," I blurt out before I can stop myself. Instantly my stomach feels wobbly. Why did I say such a stupid thing? I can't take it back now, but I've never lied to Mom before.

"You didn't need money to pay the application fees?" Mom studies my face.

"I have my credit card. I figured it was best to put the fees on that." A plan forms in my brain, a way to make this only a half lie and keep her happy. "And truthfully"—I put a hand on my heart—"they're not officially turned in yet."

"Riley!" She shakes her head at me and takes the keys out of my hand.

"But they're done. Well, not done-done. But mostly done. I'm going to..." Dad comes into the kitchen and peers over at us. "Ms. Moore always says to sleep on stuff so the mistakes pop out. I'll turn them in after I give them one last read through. No sweat."

Mom's shoulders relax. "And you're sure they'll be turned in tomorrow?"

I can finish them up tomorrow. I'm going to have to cut Brown, Cornell, and Amherst from the list, but I wasn't really interested in them anyway. "No problem. I promise." I'll tell her I decided to narrow down my choices after she's excited that I turned in the others and visions of Harvard are dancing in her head.

"And it is New Year's Eve, honey." Dad winks at me from behind her back, and I beam at him. He grabs Mom and kisses her on the cheek.

Mom sighs and shrugs. "Okay. Drive safely, and don't get in too late." She hands my keys back.

For the first hour, I distract myself by picking up the girls and finding my way to the city through the horrendous holiday traffic. During the second hour, while we sip hot chocolate in a café, a tiny agitating spur grows in the bottom of my stomach. As we walk down Market Street toward the Ferry Building, the spur grows into an ulcer that tears at my insides. By the time we hit hour four, I am in such agony that I want to go home, tell my mother what I did, and throw myself on the floor in front of her and beg for mercy. But now it's only twenty short minutes until the stupid fireworks will be over and I can go home and face the music. Anything will be better than this.

At the Ferry Building, the air is jubilant. Street performers are singing, playing keyboards, and doing creepy puppet shows and magic tricks.

"This was such a good idea!" Zoe grabs me in a hug.

I smile and try to remind myself to enjoy moments like this. Who knows where we will be next year on New Year's Eve?

Christine starts to wander off to look at a stack of paintings some guy is selling from a cart on the street, and Zoe runs after her.

"What time do the fireworks start again?" I scan the crowded waterfront.

"*Midnight*." Ana shakes her head at me. "Is everything okay?"

I slap my head and laugh. "I meant to ask what time it is, not when do they start. I'm losing it."

"Soon." Ana checks her phone. "We should find a spot now." Ana peers through the crowd at Zoe and Christine and waves at them. Zoe drags Christine away from the street artist, and they head back toward us, but they are sidetracked by a kettle-corn booth. "You ready for this?"

"For the fireworks?" I cock my eyebrow at her.

"For all of it." She loops her arm in mine, and I allow her to lead me in the general direction of the waterfront, where the fireworks will be. We walk slowly so Christine and Zoe can catch up. "For this new year and everything it's going to bring. For life to really start." I turn my head to glance at her. Ana is looking up at the sky, her eyes glazed with excitement.

Is that really how she sees it? Maybe for her next year will be a chance to start living the life she's always wanted, away from her overprotective parents, but where does that leave us?

The noisy streets are thick with half-drunk college students and families with screaming kids. Zoe and Christine jog to catch up to us, ducking through gaps here and there and spilling kettle corn as they go. It's funny. Maybe it's the huge, pressing crowd or their giddiness, but we're having a tough time sticking together tonight. Every time I turn around, we're missing a Miracle Girl.

"Soo…" Ana nudges me. "Where's Tom tonight?"

"He's out with some friends." I shrug.

"Who?"

"Some guys from college." I look away. The truth is, I don't exactly know who he's with. All he told me is that he was going out with friends tonight, and since I already had plans anyway—and it's not like we're officially boyfriend and girlfriend or anything—it didn't seem right to press him on it.

She cuts her eyes at me. "Don't you think it's weird that he never asks you to hang out with his friends?"

"Nah." I sidestep a dog in a fancy sweater. "They're in college. They don't want to hang out with a high schooler." I keep my voice steady. On top of the big lie I told Mom earlier, this barely even feels untrue.

Ana shakes her head. "You're addicted to him, Riley. You don't even see the way he—"

Just then Zoe comes up alongside us, gasping for air. "Don't you think we'd have a better view farther away from the railing?"

"Does anyone else notice I'm still here?" Christine calls from behind me. She skips to catch up.

Ana keeps her eyes focused on mine for a minute, then smiles a little sadly, shakes her head, and turns to Zoe. "There's a decent spot over there." Ana points at a small break in the crowd near the end of one of the piers. She turns toward it, and we follow her, our natural leader.

"Christine, where's Tyler tonight?" I say quickly and paste a smile on my face.

"He has a show." Christine digs her hand into the popcorn bag and tosses some kernels into her mouth. "Plus, I don't believe in kissing in public, which is what this whole stupid holiday is about."

"Christine!" Ana grabs her head like she has a headache.

We reach the end of a long, low concrete block meant for sitting and plop down.

"What?" Christine kicks her Chucks out in front and lets them slam against the hard concrete block. "Between the stupid mistletoe and the end-of-the-year countdown, I spent December avoiding Tyler."

"And Dean was busy. He had a thing," Zoe says, catching me off guard. A strange shadow crosses her face, but it passes quickly.

"A thing?" We'd be the first to know if something was going on with them, wouldn't we?

"He wanted to edit his film one last time before the USC application is due." Her easy smile returns to her face, and I shake off what I thought I saw. "Mine's in already. Maybe if everything goes right, this won't be our last New Year's Eve together after all."

My stomach sinks. The last thing I want to talk about now is those stupid applications. "Hey, only one minute until the fireworks," I say to distract them. I hold up my phone, showing them the time.

Ana leans forward to look at Zoe. "What was your essay about for USC?"

"Dreamy thought I should write about the horses." Zoe fidgets with a bracelet she bought at one of the booths. "But I'm kind of horsed out, so I decided to write about my grandma and the stories she tells about living in the log cabin."

"I wrote about how Maria's lupus is getting worse," Ana

says. "And what it's like to not be able to help someone you love. It took forever, but I based it on the one I wrote for Princeton." She stares wistfully into the dark night, which is surprisingly clear for a city known for its fog. "And then I had to organize all my recommendation letters. I thought Ms. Moore was going to kill me. She had to write, like, twenty letters."

Christine puts a hand in their faces. "You guys can't complain to me right now. Do you have any idea how hard it was to get high-res photos of my work uploaded to my application? Their Web site hates Macs."

"Thirty seconds!" I say and point out toward the water, but no one turns. The crowd is buzzing with excitement.

"Did you go with something about Michael?" Ana asks, nudging me.

I swallow. Can I tell them the truth—that I haven't even gotten an outline of my essay done? That all I've done is fill in the informational blanks? The crowd begins to chant the countdown numbers in unison. For some reason it feels like a bomb ticking down my last seconds.

"Five."

All three girls stare at me, oblivious to the excitement around us. How do I tell them I haven't even bothered to apply to the one school we thought could hold us together? What kind of friend does that?

"Four."

The milliseconds seem to creep by, and I can barely get enough air in my lungs.

"Cheerleader"—Christine stares at me—"you turned it in, right?"

"Three."

And then as if a centrifugal force beyond my control is pulling me, I feel myself do it again. It's only a little nod, a small signal of assent, but they all seem to relax. And then, before I know what's happening, it's the new year.

The crowd around us breaks into cheers, and soon we're hugging each other and screaming at the top of our lungs, and they seem to have forgotten my stupid essay topic, and applications, and Tom, and tomorrow, and forever. We sling our arms over each others' shoulders and huddle close against the damp night air as the fireworks burst over our heads.

I have the incredible urge to hide my face from the girls. Lying to your parents is one thing. Lying to your adopted sisters, the best friends you've ever had, is definitely another.

"This is our best New Year's Eve yet!" Zoe tears up, and I make a decision. I'll go home and get my applications done, and no one will ever have to know that I lied. I'll do the USC one first. No, the Ivies are all due on the second, so I'll do Harvard first. Those are the only two that *have* to get done. The rest are icing on the cake. I'll bet I can knock out four tonight alone, and there's still all day tomorrow. It'll be no sweat if I stay focused.

A loud, fast firework screeches through the air, and we all turn our eyes up to the heavens in time to see a tiny spark explode into a million golden points of light.

27

ey, Mom?" My feet slide across the floorboards as I head down the hall. She's been on the computer all day looking into different homeschooling curriculums for Michael. I have my own computer in my room, so I can work on my applications anyway, thank goodness, but I ran into a snag. A small setback.

"In here," Mom calls from the office, her voice muffled.

Okay, I'm panicking. Transcripts. I was supposed to have my school send transcripts. And there's this whole part of the Harvard application that I was supposed to have my school counselor fill out. The transcripts I can maybe get sent out first-thing tomorrow, and I could probably make it look like the school forgot to mail them or something. But the counselor thing...My guidance counselor is Mrs. Canning, and she's hated me ever since we broke into the school last year. Plus, she's clearly not Guidance Counselor of the Year. Isn't it her job to tell me about stuff like this?

"I have a question." Okay, I have to be honest. I have to tell her I lied. Then she'll know how to make it better. Moms always know what to do.

"Mmm-hmm?" Mom doesn't look up from the computer screen. The room is dark. The sun set an hour ago, but apparently she didn't notice. I wait for her to acknowledge me, but she doesn't.

"I had a question…" My voice trails off, and Mom doesn't look away from the screen. "About my applications."

"I thought they were done?" She leans in closer to the screen.

"They are. Almost. There's a…a tiny thing I could use your help with."

"Sure." Mom's usually perfect hair is plastered to the side of her head. "I'm almost done here."

"Um…" I press one foot down on top of the other and try to keep the panic out of my voice. "If you could come now, that would be—"

"While you're here…" She clicks the mouse a few times and opens her e-mail inbox. "Are you close with Asha Nayar? She's younger than you, right?"

"What?" A sinking feeling settles in my stomach. "I know her. Why?"

Mom smoothes her forehead with her thumb and forefinger. "Oh, I don't know. Mrs. Vandekamp is organizing some meeting or something about her." She clicks the screen closed and sighs. "Honestly I don't know where these women find the time. It's like I'm the only mother who—"

Mom's new timer goes off in the kitchen, and Michael shrieks. He's not used to the sound, and it's freaked him out every time it's gone off since Christmas.

"That's it! That stupid piece of junk goes in the garbage!" Mom stands up and rushes to the doorway. "I'm sorry, Riley," she calls as she brushes past me into the hall. "I'll be with you in a few minutes, okay?" She reaches Michael in the living room as the noise gets to earsplitting decibels.

I stand still, staring at the empty spot where my mom used to be. I know she didn't mean to shove me aside like that, to choose Michael over me, but for the first time since I was a kid, I really need her help.

I try to fight the panic rising in me. She'll be back. Mom will help me figure out what to do. But as I stand there in the hallway, waiting for my brother's shrieks to die down, it doesn't feel true. If I can't even get her attention now, in a real-life emergency, will I ever be able to? I'm way too young to not need my parents. But the longer I stare at the empty chair, the more clear it becomes that as far as family goes, I'm on my own. There's only one adult who can help me now.

She's a counselor at school, so that counts. And she already offered to help. I know if I called her right now, she'd drop everything to come over and fill out the forms Harvard needs. She'd do it for me.

I head back to my room to call Ms. Moore. At least there is one person I can count on.

28

"You've got to be kidding me," I grumble into my backpack. I forgot my cheerleading sneakers at home, so I'm going to be cheering on the Varsity basketball team in—I look down—knee-high suede boots. I roll my eyes, zip the stupid backpack closed, and trudge to the door. I think there might be a pair of beat-up sneakers somewhere in the back of my car. I'll have to go check.

"Riley!"

I march into the thick hallway traffic and make a beeline for the parking lot. If I hurry, I'll have a few minutes to sit there and collect my thoughts. I exit the breezeway and walk out into the cold January day.

"Riley McGee."

I grit my teeth. Well if it isn't Little Miss Never Calls Back. Just great. Exactly what I need right now.

"There you are!" Ms. Moore trots up to my side, out of breath. "I've been chasing you for five minutes. Didn't you hear me calling you?"

I keep my eyes trained ahead, scanning the lot for my car. "No, I didn't hear you calling me. In fact, I didn't hear you calling me last night either."

Ms. Moore's eyes go dull and hard. "I went to a reading in San Francisco and didn't get home until late." She draws her mouth into a thin line. "Tell me something, Riley. What do you think it means when a student calls you hours before their applications are due?"

I pick out the teal top of the RealMobile in the parking lot.

"I ask because last night I stayed up, tossing and turning, thinking about what that could mean." She plants her hands on her hips, and her face goes red. "You know, the only thing I could think of was: she didn't get her applications done." Ms. Moore puts a hand on my shoulder. It's a tight pinching grip.

I finally turn back to her, my eyes watering. "Can't you do something?" I whisper. She's the one with all those connections at Harvard.

Her nostrils flare slightly. "I can't."

I roll my eyes up to the sky and feel them fill with tears. My nose stings.

"Life is not always served up on a silver platter, but I hate that you had to learn it this way." She releases my shoulder and looks for a moment like she's going to hug me. "Even you, even someone as talented and blessed as you, have to work hard at the things you want."

I turn on my heels, ignoring her calls, and dart through the crowd. The January wind stings my nose and rushes past my ears with a high-pitched whine. I've been trying to bite back the tears, trying to ignore the truth, but here in this busy parking lot, I can no longer ignore it: I failed.

I'm crying by the time I get to my turquoise monstrosity, blinded by the tears streaming from my eyes. I grab the door handle and pull. The heavy door creaks open. Before you can drive, you look forward to a car as a way to get from one place to another. After you get a car, you realize it's so much more than that. Your car is a locker, a hangout, a sanctuary. I throw my backpack onto the floor, pull the door shut, and wipe the tears away with the sleeve of my sweater. I rest my head against the steering wheel and reach down, feeling around on the carpeted floor. There's a box of tissues around here somewhere. I knock a cardboard party hat from New Year's out of the way and find the box wedged under the seat.

I tried to make it right. I really did. I tried to get the applications in, just like they wanted me to. But when Ms. Moore didn't call me back, I realized there was nothing I could do. Without her help, my applications would be incomplete—no matter how hard I worked on the other sections.

And in a weird way, knowing that it's too late now almost feels like a relief. Somehow, by refusing to make a choice, I finally decided. I'm not going to Harvard—or Princeton or USC or anywhere else. Those schools were never my dream anyway. Tom saw that all along. They were always about someone else. No matter what my parents wanted for me, it's out of their hands now. There are probably some colleges that are still accepting applications, but I'm not really interested in finding out. College isn't for everyone, after all.

A girl from my math class walks by, talking into her cell phone, but she doesn't notice me slumped over the wheel of the car, and a moment later she's climbed into her car and is driving away. I let out a breath when she's gone.

I'm not really sad about not going to Harvard or USC, but knowing that I failed the people who were counting on me most, that's what kills. I pull a tissue out of the box and run it under my nose. I can't go home. I can't go to Ana's house or call up Christine and see what she's up to. I can't face them.

Maybe I'll sit here in the parking lot all night. I could stretch out on the backseat and sleep there, and...

Someone raps on the window, and I freeze. There is no one I want to talk to right now. The noise comes again, a light knock on the passenger-side window, and I keep my face squashed up against the steering wheel, but turn it a little to the right. Under my arm, I can barely make out a face, pressed up against the glass. I turn my head back and reach for the door-lock button, but it's too late. The door opens, and a rush of cool air comes into the car.

Ben settles into the passenger seat without a word. I peek up at him out of the corner of my eye. He swings his bag around so it rests on his lap, and then he slides down in the seat and props his feet up on the dashboard. His dusty old Vans have a couple new holes in them. He folds his hands in his lap and closes his eyes.

"Are you okay?" His words are nice enough, but he feels distant for some reason.

I gulp for air, trying to stifle my tears, and keep my head down. I didn't invite him in, and no way am I going to let this guy see my puffy swollen face. The only sound is the hard, empty thump of a basketball hitting the pavement on the courts by the gym.

"I wanted to let you know I have some new decal designs," Ben says finally. He clicks a plastic buckle, and there's a rustling sound while he digs around in his bag. He pulls a sticker out of his messenger bag and holds it out to me. I reach for it, and from here it looks like...I lift my head up a few inches, careful to let my long hair drape down in a curtain between me and Ben. It's a girl in a short skirt and a cape, long blond hair streaming behind her, one arm raised triumphantly. The word *Supergirl* is spelled out in funky type across the bottom. He peels the slick paper backing off and carefully presses it to the dashboard, just above the glove compartment. Supergirl is smiling and happy. Something about this is so completely off base that it makes me laugh.

"My mom is going to kill me for that."

"No she isn't." He leans toward me and slowly, gently, reaches his hand out and rests it on my knee. "Tell her old Ben gave it to you. Moms love the Ben."

I smile. He's probably right. My imminent doom has nothing to do with this harmless sticker. I feel myself moving, inching toward him.

"Hey, Riley?"

I turn toward him, and before I know what he's doing, he ducks his head and presses his lips against mine. I freeze, trying to figure out what to do, but he reaches behind me and gently rests his hand on the back of my neck, pulling me toward him. I start to pull away, but then let my lips part, just a little, and he lets out a small sigh. His lips are warm and soft, and I feel myself slipping closer to him. The air inside the car is still and quiet.

Suddenly Ben pulls back. My lips feel cold for a moment, and I want to kiss again, but when I lean forward, he unlatches his seat belt and throws the door open.

"That's the other thing I came for," Ben says, stepping out onto the blacktop. "To see if you felt that way too. Because I saw you at the Living Nativity. I saw you with that guy and saw that you don't want to be with him. And then you called me on Christmas, as if you wanted to talk, so I wanted to check, because if you did like me"—he turns back and stares into my eyes—"and apparently you do"—he slips his bag over his shoulder—"you should choose me or leave me alone."

I blink my eyes and watch through the open door as Ben dips his head against the wind, pulls his jacket tighter around him, and walks away across the parking lot.

I crumple against the steering wheel. "Hey, God, are you trying to kill me today?"

I reach over and pull the door shut. I don't need the whole school knowing I've lost my mind on top of everything else.

29

So, Dean, I hear you sailed the mighty seas last week." I step around a puddle in the middle of the path and take a deep breath. The air smells clean and piney, especially after working in the barn all day. Zoe's parents have always wanted to run a horseback-riding business in the woods in her backyard, and with the money from her brother Nick's Christmas bonus this year, it looks like it may finally happen. It's going to take a ton of elbow grease, though, which is why they organized a workday today. Ana and Christine left a while ago, and Mom is picking me up soon. I wouldn't be here at all if Mom knew about my college applications, but I'm going to tell her, obviously. Soon. It's just a timing thing.

"Yeah." Dean laughs, then clears his throat. He holds back a branch at the side of the path so Zoe can pass. "What about you? What'd you do over the break?"

"Oh—" I wave his question aside. "I really didn't do much of anything." That statement is truer than they realize. "But I don't want to talk about my boring vacation. I want to hear about your trip. I can't believe you sailed all the way to Mexico."

"It sounded *so* cool," Zoe says, picking up her pace. "His uncle's boat is huge—like, twice as big as his mom's—and they sailed down the coast and stopped at all these cool places on the way." Zoe reaches for Dean's hand and threads her fingers through his. "It sounds like a dream vacation to me, but Dean's family does stuff like that all the time, right, Dean?"

"It was fun." Dean glances at Zoe and smiles awkwardly at me. "But—yeah." He presses his lips together and casts his eyes around. He's obviously trying to change the subject, and my stomach sinks as I realize why. Dean's family is quite well-off. I never really thought about how that might affect his relationship with Zoe.

"I can't believe your parents are finally opening their horseback-riding company," I say quickly.

"Yeah, it's exciting." She swings her hand, making Dean's arm swing too. "But it's not as cool as *Mexico*." She laughs and elbows Dean, and I can't tell whether she doesn't realize that Dean is uncomfortable or whether she's just putting on a really good show of pretending she doesn't notice. It's like she's trying too hard to prove that the money doesn't matter. As we walk, she tells me all about the luxurious accommodations Dean's family enjoyed on the boat, and Dean nods silently a few times. I'm almost relieved when we get to the house.

"I'm gonna wash my hands," I say as we step inside the sliding-glass door. I watch as Zoe nods and leads Dean toward the living room. They *look* so right together, like they were made for each other, and yet, something doesn't feel right. I round the counter and see Dreamy chopping carrots on the scarred countertop.

"Hey there." She waves the knife as a greeting. "What a day." She shakes her head, and her long graying hair swishes around her shoulders.

"It's exciting though," I say and run my hands under the faucet.

Dreamy smiles, and her eyes get misty. "Ed and I have been talking about opening this business since before we were married." She chuckles a little. "Isn't it funny how life never quite works out the way you expect?"

I pull a paper towel off a roll next to the sink and think back over the last few months. I don't know that I'd call it *funny*.

"So what schools did you end up applying to?" Dreamy smiles, and for a split second I wonder how she knows. But she seems to be genuinely curious, not actually probing into the depths of my mind, so I relax.

"Well," I say slowly. The fine lines around Dreamy's eyes crinkle as she focuses on me. How much can I really tell her? She's a mom, so she's obligated to freak out. But then again, she's the one who convinced me that college might not be in the cards. "Do you remember what you said a few months ago about waiting? You know, to make sure you know what you're doing before wasting money on school?"

Dreamy's brow creases, and she lays her knife down. "I don't think that's what I said exactly. What happened?"

I bunch up the paper towel in my hand. "Remember how you were trying to convince Zoe to take some time off? Or to go to City College or whatever?" I barely register the sound of a car pulling into the driveway.

"Goodness gracious." Dreamy's eyes go wide, and she shakes her head. "Don't tell me you didn't apply after all."

I freeze, my mouth hanging open. Why does she seem so shocked all of a sudden?

The doorbell rings, and footsteps move toward the entryway.

"Oh, honey." Dreamy steps forward, and the smell of patchouli hits my nose. She wraps her arms around me in a weird hug. "I hope I didn't say anything to make you..." Her voice trails off. "I wasn't saying all that stuff for *you*. I was trying to convince Zoe. I didn't mean..." She takes a deep breath and pulls back. "You have so much, Riley. So many opportunities and so many unique skills. I only meant..." She studies my face, and I have the strangest urge to cover it with my hands. "I never meant for you not to apply to college because of that."

"Excuse me?"

I turn my head. *Mom.* She's standing in the entrance to the kitchen, next to Zoe, her eyes wide. "What did you say?" She's talking to Dreamy, but she's staring at me.

"Michelle, we need to—" Dreamy opens and closes her mouth.

"Who didn't apply to college?" Mom's face is white. "Zoe?" Her voice suddenly sounds hopeful.

Zoe's face has gone white too, and her mouth is hanging open.

"Um..." I let out a long breath. I really don't want to die today, but I'm not quite sure how to get out of this. "Okay. So." I shoot Dreamy a panicked look, and she shakes her head. Great. It looks like I have to be the one to say something. "Well, the truth is, I kind of didn't quite get those applications in like I thought I was going to." Mom puts a hand on the counter as if to brace herself. "But I was talking to Dreamy a while back, and she pointed out how college isn't for everyone, and I kind of thought maybe I might take a year off and—"

"You told her *what*?" Mom turns to face Dreamy.

Dreamy takes a step back. "You have . . . I had no idea that she would . . . I am so, so terribly sorry." Dreamy's voice is high-pitched and strained. "That's not at all what I meant to convey. I was trying to explain to *Zoe* that people can do fine without a college edu—"

"I can't be*lieve* this." Mom puts her hand to her head. "You told Riley she didn't need to go to college?!" Her voice is angry, but her face looks stunned. "You told *my* daughter that?"

"Mom, she was just trying—" I jump in, but Mom isn't listening. A lump forms in my throat.

"How could you do that?" Mom says, glaring at me, and all I want to do is sink into the floor. She turns back to Dreamy. "They're only kids."

I stiffen. I'll be eighteen soon—fully an adult—but in some ways, Mom's suggestion that I am a kid who didn't know any better feels good, like an absolution.

"Let's go." I pull on her arm and turn her toward the door.

Mom doesn't respond. She's staring at Dreamy, and all I can think about is a nature show Michael watched one time, where a grizzly bear threatened to rip a photographer limb from limb to protect her cub.

"I didn't mean to cause problems," Dreamy finally says, her voice warbling. "I can see now that I did. And for that I'm very sorry." Her eyes start to water, and Mom's shoulders relax a little. "But I'm not sure that . . ." Dreamy takes a deep breath, and I wait for her to go on, but she seems to reconsider. She crosses her arms over her chest. "Well, I apologize. We'll leave it at that."

Mom doesn't respond. Finally I turn and walk past Mom, toward the door. Zoe reaches out her hand as I walk by, but I pretend I don't notice.

"Riley—"

I brush past her and out the front door. My van is parked in a precise right angle to the house. I throw open the side door and scramble into the seat where Michael is waiting, like I knew he would be.

I don't know why I do it, but I lean my head gently against his shoulder, and he doesn't shrink away. Maybe somewhere deep in that beautifully complicated mind of his, he understands that I need this. Mom gets in and starts the car without looking back at us, and my brother and I sit there together on the dark padded bench, not saying a word the whole way home.

30

F amily meeting."

Mom's long shadow falls across the wooden floor, her frame silhouetted by the bright glow from the hallway. She flicks on my light, and I put a pillow over my face. I've been hiding here ever since we got home from Zoe's.

"Now."

Her heavy steps fade as I try to find the strength to pull myself out of bed. Somehow, until that moment at Zoe's, I don't think the reality of what I did had sunk in, but Mom's reaction said it all.

I drag myself out of bed and glance at the clock. It reads 8:15. I blink at it, almost unable to comprehend the digits. It's not that I fear what they'll do to me. Any punishment they could give would be a joke compared to how I'm making myself feel. It's more that I don't want to face them. By now Dad, Michael, and all of the Miracle Girls know what I've done, and I've never felt so small.

I trudge down the hall, trying to remember the last family meeting we had. Was it when the doctors gave a name to Michael's problems? Surely not. When Mom decided to become a real-estate agent?

Mom and Dad are perched on one couch, watching my

every move, and Michael is sitting on the floor, staring into space. I slump down on the other couch and bore my eyes into the wide leather ottoman. I wrap my arms around my body and squeeze hard, trying to collapse into myself.

"Riley has an announcement." Mom gestures with her hands, giving me the floor.

My eyes flash from her face to Dad's. Did she really not tell them herself? "You're an adult." Her clenched jaw shows what a struggle it is for her to hold it together. "Tell your father what...happened."

It didn't just happen. That's the problem. I wish I could blame someone else, point to Michael or my parents or Tom, anything, but there's no one to blame but me.

"Riley?" Dad grabs anxiously at his sweatpants. "What's going on, honey?"

"I..." My throat clogs with emotion. "Something happened at Zoe's." How did I let it come to this? I'm the girl who dreamed of getting out of this Podunk town and making my way somewhere else, somewhere with skyscrapers and art galleries and poetry readings. Mom stares at her lap, apparently unable to look at me.

"No matter what you have to say, it's going to be okay." Dad's cool blue eyes peer back at me, strong and steady.

I say a quick prayer for strength and decide to just come out with it. "I didn't turn my applications in. I missed the deadline."

He bolts to his feet and begins to pace in front of the entertainment center. Michael starts to rock back and forth on the floor, and Mom covers her face with her hands.

"That's impossible." Dad stops and turns to me. "We asked if you had them done before New Year's, and you said yes."

My eyes go blurry for a second, but I force myself to stay focused. "I said they weren't quite done and I *meant* to get them done."

"No, no, no, no." Dad scratches his head. "Well, this can be fixed, obviously. Riley's sorry now, and we can make this better."

"Jack." Mom pushes herself off the couch and puts a hand on his shoulder. "I've been working through it since I found out." She glances at me, then turns away quickly. "It's over for now. There's next year, maybe even next semester at some schools, but for now, it's over."

Mom's right. There are probably some state colleges that would take me, but the Ivy League has slipped through my fingers, just like that. It would be better to wait and try next year.

My hands begin to ache, and I realize I'm clenching my fists. I open them and press them into the couch, trying to remember to breathe. Michael's rhythmic rocking moves in and out of my peripheral view.

Dad's shoulders buckle, and he lets out a long, deep sigh. Mom whispers something gentle and soothing to him, and for a second I can picture them as college students, young and in love.

"I'm so sorry," I manage through my tear-choked voice. "I've been having a hard time. I'm not sure what I want or where . . . I couldn't do it." I gasp a few times for air. "I didn't mean to hurt you, but I couldn't make myself work on them."

Dad sits down again and grabs his hair in big clumps. His bald spot stares back at me. It first started to show last year, and something about it makes me even sadder.

"Everything is going to be fine." Mom places a firm hand on Michael's knee. He stops rocking and stares blankly.

Dad doesn't seem to hear her. "Does this have anything to do with Tom?" The tendons in his arms work, rising in long, taut threads. "Ever since he came back around—"

"Dad." I raise my voice, but not in anger—more to snap him out of it. I lean forward and give him a pleading look. "This had nothing to do with Tom. It's about me and my issues."

"I'm sure it will all be fine." Mom directs her homily squarely at the hardwood floor. "In the morning, we'll think about our options, but for now, it's best if we go to bed. Everything will look better tomorrow."

I find myself staring at her spot on the floor. One minute of silence bleeds into the next, all of us listening to the faint hum of the heater. Has it always been this loud? How do we go about our daily lives and not hear it?

"Sorry, Riley," Michael blurts out.

"Thank you," I whisper, and tears begin to roll down my face. He leaves the room without acknowledging me, and I cry harder.

Mom follows after Michael, as if to comfort him, but she goes straight to the master suite instead.

They had so much faith in me, and I blew it. I understand that. But I've also never been so humbled by regret in my life. Doesn't that count for something?

"It's late," Dad announces to no one at all. He rises and heads for the back of the house too.

Mom and Dad need time to process what I've done. I know they love me no matter what. They must have said it a million times when we were growing up. But as I trudge to my room in the dark, it's hard to make myself believe it.

31

The noise from the gym grows fainter as I make my way through the parking lot. The basketball game lasted longer than usual, but that means it trimmed a few hours off my unbearable evening at home, so it's all right with me.

An automatic light flickers on over the parking lot as the cold January night settles in. I look at the RealMobile, then pause. Christine's boxy silver Volvo and Ana's candy-apple red Audi are parked next to my car. Why are they still here? Classes ended hours ago. I got to school late and avoided them at lunch and thought I had made it through the day without facing them, but I squint and can see them lounging on the hoods of their cars.

An ambush. I adjust my bag. There's no way to avoid them now if I want to get to my car. I sigh and head toward them.

"Hey," I say quietly as I approach the circle. Ana is leaning against her car with her arms crossed over her chest, and Zoe and Christine are lying on the hood of the Volvo staring up at the sky. Their arms are splayed, and they appear to have been hunkered down for the long haul.

I wait for one of them to say something, but no one does. I zip up my cheerleading hoodie to fight off the chill.

"Guys, I'm really sorry."

Ana shows me a weak smile, giving me the strength to try to push forward. "I really, really meant to apply to USC, but I choked."

Christine hops off the hood and levels her eyes on me. "Why didn't you come talk to us? Let us help you?" Her voice gets louder at the end.

"I tried to..." Did I? All year they reached out to me, did everything they could think of, but I kept pushing them away. Why did I do that?

"No you didn't." She takes a few steps toward me. "Why can't you accept help? That's what I don't get."

"Christine." Ana moves toward her and touches her shoulder gently. "Riley's sorry."

"She *should* be sorry." Christine turns back to me, her eyes narrowed. "You messed everything up, all of our plans."

"Christine." I don't know what else to say, so I let the word hang in the air. I peer around her and try to see Zoe's face, but she's still staring up at the sky, as if she can't hear what's going on.

"She didn't mess up *everything*." Ana gives me a sympathetic smile, and it seems like the nicest thing anyone's ever done. "And she's trying to apologize."

She, she, she. The way they're talking about me makes it sound like I'm not here, but I try to ignore that. "Guys, I'm so sorry." I push my fists down deep in my hoodie pockets. "You have no idea how wretched I feel. I'm sorry for lying, I'm sorry for—"

"And why are you avoiding us?" Christine takes a few steps backward, putting more space between us again. "We shouldn't have to hear about this from Zoe and then wait for you in the parking lot."

Zoe sits forward into the light, and I see the tears streaming down her face. It feels like a punch in the gut. Christine is mad, but she'll cool off; hurting someone as pure and loyal as Zoe—that's low. How can I ever forgive myself? Are they going to be able to forgive me?

"Christine, knock it off." Ana throws her hands up in the air. "We're Miracle Girls, and that means that we forgive, no matter what. We've forgiven you plenty of times."

Christine starts to say something else, but nothing comes out.

"No, it's okay. She's right," I say quietly. "I've been a bad friend, but I didn't do this to hurt you on purpose." They all turn their faces toward me, and I look down. "That's the last thing in the world I'd want to do. I'm going through something...." Zoe wipes a tear away, and I almost lose it myself. "But I should have reached out to you guys for help. I don't know why I couldn't. I think I told myself you wouldn't understand, but maybe I thought you'd look at me differently."

"You did the best you could." Ana walks over to Zoe, sits on the hood of the Volvo, and puts an arm around her. "I know you wouldn't hurt us intentionally."

Christine turns her back to me and crosses her arms over her chest. She stares at the school gates in silence.

I guess I always thought USC was Zoe's dream, but somehow during this year, it became Christine's too.

"I couldn't picture myself at USC. Well, at any college,

really." I shake my head. "I really wish I could take it back, take everything back, and apply this time. I don't want to lose you guys."

"But it's too late," Christine says quietly without turning around.

32

Tom gets off work in five minutes, so I'm standing outside Velo Rouge Café trying to look nonchalant. An
old bicycle hangs over the entrance and several skinny
bikers with scraggly beards are smoking outside. The lights
inside the café go off, and I brush my fingers through my hair
and stand up straight. A moment later the door opens, and
Tom steps out, laughing, followed by a girl with long curly
hair. She grabs his arm and pulls him back toward the door,
then turns and slips a key into the front door. Tom swats her
playfully. I clear my throat.

"Tom?"

He blinks, and then his face breaks into a smile. "Riley!"
He waves for me to come closer. "What are you doing here?"

"I wanted to talk to you," I say, trying not to let the horror
show in my face. Who is this girl? She seems older, like she's in
college, and they looked mighty friendly there a minute ago.

"Riley, this is Jen." Tom slips his arm around my shoulder.
"She's my manager, and we close together. Jen, Riley."

Jen puts her key into her pocket and gives me a halfhearted
smile. "I've heard a lot about you." She smirks at Tom.

"Jen was just leaving," Tom says, and for some reason that
cracks Jen up.

"All right, all right. I'll go, cradle robber." Their eyes meet for a second too long. "See you tomorrow." She zips up her leather jacket and starts to walk away, but casts a glance back over her shoulder and winks at Tom, then disappears around a corner.

"What was that about?"

Instead of answering, Tom pulls me in close and plants a kiss squarely on my mouth. Instantly I forget why I'm here. I press against him, and his strong arms wrap around me. This feels so right. And Tom's always had plenty of girl friends. Why would that bother me now? I guess I'm feeling vulnerable with all that's going on.

Eventually, I have to come up for air, giving me a chance to remember what I came here for in the first place. I pull back and take a deep breath.

"Hey, Tom?"

He smiles at me, his face only a few inches from mine, his eyebrow raised.

"I didn't apply to college."

"What?" He takes a step back. "You didn't?"

"I don't know what I'm going to do next year, but I'll probably be around here or whatever, so I thought you should know."

"Riley, that's fantastic." Tom leans in again, pulling me in for another kiss. He brushes his fingertips against my neck, and I shiver with pleasure. "That's so amazing. I can't believe it." He presses a light kiss on my lips and another on my cheek.

"Tom?" I need to get this out before I forget. "I also wondered if you could help me with something."

"Anything," He whispers, his breath warm on my ear.

"I want to find out how to get in touch with a doctor at the UCSF program. All I know is that his name is Dr. Matt."

"Dr. Matt, huh?" Tom laughs. "Sure, no sweat. But first I need something from you." He puts his hand on the back of my head and pulls me close.

I nod. "Anything."

"Shut up and kiss me." He presses his lips against mine, teasing me, and I feel my body respond. I don't know how long we stand there, making out on the street for the whole world to see, but I don't care.

"All this time I thought I was going to lose you, and now," Tom whispers, "I don't have to lose you at all."

Somewhere in the dark recesses of my brain, I wonder why he's the only one who is happy for me, but then he pulls me close again, and I wrap my arms around his strong shoulders like I'll never let go, and it doesn't seem to matter.

33

"What do you think of this one?" I tap on the window of a red Volkswagen Bug. I don't have the slightest idea why Zoe thought I would be helpful shopping for a car, but I'm trying to be useful.

"Ed says Beetles are a pain to repair." She walks farther down the row and stops at a red Toyota Camry. It's got to be at least ten years old, and it has that light tan interior they loved so much in the nineties. She squints at the paper taped to the driver's side window. "The mileage on this one isn't too bad."

"It's . . . nice."

This place is huge. They've got row after row of used cars of all kinds, lined up as far as the eye can see. Colorful flags whip in the breeze above us, and canned pop music plays out of loudspeakers scattered around the perimeter. Three different salesmen emerged like sharks from a small dumpy office at the back when we pulled up, but we finally convinced them to let us browse on our own for a bit.

"It looks dependable. And, uh, safe." I have no idea what I'm talking about. I assumed we'd come here and pick the coolest-looking car, but Zoe's being weirdly methodical, poring over crash test ratings and gas mileage figures.

She walks around and studies the back of the car. "You don't think it's too soccer mom?"

I run my fingers over the gold-colored trim. "It goes with your hair."

Zoe rolls her eyes and moves down the row, stopping in front of a white Ford Focus. She checks the price tag.

I guess it makes sense that she's being smart about this. I can't count the number of hours Zoe's slaved away at El Bueno Burrito to save up for this car. And I'm excited for her, I really am, it's just that all of this suddenly makes her seem so... I don't know. Grown-up. While I've been busy painting cheerleading banners and writing stupid stories, she's worked toward, saved up for, and researched cars. She'll walk out of this lot with a loan and insurance and all kinds of other things that feel way too adult for me to conceive of.

"Zoe?" She sizes up a black hatchback and turns to me, smiling. "Why didn't Dean come with you today?" I sidle between a massive Ford pickup and a smaller black Chevy and walk over to her. "Or Ed? Doesn't he know a lot about cars?"

"Ed told me all kinds of stuff about what to look for," Zoe says, squinting at the paper on the car window. "But he wanted me to do this on my own. And Dean had a... Dean had to help his dad." She bites her lip and runs her finger down the column of figures on the paper. "Besides, how often do we get to do stuff like this, just the two of us?"

"Buy cars?"

"Hang out." Zoe steps away from the car and slings her arm around my shoulder. "You know...talk...about everything."

Her smile is determined and a little familiar—and suddenly I get a sinking feeling in my stomach.

She unzips her bag and roots around inside, then looks up at the long row of cars and shakes her head. "Let's sit. I want to show you something."

"Sit?" I look around.

"Come on." She lifts the door handle of the black hatch-back and swings the door open, then slides into the driver's seat.

I study her face through the grayish glass. She's so earnest, so hopeful.

"I figured out some options for you."

I sigh and climb into the front seat on the other side. "Options?" I slide the seat back as she unfolds a crumpled stack of papers.

"I looked into colleges that have later application deadlines, and I found that several of the public schools in Southern California are still taking applications for certain majors. So Northridge, Fullerton, Dominguez Hills..." She hands me a printout of application information. "They're all within a short drive of USC, and with your grades I bet you wouldn't have to pay."

"I don't want to go to those schools." I try to catch her eye, but she keeps going.

She scans the printout. "I pulled up the classifieds for the *Los Angeles Times*, and there are tons of jobs available so you could work for a while." She shoves another paper into my hands. "But here's what I think is your best option. I found all this stuff about how to spend your 'gap year.' That's a real term, and lots of people do it. There are all these sites to help you do something good for the world before you go to college."

"Zoe."

She stops talking, her eyes wide as she tosses the rest of the papers into my lap.

"I..." I don't know what to say. I don't know how to process what she's saying. "Thank you." I tuck the papers into my purse. "I appreciate it."

She bites her lip. "I just, you know, I want you to be happy. And since Dreamy said...well, I wanted to make it right somehow."

I study my bitten-to-the-nub fingernails, then sit on my hands. "It isn't Dreamy's fault."

A Beyoncé song plays out over the lot, deadened by thick layers of glass. It sounds so incongruous I almost want to laugh.

"I don't want you to get stuck here." Her eyes well up with tears for a minute, but she manages to blink them back. "Not for us or for Tom or for anybody. You need a fresh start....We all do."

"I don't know what I'm going to end up doing next year," I say quietly. "I don't know if you can really help me there. But maybe you could pray that God would help me figure it out."

"I already do. Every night, every time I think about it." Zoe's cheeks burn red, making her faint freckles stand out. "I've been at it all year."

I lean over and give her a hug, her soft hair tickling my face.

I press my eyes shut and smell a faint whiff of patchouli and some kind of cooking spices—cardamom, maybe, or coriander—and it smells like heaven. "Zoe Fairchild, how am I ever going to survive without you?" My voice breaks off at the end.

34

O h hey." The annual Valentine's Day dance is this Friday and Ashley's been keeping the squad late to work on decorations, but I'm cutting out early today. Still, the school is mostly deserted, so I wasn't exactly expecting to see Asha hanging around the parking lot. She's wearing a big, loose top, and her belly protrudes in front of her tiny frame, so she looks further along than she is. I glance around the school parking lot, then back at her. "Do you need a ride or something? I don't mind dropping you."

"Gosh, thanks." Asha's voice is laced with sarcasm, taking me off guard. "But my brother's taking me home." She pushes a strand of dark hair behind her ear.

Am I missing something here? What did I do wrong? "Listen, I know what Jandel's been up to. When Ben and I were talking about it, I said—"

"*You* were talking to Ben? I doubt that."

I take a step back. "Asha?" I tilt my head. "Is everything okay?"

She rolls her eyes and glares at the gates at the end of the parking lot, refusing to acknowledge me. I wait a few minutes, and the silence grows awkward. I don't know what's going on here, but I can't actually make her talk to me or accept a ride—pregnant or not.

"Well...I'll see you around then." I clear my throat, but she doesn't seem to hear me, so I start walking for my car. Maybe I should call Ben to make sure everything's okay with her.

"I really liked you, you know."

I freeze but don't turn around, my heart beating faster.

"When we first moved here, I heard a lot of rumors about you, but I never believed them. And when you and Ben started talking, I was actually happy about it."

I turn around and look up at her, standing on the front steps of the gym.

"You seemed really cool. Maybe it was because I knew you went to church. But now..." She brushes a lock of hair away from her face. "Maybe you're just like all the other hypocrites."

I shake my head slowly. "Asha, if this is about the way the youth group moms—"

"They 'suggested' I might be happier in the young parents group instead of the youth group." She glares at me. "Did you know that?"

"They—what?" I hitch my bag higher on my shoulder. "They kicked you out of youth group?"

"Technically, I'm still allowed to come." She rolls her eyes. "But Jandel thinks the *support* from other moms might be good for me. Whatever." She plays with her brilliant gold necklace, the small sapphires in it sparkling. "I wasn't talking about them anyway. I was talking about the way you treated my brother."

"What?"

"He really liked you, but now he's moping around the house, half-dead." She puts a hand on her stomach.

"Things got…complicated, and I wasn't sure what to say to him."

"Look, obviously I'm not in a position to be telling people how to behave." She slides her hand to the other side of her belly. "But Ben is a good guy, and he at least deserves an explanation."

I shield my eyes from the afternoon sun and stare at her. I could stand here and try to justify what I've done, weasel my way out of things again, but she's right. All year I've been avoiding my problems, hoping they'll magically solve themselves. Ben got caught in the cross fire. Maybe it's time to take some responsibility for my actions.

I drop my hand. "Where'd you say he is?"

When I step into the auditorium, a few of the kids from Mr. Dumas's art class are putting the final touches on some kind of castle backdrop. The art kids often help the drama class with their scenery, and it looks like there must be some Shakespeare in our future. I scan the stage and pick out his familiar black hair easily.

"Ben."

At the sound of my voice, he stiffens. A few long seconds pass while he stays crouched over, his paintbrush stuck in the can. He turns to me, his face a mix of emotions I can't quite read.

"Are you…"

The other art students on the stage seem to sense the awkwardness and immediately begin packing up their paint supplies.

He nods. "Yeah, I'm done here." He dusts off his hands, mumbles good-bye to a few people, then hops off the stage with an easy lunge.

"Maybe we should grab a seat." I gesture at the empty auditorium and start heading toward the back, where no one has even bothered to turn the lights on.

He follows wordlessly behind me, and I stop a few rows from the back exits, then shuffle down to the middle of the row. I flip down the seat and slide low, trying to steel my nerves. What's one more person yelling at me? I'm kind of getting good at taking my lumps at this point. Plus, after I apologize to Ben, I'll have officially begun to make amends for the royal mess I've made of this year. That's progress, I guess.

Ben sits next to me and swings his legs over the row in front of us and waits. He's definitely not going to make this easy on me, and I don't blame him.

"I'm sorry I've been horrible to you lately. I've been having a rough couple of months."

He nods thoughtfully, keeping his eyes on the stage. The remaining art students wave good-bye to each other and disappear in different directions, leaving us alone. "I think I heard about that." Ben's voice is quiet. "Something about college. My friend told me, but I said it couldn't be true."

He glances at me, and I nod to confirm the rumor. I guess it was stupid to think he wouldn't have heard. Even though I didn't tell many people, these things have a way of traveling. I'm sure it's all over school by now.

"What happened?"

"I don't know. All the schools seemed like somebody else's dream." In the front of the theater, someone peeks in the door, looks around, then goes back out again. "But I know you've had a bad year too. I'm sorry. I didn't mean to make you think...anything. I like hanging out with you, but I didn't mean to use you or anything."

He sighs deeply and waits for a moment. "It's okay."

"That day in the van..." How can I put this into words? I'm really not sorry he kissed me. "Tom and I go back a long time. We've been together in some form or another for two years now." Ben is so different, so unexpected, but Tom and I have history, and our attraction to each other is impossible to resist. "You asked me to choose, and it wasn't easy, but ultimately, I made my decision."

Maybe if we had more time together things might be different, but Ben's going off to college and I'm sticking around and Tom is...well, he's here. He knows about my messy family, and he's used to my faults.

"I see." He clenches his jaw tightly and twists his watch on his wrist. "That's a shame. I really thought we made a lot of sense together." A silence passes between us. "My friends said I was crazy, that you never dated guys like me, but I don't know. It felt possible somehow."

I put a hand on his knee. "We had a connection. Definitely." I smile. "But it's not right, at least right now. And I don't know if it ever will be."

Ben nods slowly. We both stare at the stage, and I realize the play must be some kind of romance in honor of Valentine's Day. Did Shakespeare write any romances that don't end badly?

"Here." Ben pulls a small package wrapped in brown paper out of his bag. I take it from his hand gently. "I was going to give this to you anyway. I'm not normally into this made-up holiday, but this year . . ."

"Ben, I don't know if—"

"Don't worry. I understand." He holds up his hands. "But either way, this should be yours."

I search his face for some indication of what this means, but something in his eyes forces me to turn away. I slide my finger under the edge of the paper.

"Wait." He grabs my hand tightly. "Open it after I leave." He stands up and begins gliding down the aisle. "I need to get going anyway. Asha's waiting for me."

I watch him go, walking down the long narrow aisle, his head held high. When the door shuts, I slip my finger under the flap, pulling the Scotch tape up. I unwrap it quickly, careful not to tear the paper, and pull out a simple black picture frame. I hold it up and suck in my breath.

It's me. A black-and-white picture. My face is silhouetted against a dark gray sky, and I'm staring off toward the horizon, not really smiling, but not really not. In the bottom left corner, you can see the base of the cliffs and churning gray water in the distance. It must be the one he took at Mavericks.

There's something almost arresting about the shot. The bright white flash of the setting sun in one corner catches my attention, then my eye travels down, tracing the stark contrast of the dark cliffs. But the more I look at it, the more I realize the real beauty of the picture isn't the absolutes. It's what's going on in the middle, in the dozens of different shades of gray that make up the real subject of the photo: the silvery light on the tip of my nose, the darker shadows under my eyes, and the varied and layered patterns of the hazy clouds in the sky. When I study the shading, I can see that underneath the halfhearted smile, there's something in my face that looks... lost. I'm not really watching the tiny specks of white below at all. I'm looking for something and not finding it.

35

The door to the classroom opens, and Mrs. Benassi scurries into the room, holding a dozen long-stemmed red roses.

"I don't mean to interrupt, but it's for a noble cause."

"Yes?" Ms. Sanchez stops reading midsonnet and peeks over the top of her wire-rimmed glasses.

Mrs. Benassi's skirt rustles as she makes her way through the maze of desks toward me, grinning. "For you, Riley."

Several people in the class whistle as she hands me the flowers. I bend forward and inhale the sweet perfume of the roses. The scent is light and lovely, intoxicating.

"Now you be nice to your young man," she says, winking. "By the time you get to my age, they've all stopped trying, but this guy, he's a keeper," she says under her breath. She nods deferentially at Ms. Sanchez, then turns and waddles back toward the door in her orthotic shoes.

Everyone is looking at me. I can feel it. Lots of girls have flowers on their desks—it's Valentine's Day, after all—but no one else had their flowers delivered in class. I try to be inconspicuous as I peek at the card:

Happy Valentine's Day.
Love, Tom

"Are we ready to move on?" Ms. Sanchez asks, clearing her throat, her short hair gelled into place. "Riley, since you seem to know so much about the Shakespearean art of wooing, perhaps you could continue with the hundred and sixteenth sonnet?" She eyes me over her glasses while people around me snicker. Ms. Sanchez isn't bad, really. She just takes AP English way too seriously.

"Sure." I look down at my book and try to focus on the words, their dark shapes contrasting sharply against the stark white pages, but my stomach is jumpy and I can't seem to make my mind stay on anything today.

"From the top please." She waits, a smirk on her face.

"Right." I bite my lip and look down. This is the most romantic thing anyone has ever done for me. "Sonnet one-sixteen." I clear my throat. "'Let me not to the marriage of true minds admit impediments.'" Out of the corner of my eye, I see Ms. Sanchez nodding.

Tom and I have had our ups and downs, yes, but he still loves me. That's obvious. And that's all that matters.

36

I open Ana's door, see her tear-stained face, and grab her in a tight hug. I hold her and rock for a moment, whispering shushing noises because I don't know what to say. She found out this morning that Maria is slipping away.

I pull back and squeeze Ana's hands. Her face is ashen, and her eyes are red. Christine is sitting on Ana's bed, and Zoe is next to her, gripping one of her throw pillows with all her might.

"I want to try to fit it all in a carry-on so I don't have to wait at baggage claim," Ana says, studying the neat piles of clothes lined up in front of her suitcase. We all nod. We know what this means. Ana wants to be there with Maria at the end, and Maria doesn't have much time left. "It's going to be tight." She starts placing her clothes inside in precise piles, her movements quick and efficient.

Zoe slips off the bed, walks over to Ana's desk, and lifts a piece of paper off the surface. "Why do you have an electric blanket on your list?" Zoe cocks an eyebrow.

"Pneumonia gives you the chills," Ana says and starts digging around in her closet. She pulls out a dark blue blanket with a cord and puts it in the suitcase. "Also, I can't forget to bring my digital thermometer. I don't know if Maria's niece has one, and we'll want to have accurate readings," Ana says, almost to herself. "Can you add that to the list for me, Zo? Oh, and I need to grab the vaporizer." Ana rattles off five more gadgets and medical doodads that only she would have heard of. This is Ana in crisis mode: focused, organized, and hyperefficient.

She leans back on her heel, surveys the already-overflowing suitcase, and shakes her head. "This is never going to fit." She pulls a giant piece of black luggage off a high shelf in her closet, unzips it, and puts it down next to the other one so she can transfer her things over.

"You're doing a great job." I smile at her warily, not sure why I said it. Maybe it's because for the first time in her life Ana isn't in control of a situation. I sink down onto the floor next to her.

"She'll be so excited to see you." Zoe joins us, sitting cross-legged next to me. I fight the urge to glance at Christine, who's boring her eyes into Ana's duvet. Christine knows what it's like to lose someone you love, and though her mom passed away before high school started, before we even knew each other, I'm sure it still feels like yesterday. She'll come over and join us when she can. "I still can't believe your parents are letting you go to Mexico by yourself."

"Seriously, when you told me that, I thought the earth was off its axis." We all turn at the sound of Christine's voice. She raises a wry eyebrow at us and comes over and joins our circle.

"Actually, I didn't give them much choice." Ana laughs. "When Graciella called and told me they were moving Maria to hospice care, I just sort of told Mom and Papá that I was going to be there by her bedside."

"Really?" I can feel my eyes bug out of my head. "And they went for it?"

Ana grabs a pair of tennis shoes from the closet floor. "I had to promise to stay in constant contact," she says as she chunks them into the suitcase. "I'm supposed to video chat with my parents every day, and I promised to upload photos and text messages every few hours so they'll know I'm alive."

"Wait, you're going to be all ET blog home in the Middle of Nowhere, Mexico?" Christine shakes her head.

"Guanajuato is hardly the sticks. Graciella has high-speed Internet at home. I called to double check."

My head swims thinking about how efficient and driven Ana is. Why couldn't I have been born more like her? When she's faced with an insurmountable task, it somehow makes her more capable. She doesn't hide and hope it goes away.

Zoe grabs her hand and squeezes it. "What are you going to do about school?"

"Mom filled out the long-term absence form, so that buys me a week or so. Then it's spring break. After that, I'm really not sure." Ana shrugs nonchalantly. What a far cry this Ana is from the underclassman who lived and died by her class standing. I wonder if she even realizes we're currently tied for number one. "I'll cross that bridge when I get there."

Her face goes dark, and my heart breaks for her. I take Ana's other hand, and we draw them all together. Christine throws her hands in too, and we're bound into a tight knot.

"Thanks, guys." Ana smiles at us. "For coming over and for this." She squeezes us and then lets go. "Now, if you really want to be there for me, you'll help me pack. I'm leaving in two hours."

We all rise to our feet and throw ourselves into the task at hand. Christine takes Ana's packing list and calls out items. Zoe pulls things off the shelves, and I run back and forth to the medicine cabinet, locating bizarre medical equipment. And before we know it, we've got our friend ready to face one of the hardest times in her life.

Christine lowers the top of the huge suitcase, which is stuffed to the brim. "I really don't think that thing is going to close."

Zoe sits on it, and they goof around, trying to get the zipper to slide in a variety of ways. I take a few steps back and watch the scene. If you squint, if you move forward a few short months in your mind, this looks like something else entirely. This is how it will be when they pack and leave—and I stay behind.

My knees want to buckle, and the air whooshes out of my lungs. I stumble backward and sit on the bed.

"You okay, Cheerleader?" Christine stops trying to zip the suitcase and looks at me.

"Oh, I'm fine. Totally fine." I fan my face, trying to get air. "It's just... I'm going to miss you guys."

37

I unlock the door and peer in like I'm expecting the boogey-man to jump out. The clock reads 3:15. For the first time in an eternity, the stars of high school extracurriculars have aligned to set me free right after school.

I walk in the front door, set down my backpack, pull off my shoes, and wander through the rooms one by one. Mom and Michael should be home. I hear a muffled noise from the formal dining room and head in that direction. As I turn the corner, I jump.

"What's wrong?"

Mom's forehead is pressed to the glass top of her formal dining table, the one I'm not allowed to leave fingerprints on, and Michael is sitting in the corner, tapping his head on the wall, mumbling to himself.

Mom pulls her head off the table. "We're taking a short break."

Michael doesn't seem to notice I'm in the room, but his repetitious mumbling gets louder so I know he sees me.

"You're home early." Mom is only wearing one earring, and her shirt's untucked. I try not to stare.

"Yeah, kind of a fluke." I begin to edge out of the room. This whole scene is weirding me out. Maybe I'll give them a moment. "Just wanted to say hi. I've got some stuff to do."

Mom nods and lays her head back on the table.

I head down the hall, my feet slipping across the hardwood floors, as I hear her pleading with Michael to sit at the table again and finish his work. Michael's mumbling gives way to full-on screeching, and that's when it hits me. This is my chance.

Michael's tantrums never last too long, so I only have a little while to find out more about Dr. Matt. Tom was able to give me his last name and e-mail address, but I still need a few questions answered before I e-mail him.

I flip on the light and walk into the office. No one seems to notice, and for once, I'm thankful. I lower myself into the padded desk chair and pull open the bottom desk drawer, my pulse pounding in my ears. I'm not sure what I'm about to do is the right thing. I hate to sneak around behind Mom and Dad's backs, but I'd do anything to help Michael. It's worth it if I can save my brother. God can see that, right?

I used to think my mom was really organized. She has an elaborate filing system with color-coded labels, but it's been months since she's actually had time to file anything. I flip to the folder labeled MICHAEL, then to the subfolder UCSF, but as I suspected, it's empty. That means the records are buried somewhere in—I shove the drawer closed—there. I pull a wire basket stacked with papers toward me. I flip through the papers on top. Phone bills, address labels from Christmas cards, receipts. Nothing that looks like medical records. I'm going to have to go through the whole stack. I take a deep breath and start to rifle through.

A few minutes later, with Michael's screams still echoing through the house, I find a yellowing envelope. Tucked inside is a stack of my old report cards. I pull one out gingerly and see it's from third grade. I made A's in math, science, reading, spelling...pretty much everything. Except—I peek over at the right side, where Mrs. Mickelson graded other things. Maturity: C. Self-control: C+. Decision Making: D.

I fold the paper and shove it back into the envelope. What kind of cracked-out school grades kids on maturity anyway? Of course I wasn't exercising good judgment. I was nine. I toss the envelope back into the pile and keep digging. I have to keep focused, searching for anything that looks vaguely medical, but still, I can't stop wondering why my parents were looking at my old report cards.

The wailing in the other room stops, but Mom's voice is a steady hum. I don't have too much longer now. I turn back toward the stack of papers. Records. What I need is Dr. Matt's records, and they're not here.

There are a bunch of other medical papers in the bottom of the basket, but no records, so I turn to the computer. I drum my fingers on the keyboard while it boots up, and then poke around in the virtual files, but I don't find anything that looks likely. It has to be in her e-mail.

What would her password be? I open her e-mail program and type in Mom's username. *MMcGee*. It's the same for everything. For her password I type in *RealEstate*. No luck. I try *HalfMoonBay*. Nothing. Okay. How about *Indiana*? That's the name of the dog we had when I was a kid. I try a few other likely combinations, but nothing works.

They have to be in there. I've got to get into her e-mail somehow.

I press my fingers against my eyelids.

"Riley!" Mom yells from the kitchen. "Could you come give me a hand?"

"Hold on." Okay. I need a Plan B. I open a separate tab and log into my Gmail. If she comes in here, I'll close out of her e-mail quickly and say my computer is acting funny. It *has* been crashing a lot recently. But as soon as my e-mail loads, a message from Ana catches my eye, and I can't resist clicking on it.

> *Hey guys,*
>   *I made it. Maria's not good, but she's peaceful. More soon.*
>
> > *Ana*

I know she'll write more when she can, but even her few terse words make it clear that she's hurting. I whisper a prayer for Ana and for Maria. I remember what it was like to face death, how terrifying it felt to know that my moments on earth were numbered, and I pray for peace for Maria's soul.

"Riley, I need your help getting dinner started."

"In a minute!" My heart begins to race, and I click back to my mom's ancient AOL account. What's her stupid password? How hard can this be? *Think, Riley, think.*

I type Michael's name into the password line. No luck. I move to close down the window, then pause. I might as well try. I type in *Riley* and hit return.

A moment later, her inbox pops up onto the screen, and I pump my fists in the air.

Quickly, I search for the words *Matt Nguyen* in her messages. A message pops up from him from last summer. I click on it and see that at the bottom of the screen is an attachment called McGee_Eval. *Bingo.* I double-click it and download the Word document.

It opens, and I know I've found it. It's got the logo from the UCSF program there at the top. I scan the papers, dated from a year and a half ago, when Michael left the program.

Michael lacks self-control and self-discipline.

Apparently it runs in the family. I run my eyes down the evaluation form.

Seems not to notice certain external stimuli.
Methodical and repetitive.
Prone to violent outbursts.

Dr. Matt's evaluation goes on for several pages, but the more I read, the more I wish I hadn't. It's nothing I didn't know, and it's all true, but somehow, seeing it there in black and white makes it feel so cold. In these notes Michael isn't a living, breathing person, he's a case number, a problem to be solved. On the last page, there's a note.

I strongly recommend that Michael stay at UCSF for further therapy.

The scrawled signature at the bottom reads *Matthew Nguyen*.

I stare at the screen until the words become blurry. I guess I knew they wanted to keep Michael there at the program longer. I remember my parents discussing it and deciding to bring him home at the end of the summer. I remember being excited about him coming home. I made him a Welcome Back cake, but he refused to eat it because it had melted chocolate chips, which he hates because...Well, who even knows why. I remember that it was the start of junior year, and Tom had recently left for college, and I was frustrated by the chaos our lives were plunged into when Michael came home again. I remember just wanting things to get better.

Did we do the right thing? If he had stayed at UCSF longer, like Dr. Matt wanted, would Michael be better off now? I lower my head into my hands. It never occurred to me that we were being selfish in wanting him to come home again. He was fourteen, and he'd been gone for three months, and he said he wanted to come back home, but now, I don't know. I can't help wondering if maybe he would have been able to survive at Marina Vista if he'd stayed at UCSF longer. Maybe it would have been kinder to him, in the end, to let him go.

I open a blank message and write Dr. Matt a brief note, chronicling what's been going on all year and asking for his help.

Soft footsteps sound in the hallway, getting closer and closer.

I sign it *Michelle McGee* and hit send. Then I shut the report document, move it to the trash, and quit the browser window in a matter of seconds.

"Riley?" Mom appears in the doorway and raises her eyebrows. "What are you doing on my computer?"

"Coming." I push myself out of the chair. "Sorry. Mine's acting funny, and I wanted to check up on Ana." I ask God to forgive me for lying to her and snooping around and pray this doesn't technically count as a sin. Do you get any credit for having good intentions?

38

t's like God dumped dirty bathwater all over Half Moon Bay. The rain pours down in thick sheets, soaking the dark streets and pooling on the soggy grass. The spot where the Living Nativity stood at Christmas is one big mud puddle, scarred and raw in the otherwise perfect lawn in front of the perfect church.

Michael throws open the car door and takes off across the dark lot, flapping his arms. He's mad because I wouldn't drop him off in front of the youth room door, and maybe I'm being passive-aggressive, but it's his fault we're late anyway. He was the one who had to count all five hundred puzzle pieces before we could put the stupid box away. I watch his blond head disappear inside the church doors.

Maybe I should stay out here where it's quiet. I'm not in the mood for tied-up-with-a-bow sermons about Jesus helping you battle cliques and God being there for you when you get a zit. Why does church boil stuff down to baby food? Real life is so much more complex, and baffling, and lonely. I lean my head against the headrest and close my eyes, but all I can think about is why I came tonight.

Ugh. I tap the steering wheel a few times. I have to go in there for Ben. No matter what has happened between us, he needs a friend right now. I force myself to climb out of the van.

The lights from the youth room spill out into the dark lot, reflecting across standing pools of water. Through the window, I can make out Dave and Tommy on the small stage. They must still be doing worship time. Which, now that I think about it, is kind of a ridiculous concept. Aren't we supposed to worship God all the time? My foot lands squarely in a puddle, and a bit of water splashes over the rim on my shoe and creeps into my sock. I decide to make a run for it.

I duck under the eave as the band finishes a song, the long, low notes hanging there, only partially muffled by the thin walls of the youth room. I shake the water off my jacket and comb my fingers through my hair, then walk toward the door, clinging to the side of the building, out of the way of the rain. I'm almost at the corner when something in the shadows moves.

"Aah!" I jump back.

"It's just me, Riley," Ben says.

I lean back, pressing my back against the hard wooden shingles that cover the walls of the old wing of the church. Inside the youth room, Fritz is reading from the Bible.

"You gonna hang out here all night?"

He shrugs. "I'm working up the guts to go inside."

"So why are you here?" Rain splashes down onto the black asphalt in sheets, but it's dry and almost cozy here under the eave.

"For Asha, I guess." He kicks at the cement. "She couldn't face them, but I wanted to go in there and do it for her."

I tilt my head and shove my hands into my pockets. "Am I

supposed to say something about how everyone is wanted at church?"

"Nah. You'll get in trouble for lying." He peeks his head around the corner to look inside the youth room. From where I'm standing, I can see Maddie Barrow bowing her head in prayer.

"You're right. They're a bunch of hypocrites." I study his face. There are dark circles under his eyes, and his cheeks look a little sunken, like he's lost weight. "Please tell me Asha knows that."

"Church is supposed to be the one place where your past mistakes don't matter, where forgiveness means a clean slate," Ben says, his voice flat. "I used to really believe that. But now..." He shakes his head. "You ever feel like God is one thing, and church is something else entirely?"

I nod. It's funny. Maybe it's because of the changes I've seen in my church recently, or because of the mistakes I've made, or maybe it's simply a part of growing up, but the church I grew up with looks less and less like the body of Christ these days. The more I stare at it, the more it looks like a bunch of messed-up people trying to look like they're doing the right thing.

"I still believe God is out there." Ben leans forward and points up at the night sky. "I'm just not so sure he's in there." He tilts his head back toward the youth room again. "I've never felt more judged anywhere than I have these past few months in 'God's family.'"

I rest my hand on the wall and rub my finger along the grooves in the cracked shingle. It feels solid and natural.

"Come on." I reach out and grab Ben's arm. I start to pull

on his arm, but his feet don't budge. "We can't let them do this. Let's go in there for Asha. We'll do it together."

He rolls his eyes and digs his shoe into the soft muck of the earth. "They don't want me in there. Me or Asha. No one from our messy family."

I sigh and peer through the window again. A couple of freshmen girls in the back row are giggling at something on their phones while Fritz is talking. A group of guys is sprawled out on the couches near the front of the room. I have no doubt that Ben is right, actually. These people don't want ugliness or messiness traipsing into the middle of their church. But then off to the right, near the front, I catch a glimpse of red hair. Zoe. She's looking toward the door, biting her lip, and I know, in a way I could never explain, that she's looking for me. Waiting for me to walk in. Worried that something happened to me.

"My friends and I want you in there. You're welcome with us." I pull his arm again and take a step toward the door. "And after everything we've been through this year, I want to be here for you."

"I forgave you, Riley. I really did. But you chose him, remember?" He takes a deep breath. "I'll figure this out on my own."

I watch Zoe for a second more. She turns back around and leans in to whisper something to Christine, who sits up straight and starts to look around the room.

"I hope we can be friends again someday." I take a few steps to the door and hold the handle, listening for a moment, praying that he'll follow me, but he doesn't. I hear him walk away and turn to see him climb into his car.

I contemplate giving up and going home too. Almost nothing sounds better than pulling the covers over my head and trying to forget about everything, but Michael's already in there. Plus, if there's some way to help Ben, I'm going to need the Miracle Girls. And I'm going to need one more thing too. I pull on the handle. Who knows, maybe I'll finally get through to God at church of all places.

39

I sigh and push my duvet back. Obviously I'm not getting to sleep anytime soon. I stumble across the cold hardwood floor, bleary-eyed, and move my mouse. My screen comes to life. I type Mom's password into her e-mail account and shut my eyes while it loads. "Please, please, please."

I synced Mom's e-mail account to my phone, and I've been watching her inbox like a hawk all day, but doctors keep weird hours, and he could have written me back tonight. Good thing Mom has the computer skills of a grandma or this plan would never work. Her inbox finally loads, and I scan her new messages quickly. Nothing from Dr. Matt.

I close her e-mail account and open up Gmail. I delete a few junk-mail messages, get rid of a gazillion Facebook updates, and then my eyes catch an e-mail from Ana. My stomach drops. I haven't heard from her in days.

My Miracles,

By now you've probably figured out that Maria has passed away. I meant to take a few moments right away to tell you it had happened and that I was doing okay, but the words wouldn't come. I hope it's better late than never.

On Tuesday, Maria was feverish and hallucinating. It was hard to watch her fight against the disease. Her cough

*was scary and chilling—and I probably should have
known then that she was passing away.*

*At noon, she woke up suddenly and asked for a glass
of water. After a few ice cubes and a little soup, she laid
back, shut her eyes, and took my hand.*

"Anita," she said. "Talk to me about home."

*I started telling her things, stupid little things to help
her relax. I told her about my writing class and how the
teacher really encouraged me. I told her all about Mom's
hideous attempt at redecorating our house and how Papá's
law practice is booming. I talked about you guys, and I
mentioned all the pressure we're under and how it feels more
important than ever to stick together. And we talked about
Dave, how long ago all that seems now and how excited I
am about next year, being on my own and trying out my
wings. I even told her about my secret dreams for the future,
some half-formed ideas I've been having lately, things I
haven't been able to tell anyone yet. Yes, even you guys.*

*Around dusk she called for Graciella and the rest of
her family to gather around. We all grabbed a hand or a
foot or an arm or a leg, and the priest began to pray. It
was one of the most beautiful things I have ever seen. The
sun spilling across her bed, the whispered prayers in Spanish, the heads bowed and hands lifted over this mighty
woman. And with all of us around her, she slipped away.*

*It's been hard for me to let go, but her family has basi-
cally adopted me, and having them near me right now is
exactly what I need. But I miss my Miracle Girls family
too. I'll be home in a few days, and I have so much to tell
you guys. There are big changes afoot for me, but I want*

to discuss them in person. Please know for now that I am
okay, that Maria is finally better, and that I love you. (Is
that stupid to say? I'm not sure I ever had the guts to say it
out loud, but suddenly, now, it feels important.)

Ana

I grab the box of tissues and blot the rivers of tears running
down my cheeks. I was hanging on her every word without
realizing it. Somehow she brought the whole scene to life, and
I could almost feel the moment of Maria's passing.

And then, slowly, so gradually I almost don't notice it at
first, I begin to pray. I beg God to hold up a lamp in the darkness and cast some light down my path. I mumble my words
in the silence of the still house, and for the first time in a long
time this feels right. Someone or something out there seems
to be listening.

40

Dear Mrs. McGee,

I was distressed to get your e-mail and would love to schedule an assessment of Michael ASAP. I'm afraid I'm traveling at the moment. Would next weekend work? I have an opening at 11:30 on Saturday. Let me know at your earliest convenience.

Sincerely,
Dr. Matthew Nguyen

My heart races, and I hit reply. Technically I told Mom I'd be working on my calculus homework when I left the dinner table, but I had to check to see if there was anything from Dr. Matt. I hate to do this to Mom and Dad, but I've got to figure out how to help Michael. They saw Dr. Matt's recommendation, and they still brought Michael home. They heard Ms. Moore's advice and didn't listen to it. What I need right now is access to someone who understands the situation, someone who isn't afraid to tell me the truth and help me help Michael.

I type out a reply, trying to write in Mom's formal Realtor tone as I assure Dr. Matt that next Saturday is perfect. I'll tell Mom and Dad that I'm taking Michael to the new Academy of Sciences in San Francisco. He's been dying to go. And once Dr. Matt sees Michael, he'll have to go through with the assessment. That kid has an angelic face that could melt the hardest of hearts. I scan my message and decide to add a sentence about how the whole family appreciates his quick attention to the matter. I smile. That end part is brilliant. Mom loves to thank people for their "quick attention" to matters.

I click send and then erase the message from her sent folder. I doubt she even knows that she has a sent folder, but you can never be too careful. I log out of her account and tap my fingers on the keyboard.

What did Zoe say it was called? A gap year? I type that into Google and click on the first link. The site has all kinds of information about programs I can do all over the world. Kids like me are taking time off before college to build houses in Ecuador and learn Italian in Florence and work with elephants in the Congo. That could be cool. I click on a few links and try to imagine what it would be like to work with a marine biologist in the Galápagos Islands. I like turtles. But then I notice a tiny little number at the bottom of the screen, and my heart sinks. These programs all cost thousands of dollars. A few weeks ago I suggested a backpacking trip through Europe to Mom and Dad, and they made it pretty clear that their sponsorship of me ends the day I graduate from high school.

The image of Ana holding Maria's hand flashes in front of my eyes.

Well, so what if they're not going to support me financially. I can get a job and find an apartment and still do something meaningful with my year. I could help sick people. I could save up and hike Kilimanjaro. I could dig wells in developing nations. I could...do this thing with elephants.

No. No elephants.

I keep researching, and with each click of my mouse, I feel better and better. *Click, click.* Yes, the sound seems to say. *Click, click.* This is what you're supposed to do. Take charge of your own future. Grow up, get over yourself, and use your talents. I lean back in my desk chair. Maybe I'm not going to college right away, but I'm going to do something better. Instead of burying my nose in a book, I'm going to use my time to make the world a better place.

I sit forward again, open Facebook, and start typing an update. Let's see. What should I say? *Finally figured it out.* No, that's not really right. *On my way.* Well, yes, but that doesn't exactly convey the excitement I feel. Hmm. I'll think about it.

I click over and approve a few new friends, not really looking at who they are, and then click over to my wall. Emma is updating her status every few minutes as she watches *Gossip Girl*, Ana is apparently eating calculus for dinner, tons of people have uploaded photos from an epic party on Saturday, and Ashley...What?

I lean in close to the screen and blink my eyes. Ashley's message on my wall says, "Heard about what happened with T. I'm so sorry. Call me night or day if you need to talk."

Need to talk? What on earth is she talking about now? I see that she's online and IM her.

Riley
What's up with the graffiti?

Ashley
*Are you embarrassed? I'm sorry. I'll take it down. Should
have thought of that. Just wanted to say I was sorry.*

Riley
WHAT ARE YOU TALKING ABOUT?

Ashley
Oh.

Riley
Very close to pummeling you right now.

Ashley
I thought you knew.

Riley
KNEW WHAT?

I hold my breath, waiting for her to answer. Somewhere
deep in the recesses of my mind, my brain keeps tossing up
an answer, but I block it out, push it down so deep that I can't
really hear it.

Riley
*I'm serious, Ash. You've got me scared. Please tell me what
you're talking about.*

Ashley
Please, call Tom. This can't come from me.

I close the Facebook tab, then click back to my e-mail

to write the girls and ask if they've heard any fishy rumors about me. My heart races, my head jumping from one horrible scenario to another, skipping away from me. After a few lines my typing gets harder and harder until I'm banging on the keyboard and my message becomes an angry jumble of letters.

"Augrhe!"

I stand up suddenly, knocking my plastic IKEA chair onto the hardwood floor with a loud thwack. I dig through my jeans pockets looking for my car keys. It's a school night, but who really cares anymore? I'm keeping my grades up without even trying.

I grab my purse off the bed and take a few steps toward the hall, then dash back into the bathroom to make sure I look at least somewhat sane. If I'm going to really do this, then I'm going to do it looking good. I brush my hair until it shines, slick on some lip gloss, and dab a little powder on my shiny forehead.

I walk down the hall and hear muffled angry voices coming from Mom and Dad's room. Oh well, I'll leave them a note. I grab the notepad Mom keeps on the kitchen counter and scrawl:

Back by 11 p.m., I promise.
—Supergirl

I park the car, slam the door shut, and begin marching toward Velo Rouge Café. I swing the door open, and my eyes immediately go to the small barista bar, but I don't see him. Spinning slowly on my heels, I look from table to table until finally I spot the back of his head at a spot in the rear of the café.

As I storm back there, I have a moment of recognition about how stupid I'm about to look, like some silly high school girl, but there's no turning back now. If one of his little "friends" wants to have a good laugh at my expense, let her.

"Can I talk to you?" My voice is high and thin. I angle my body away from the girl at the table, pretending she is nothing more than a speck of dust to me.

"Riley?"

"Now!" I cross my arms over my chest and dig my fingernails into my arms.

"I can't right now." He gestures at the curly-haired girl he's sitting with, and now that I'm closer to her, I see that it's Jen. On the table in front of her is a clipboard with the words *Staff Schedule* at the top. My face begins to burn red. "My break is in—"

"It's okay, Tom." Jen tucks a pen under the clipboard's clasp and smiles at me. "Take your break early, and we'll do this later." I try to make eye contact with her to show her how much this means to me, but she's checking something off her list. "But please, do this outside."

"Thanks, Jen," he calls after her. She walks away and inspects the milk and sugar station. Tom turns back to me and starts to say something, then shuts his mouth firmly and walks to the front.

I follow after him, checking to see if anyone noticed, but everyone is too wrapped up in their own lives to care. Why

I drop my head, letting my hair hide my face, and hold my sides. "Tom." I need to get him to let his guard down. "I know you've been cheating on me." After I utter these words out loud, the weight of them hits me, and my head begins to spin.

"Rye." He reaches out and touches my hair. I flinch like he's hit me and take a step back. "I don't know what you know or what you *think* you know, but it was only that one time."

It doesn't hurt as much as I thought it would to hear him admit it. I suppose I already knew on some level anyway.

"It was a total mistake." His voice cracks at the end.

And suddenly it dawns on me what that slight waver in his voice is—the one I used to think was an endearing sign that he still got nervous around me. He's lying. His voice wavers when he lies. He's probably been lying the entire time we've been together.

I hold my head and stagger toward the sidewalk, stopping to press my face to the cool brick. The way he canceled on my homecoming; Jen's smirk when I met him here last time; all those nights he missed his call with me; the over-the-top dates and gestures. Everything begins to fall into place, and I feel nauseated.

"Riley." He puts a hand on my shoulder and nuzzles his face into my neck. He smells good, like freshly ground coffee beans and soap. I allow myself one last intoxicating breath of him. "I'm so sorry."

It would be stupid to think I won't miss this. In so many ways he's the perfect guy for me: sexy, smart, kind. He's the first guy I ever loved.

"I'm begging you to forgive me. I'll do anything." He mas-

doesn't Tom seem surprised to see me here on a Wednesday night? Why isn't he shocked at how mad I am?

Tom shoves his hands into his pockets and walks around the side of the building, past the cluttered bike rack. At the end, a lonely tire is locked to the rack, rusted and weather-beaten, the chain hanging onto something that doesn't matter anymore. Tom leans back against the wall and drags his hands over his face.

I join him in the shadows and wait.

A car turns down the street, and for a moment Tom's face is lit by the warm yellow beams. Even now he is insanely beautiful to me, so I turn away.

"Really? You're not going to say something?" I almost don't recognize my own voice.

"It seemed like you should start things off." He's angry, and that makes my pulse quicken. I take a step toward him.

"Me? Really?" It dawns on me what he's trying to do here. "So I guess you're not sure exactly what I've heard."

"I don't know what you're talking about." Tom runs his fingers through his hair and scratches a few times. "What I know is that you showed up at my job tonight and annoyed my manager."

"No." I try to make eye contact, but he's staring across the dark street at nothing. How long has it been going on? Was it only one girl? Or were there many? "I think you know more than that. You know it'd take something pretty big to make me do something like this." Does everyone know? Have they been laughing behind my back all this time? How do I get him to admit it?

sages my shoulder and keeps whispering reassurances in my ear.

But I know better. Tom is, well, it's like Ana said: He's my Kryptonite. But that doesn't mean I have to keep letting him hurt me. I say a prayer for strength and feel emboldened with every silent word.

"Stop." I shirk loose of Tom's hand and turn to face him. "I want this to end, now."

Tom's eyes water in an almost-convincing way. "That's crazy. We have something other people don't. You're going to throw it all away for one little mistake?"

I hold up a finger. "It's not once. I can see that as plain as day—just like I can see that you're going to do it again." I wait as a red-haired guy unlocks his bike and pops it off the rack, clearly hurrying to get away from the fighting couple. I take a few steps away from the café, toward the beckoning darkness of the sidewalk. "So in case it wasn't already obvious, we're done."

"Riley, wait." Tom chases after me, but the RealMobile comes into view up the block.

I turn back on my heels and level my eyes at his sorry head. "What I need from you is to forget I ever existed."

He laughs and reaches out for me. "Stop acting like such a *baby*."

I dodge his hands and keep walking backward. How could he have pulled the wool over my eyes? Now that the scales have fallen away, he's so transparent. "Don't call. Don't write. Don't contact me in any way."

"Fine. You're too immature anyway."

I open my mouth, thinking up a thousand insults, but I stop myself. He's trying to draw me in, get me to scream and yell at him until I feel better, and then he'll weasel his way back inside my heart.

"Bye, Tom."

His mouth hangs open in shock.

I leave him standing in the dark, looking scared, alone, and lost. But for a change, I feel found.

41

I yawn and twist on the hard plastic chairs in the waiting room. We woke up early and did the world's fastest tour of the Academy of Sciences, then came straight here. It seemed easier to really go than to answer all of Michael's questions about why we weren't going. I don't need a meltdown today of all days.

"I'm sorry, who did you say you are again?" A small line forms between the receptionist's eyebrows as she studies me.

I gulp. "We're here to see Dr. Matt." I motion at Michael, who's happily counting to himself. "Michael McGee. Dr. Matt's expecting us."

"Yeeees." She tilts her head to the side and makes a mark in her appointment book. "I'll tell him."

"Thank you." I nod at her, trying with every inch of my being to look twenty years older.

"Is Chase coming too? How about Jamal?" Michael rocks back and forth in his chair. The sound of kids playing drifts down the hall, and he rocks faster.

"No, we're only going to see Dr. Matt today." I block all doubts out of my mind. We've made it this far. It's got to work, for Michael's sake. "I thought it'd be nice to say hi."

We both turn at the sound of footsteps in the hall, and Michael is on his feet in seconds. He flies down the hall and yells hi at an Asian man wearing glasses.

"Michael, it's good to see you." Dr. Matt does not reach for Michael or wave. He smiles and searches for eye contact with him.

Michael blinks and starts flapping his arms by his side. The arm flapping was one of the first signs that my baby brother was different from other kids. At first we thought it was kind of cute and even called him Birdie, but once the doctors told us what it was about, the flapping became a sign of the struggles he would always face.

"I've missed you this year. All your old friends miss you."

I smile as I hold out my hand to Dr. Matt. "Riley McGee."

He shakes my hand and then peers behind me. "Did your mother step out for a minute?"

"Duh! She's not here." Michael's tone is teasing, and he waits for Dr. Matt to get the joke.

I motion down the hall and begin walking. "Can we talk for a moment in your office?" Dr. Matt is frozen in place, but I keep wandering down the hall, hoping to pass a door labeled something obvious like "Dr. Matthew Nguyen." I stop several yards away. "Please? I'll explain the situation in private."

Michael runs down the hall after me, oblivious. "Come on, Dr. Matt."

Dr. Matt glances back at the receptionist, who is doing her best to look like she's not paying attention, but her *People* magazine is drooping. He sighs and walks down the hall, then stops short and walks into a room I already passed.

Michael and I wander in behind him. He motions at two chairs on the other side of a modern white desk, presses the heel of his hand into his right eye, and sits down.

"Look, I can explain everything, but…" I glance nervously at Michael. It's tempting to try to talk over his head, but even though he misses social cues, he's not dumb. I know he understands a lot more of what's going on at home than he lets on.

Dr. Matt clears his voice. "Michael, I need your help today. Can you help me?"

This is a mere formality with most people, but this question is full of meaning for Aspies. On good days, Michael can help. But when he has sensory overload, when he's having a bad day, when something is unnerving him about his surroundings, he really can't help. Dr. Matt really wants to know how he's doing today.

"Yes," Michael says into his lap. "I'll help."

"Wonderful." Dr. Matt stands up, circles around the desk, and opens the door of his office. "We got a new game for the PlayStation, and the guys are stuck on level three."

"Okay." Michael joins him at the door. As they walk down the hall, I hear him say, apropos of nothing, "The albino alligator had seventy-five teeth. That's about average." I smile to myself. I thought I'd never tear him away from the alligator at the Academy.

When Dr. Matt comes back into the room, his face is sour. He sits down behind his desk and sighs. "Your parents aren't here, are they?"

I shake my head. Though Dr. Matt's appearance is impeccable, with short nails, a neat haircut, and a crisp white doctor's coat, his office is messy and disorganized. There are tall stacks of manila folders on his desk, his computer is from the dark ages, and there are books stacked all over the floor.

"And it wasn't your mom who contacted me?"

I shake my head again.

He peels off his wire-rimmed glasses and pinches the bridge of his nose. "I should have known. They didn't exactly part on the best of terms with me or the center."

"Really?" I remember the day we picked Michael up as being tense, but I thought it was because we'd all missed him so much. "What happened?"

"Riley..." Dr. Matt hesitates as if he's not sure if he has my name right. "I can't discuss a patient with anyone other than his parents or his legal guardian. And I'm afraid that I'm going to have to ask you to leave. There's a better way to do this."

"No, wait!" I bolt to my feet. After everything I did to get us here and all that's on the line, I'm not going to let him shuffle us right back out again. "I'm his sister, which means that someday I could be his legal guardian. Did you ever think of that?" I gulp at my own words. I'm not sure if I've ever admitted that to myself before. After Mom and Dad are gone, I will be Michael's keeper. The responsibility sends my head spinning.

"But you're not now, and the law is very clear on this point." Dr. Matt takes a folder labeled *McGee, Michael* and shuts it. "Please, encourage your parents to give me a call."

"Don't you think I thought of that? It won't work." I press my hands to the desk and lean across it. "I'm sorry I tricked you. I knew it wasn't the right thing to do, but I can't watch

Michael flounder like this anymore, and Mom and Dad are in denial or something."

Dr. Matt stands, pushes his chair under his desk, and motions to the door. "I wish I could help you. Please know how much I wish I could." He takes a few steps toward the door.

"Okay, wait." My brain runs a million miles a second. There has to be a loophole in here somewhere, and I'm going to find it for Michael's sake. "All I'm asking is that you go in there and talk to Michael. You're allowed to talk to him, right? You don't have to do an official assessment or anything like that—just talk to him like a friend. Ask him how he's doing and stuff."

Dr. Matt's back is to me, and he's holding the brass doorknob in his hand. His shoulders slump, and I hear him draw in a long breath.

"He asks about you a lot," I say quietly. I squeeze my eyes shut and send up silent prayers, begging for a miracle.

"Stay here," Dr. Matt finally says and walks out of the room carrying my highest hopes with him. Twenty grueling minutes later he returns. He seems shaken, and his eyes are a little watery.

"Riley, I'm going to level with you." Dr. Matt sighs. "Not as a doctor, but as a friend. I'm telling you that he needs to be in a special program."

"Did you see the hand flapping?" I stand and take a few steps toward him. "When he first came home from UCSF, he almost never did that anymore."

Dr. Matt nods slowly. "I noticed." The sound of a meltdown happening a few doors down drifts into the room. "But more importantly, he's deeply unhappy. It broke my heart to hear him talk about high school."

"I couldn't watch him all the time, but I really tried." A lump forms in my throat, and I swallow hard to push it down.

"It's not only that. The way the classes are taught doesn't fit his needs. He can't follow what's going on in half of them." Dr. Matt goes over to his bookshelf and rummages around. He finds a book with a thick spine on the third shelf and hands it to me. *How to Teach Autistic Kids.* "Here, take this. I think you'll find it really interesting."

I take the heavy textbook from his hands. "Thank you." I wait for him to say more, but he stays silent. Am I supposed to leave now? This is all I get? A book?

No, no, no. I can't leave now that we've agreed that Michael is totally depressed. I flip idly through the book, wondering how to push the issue.

"Riley, is there someone your parents might listen to?" Dr. Matt takes his glasses off and begins to polish the lenses on his shirttails. "Can you reach out to someone, explain what's going on, and ask them to make your parents listen?"

Tom's mom is on the board of directors. Surely Mom and Dad would listen to her, but that might not be such a good idea unless I want that creep back in my life. Hmm...I could read this book and sit Mom and Dad down and try to make them hear me. But they'd never listen to a teenager, especially one who's not going to college.

"I'd do it myself, but they were quite upset with my assessment of Michael last summer." Dr. Matt puts his glasses back on. "They made it pretty clear that my opinion was no longer wanted."

What I need is some kind of expert they trust. An impartial observer. Then it's as though there's a break in the clouds. All of a sudden the answer is as clear as day. I grab my purse off the chair and loop it over my arm.

"Actually, I do know someone."

42

I wait till I'm back on the freeway to make the call. Michael stares out the window as the suburbs of San Francisco fade away. When the phone rings, I pray that my luck hasn't run out quite yet.

"Riley?" Ms. Moore's voice is a little high. "Is that you? Is everything okay?"

Maybe she sounds weird because I'm calling on a Saturday afternoon, or because we haven't really talked in months, but I kind of doubt it. Ms. Moore has a way of reading minds or something. "I need to talk to you. Do you have time, um, now or maybe today?"

"Yes, of course. Where are you right now?" I can hear wind whipping around in the background. It's been an especially stormy April, and the sky is overcast and moody today.

"I'm coming back from San Francisco."

"Do you have a pen? Let me give you the address."

I find a pen and piece of paper in the console while Michael reminds me that talking on the phone while driving is illegal. It's not a threat that he's going to tattle on me, just a fact. "Okay, I'm ready."

She reads out an address to me. I know the general area, but what on earth is she doing all the way on the south side of town?

"Are you sure now is fine?" I try to sound extra desperate, even though I'm giving her a chance to wiggle out of it.

"Of course." She takes a deep breath. "I've been hoping you'd call."

A small sign at the end of the driveway says *The Mackinaws* and has a horseshoe nailed to it. The closest neighbors must be a mile down the road. I turn down the long dirt driveway, not really sure where I'm heading.

"Where are we?" Michael rolls down the window and studies the tall trees that form a semicircle around the low, no-nonsense brick structure.

"I need to talk to Ms. Moore really quick, then we'll go home." I stop at the end of the driveway and shut off the van. There are no signs of life anywhere. "Ready?" I smile and pretend I know exactly where I'm going. Michael shrugs, and we both get out of the van. I slam my door hard, hoping someone will hear the noise and come find us.

I take a few steps toward the front door, then stop. Ms. Moore was obviously outside when I called. Maybe we should circle around to the backyard?

"I want to go home." Michael scowls, and I see that he's had enough for one day. I'm probably five minutes from a meltdown.

"But then you'd miss the surprise I have for you!" A familiar man's voice says.

"Nick?" I turn in time to see Zoe's brother walk around the corner of the house.

"In the flesh." He clomps toward us in his giant work boots.

"Natalie's around back with the surprise." He motions for us to come with him, and within seconds Michael is at his side, peppering him with questions. I follow behind them, lost in my thoughts. Is Nick dating Ms. Moore? Does Zoe know? And what is this surprise?

As we make our way back, we pass misshapen hedges and lumber through high grass until we finally reach the expansive backyard. Well, it's more of a back lot, really. How many acres do these people own? To the left, past an old, sagging badminton net, there's a barn. I see Ms. Moore standing in front of it, smiling and waving, and I'm filled with remorse. She's clearly on some kind of weird horsey date with Nick, and we're interrupting it. It was not a good time for her, and she didn't hesitate to say yes.

Michael walks over, says hi to Ms. Moore, and wanders into the barn. Nick disappears in after him.

I linger at the door of the barn with Ms. Moore. The afternoon light is fading already, casting long beams across the hay-strewn floor. I swallow back a lump in my throat and give myself a pep talk. Why is it so hard to say those three little words?

"Listen," I say, mustering as much courage as I can. "I wanted to tell you how sorr—"

"I know." Ms. Moore holds up a hand. "I appreciate what you're going to say, but it's not necessary. We all go through rough periods."

"But that doesn't mean it's okay to abuse the people who

are trying to help you." I cringe, thinking back to all the ways I shut her out this year, all the quiet betrayals of my thoughts. "It's no way to treat a person, and I'm really sorry."

"Well, thanks. You're long forgiven, but I am cheered by your apology. It shows you've grown this year." She stuffs her hands in her pockets and begins to wander away from the barn door.

I follow a few steps behind her and chew on my lip. "I don't know if you're going to think I'm all grown-up once you hear what I've done."

A loud, happy neigh peals across the empty expanse.

"Whatever you did, you can tell me, and I'll try to help." We stop at the edge of a fenced-in ring, and I loop my arms over the highest wooden plank and stare into the distance. Ms. Moore leans her back against a solid wooden post and looks off in the other direction.

"I did some things that were technically wrong, but kind of right too."

Ms. Moore nods, and I try to explain everything, about how my parents didn't really want her advice and neither did I, but then Michael didn't get better and I felt him slipping away. I talk about finding Michael's medical records and breaking into Mom's e-mail account. Finally, I confess everything about our visit with Dr. Matt this morning and how he saw how serious the problem is.

"I know I shouldn't have lied and snuck around and all that other stuff, but right now I need your help with my parents." The sun begins to slide behind the tops of the trees in the distance, and the breeze kicks up again. "I can't watch Michael be unhappy anymore. It's killing me."

Ms. Moore casts her eyes to the barn on her right. We can hear the muffled voices, the jingling of the bits, and the occasional horse nicker from inside.

"That's the funny thing about right and wrong," she says quietly. "As you get older, the lines get kind of blurry. What is wrong in one situation can be a hundred percent right in another." She pushes herself up and sits on the top rail of the fence. I follow her, pulling my arms down and hugging them to my body.

What's she saying? That right and wrong can change? Sometimes the best you can do is a little of both? Choose the least terrible option? "I hate this. I really don't know if I'll ever get it right."

Ms. Moore smiles and laughs. "That's how you know you're getting it right. It's when you stop questioning that you have to worry." She jumps down off the rail, takes a few steps back toward the barn, and motions with her head. "C'mon. We've got a lot of work to do."

I jog to catch up to her. For being so short, she's surprisingly quick. "Does that mean you're going to help me?" Surely Mom and Dad will listen to her if she confronts them a second time. How stubborn can they be? "I know you can convince my parents."

She links her arm through mine and ushers me to the barn door. "Not me, Riley. *We* are going to change their minds. Together."

"They won't listen to me. Trust me, they think I'm still a little kid. They won't go for it unless you convince them."

"Well then, we'll just have to show them that you've grown up." Before I can ask what the plan is, she's pulling me into the dark barn. Nick is standing next to my brother in front of the second stall on the left. A middle-aged couple is hovering there too.

"Riley!" Michael flaps his arms. "There's a baby horse over here. She's a filly. The girls are called fillies, and the boys are called colts. She's only four weeks and three days old."

I walk to my brother's side and peer over the top of the stall door. A brown horse with three white socks looms over a tiny version of herself. The filly is standing on all four legs, but they're splayed in a funny, unsure way.

"Wow," I whisper. The filly turns in my direction and stares at me with rich brown eyes and long, thick lashes. "She's so tiny." It's the most obvious, mundane thing I could have said, but I can't move past how frail and small she is. It seems impossible to think that she will grow up to be as tall and strong as her mother.

"Do you think Zoe will like her?" Nick asks, grinning from ear to ear.

43

"Zo, did your parents freak out when you got the acceptance letter?" Ana takes a paper bag from her backpack and pulls out a bagel.

"You got in?" I jump up and run around the table to grab Zoe in my arms. She worked so hard for this. This is huge. "Oh my gosh. Congrats!"

Zoe pulls away. "Thanks. They got in too." She gestures at Ana and Christine.

"You guys all got in? To USC?" I feel my mouth hanging open. I'm not surprised, really, I'm just...Wow. They really might do this crazy thing, going off to college together, leaving me...where? "That's so awesome!" I try to sound upbeat and run around and hug the others.

"So you're really gonna go?" I sit back down on the bench and look around, praying they can't hear the fear in my voice. Ana shrugs, and Zoe looks down at the table.

"I didn't get much financial aid," Zoe says quietly. She pulls a cheese sandwich out of her bag. "Dreamy and Ed were really excited for about five minutes, but then we read the fine print. Ed is going to call the financial aid office and talk to them, so we'll see."

"That's ridiculous!" Christine's nostrils flare. "You filled out those forms perfectly. Even Ms. Moore said so."

"I know. But Ed's landscaping is back on track, and Dreamy's got her part-time thing. They make a little too much for me to qualify for any significant help."

Something buzzes in Ana's purse. She reaches in and pulls it out to switch it off, but she freezes when she sees who's calling.

"Right back." She chucks her bagel down and stands up quickly.

We watch her go, and for a minute we're all quiet.

In the far corner of the courtyard I see Ben and some of the other skaters he hangs out with at their usual table. I crane my neck to try to catch his eye, but he's talking to a redhead wearing a pair of hot-pink Vans. I wonder if he's heard that I broke up with Tom.

"Did they say you couldn't go if you didn't get more financial aid?" Christine asks, snapping me back to attention.

"I'm totally still going." Zoe shakes her head. "I'll figure it out somehow—take out big loans or whatever. How often do three best friends get into the same school?"

"Seriously." Christine lifts her bottle of green tea in a toast. "SoCal, here we come!"

It is pretty incredible that they did it, actually, but it didn't happen in a vacuum. Zoe got her grades up this year and really worked hard on her application. Christine's grades weren't awesome, but she turned out to be one of those closet SAT geniuses. And Ana, well, they're probably going to pay her money to attend USC.

"WHAT?!" Ana screams into her phone. Even from across the courtyard I can hear her perfectly. "Are you serious?!"

"I hope everything's okay." I turn back to the table and see a strange look on Zoe's face. Ana shrieks, and a moment later she's at our table, jumping up and down.

"That was my mom." Ana's face is flushed, and her eyes are watering. "I got into Princeton!"

Without thinking about what I'm doing, I tackle her in a huge hug and feel my own eyes well up with tears. "Oh my gosh! Congratulations! This is so huge!"

Ana looks like she's about to hyperventilate. I hand her my water. She takes a sip and starts laughing. I watch her, thinking of all the late nights, her unwavering devotion to such a far-off goal, her pure determination. She did it. She really, really did it. She got into the best school in the country. I look down at the table.

"So you're not just a pretty face." Christine walks over and gives her a hug. Is that the first hug she's ever initiated?

Then, for some reason, I turn to Zoe. Her face is plastered with a huge smile, but there's something sad about it, something lingering around her eyes. "I'm so proud of you, Ana." She shakes her head and rolls her lips in. "It's really happening, just like you've always planned."

Ana squeals, then takes a deep breath and tries to get herself under control. "Well, not *exactly* like I planned," she says, laughing a little. "I mean, mostly, but not totally." I widen my eyes, and she smiles nervously and goes on. "Remember when I said I had some things to tell you guys? Some harebrained plan I'm cooking up?"

For some reason, I'm not sure I want to hear whatever it is she's about to tell us, but I nod anyway.

"It kind of happened because of Maria. But then, I don't

know. I guess it started before then, really. Maybe it had been building for years, and I never realized it."

"Ana," Zoe says with uncharacteristic exasperation, "use your words. What on earth are you trying to tell us?"

Ana takes a few breaths and pushes her palms in a downward motion, like some kind of weird yoga move. "Okay, that call." She holds up her cell phone. "That was my mom. Do you know what she did? She saw this huge envelope from Princeton in our mailbox so she opened it and read it."

"She opened your mail?" It's hypocritical of me to be judgmental, given that I've become a grade-A snoop, but still, that's kind of crazy.

Ana points at me. "Exactly. You know how intense they are. And that's my problem."

"They've always been bonkers. What's the deal?" Christine narrows her eyes.

"I'm not going to be a doctor. And I think they might kill me."

This time it's our turn to scream. "WHAT?!" We ask her rapid-fire questions. How can she be so sure? What made her decide? Will her parents still pay for college if she's not premed? What's she going to do if she's not a doctor?

She laughs at us and holds up her hands. "I don't know the answers to all of your questions. But I can tell you a few things." She peels the crust off the edge of her bagel and seems lost in thought for a moment. "When I went to Mexico, I kind of thought I could save Maria with round-the-clock medical attention. I knew the doctors had sent her home to die, but I still believed." She pinches off a section of dough and squishes it between her fingers. "But nothing I did helped—or even made her feel better. The only thing that actually comforted her was spending time with her, chatting together, telling her stories." She stops, her lip trembling. I give her a squeeze.

"I guess that's when I realized I'd been looking at healing the world in the wrong way." Zoe rummages through her purse and finds a small package of tissues. Ana takes one and mops up her eyes. "My goals are the same, but I don't want to do it through medicine anymore." She nudges me. "God knows that math and science really aren't my strengths anyway."

"What are you going to do then?" I stare at her in wonder. Our rock, our sure-footed Ana did something I didn't think she was capable of. She moved.

Christine and Zoe peer across the table at her, hanging on every syllable.

"Well…" She collects her shredded bagel and shoves it back into the paper bag. "I guess this is where I need your help. Can any of you tell me how I'm going to make Mom and Papá understand I want to be a writer?"

44

I slip out of the youth room, but nobody notices. I drag my hand down the wall as I make my way to the bathroom. There's a bigger restroom in the new wing, but the old handicap-access two-holer is closest to the youth room.

I swing open the door. There's a dark shadow in the first stall and an Out of Order sign on the other. I sling my purse onto the counter and dig inside for my powder and lip balm. It's probably one of the old ladies from the quilting circle, which means I'll be waiting forever. They meet in the bridal parlor on Sunday nights, and they're notorious for gassing up the place.

I slick my Chapstick on and pucker my lips a little. Ben and I aren't exactly on friendly terms again, but it did seem like a good sign that he showed up tonight with Asha. Fritz must be making progress with all the gossipy old busybodies at church.

A low moaning comes from the stall, and I grimace in the mirror. Okay, that's just gross. I know they're old ladies and they probably can't help it, but still. Maybe I should haul my lazy bones across the church and use the other restroom and leave this poor old gal to her business.

A ragged gasping breath comes from the stall, and I pause. Is she crying? I shift a few inches to the right and catch a glimpse of the shoes underneath the stall door. Hey, wait a minute. This isn't some old lady. Who did I see wearing gold metallic ballet flats today?

There's another moaning sound. I'm going to have to do something. I don't want to embarrass this girl if she's got a stomachache, but if there's something seriously wrong, I can't walk away either.

I take a deep breath, walk over to the stall, and knock quietly. "Are you okay?"

"Riley?" A desperate, hoarse voice whispers.

"Asha?" I knock on the door again. "Are you stuck? Do I need to...go get help?"

"No." I hear her moving on the other side of the door. "Don't do that. I'm fine." Through the crack between the door and the frame, I see her unroll some toilet paper and blot her forehead. "I've got a stomachache, and I certainly don't need your help."

I study her for a moment. There's something not quite right about this situation. Asha is acting really out of it. I know she's mad at me, but this is something else. Why won't she get up?

"When are you—"

"One more month." She moves around behind the door, rustling her clothes, like she's pulling up her pants, then pushes the door open. I grab her arm. "Look, I'm fine. You can use the bathroom now." She leans over and glances at the back of her jeans.

"Asha?" I peer behind her and blink a few times. The back of her pants is wet. "Are you sure your water didn't break?"

"No, it couldn't have." She turns around and tries to get a better look at the back of her pants. "I went to the doctor on

Monday, and everything is fine," she says louder. "The baby's coming during summer break. It's all going to work out, okay?"

"Okay, okay." I flush the toilet, noticing the water is a little pink, lead her to the sink, and lean her against the counter gently. "You're right." I try to steady my own nerves as I calm her down. I don't know much about babies and pregnancy, but I am pretty sure she needs to go to the hospital. How do I convince her of that when she pretty much hates my guts? "I'm sure you're right. But why don't I go and get Judy and we'll see what she thinks."

"You can't." She starts shaking her head violently. "Oh jeez." She scrunches her face into a ball and clutches her stomach.

I grab her hand, and she squeezes it hard. I stay silent and pray like I've never prayed before. I can do this. With a little help from above, I can make it through this. I can be strong right now. Asha needs me.

Her grip on my hand relaxes, and she stares up at me, her lip quivering. "Please don't go tell all those people, your popular friends. I'm already a joke to them."

I shake my head. "I would never. I swear I'm not one of those people."

"Promise?"

And then it comes to me—what I need to do. It's so simple.

"I promise." I hold out my hand and take a deep breath. "Can you walk to my car?" She nods and allows me to slowly pull her away from the counter. I put my arm around her and lead her gently, carefully into the hallway. Once I get her in the van, I grab my phone out of my purse as fast as I can.

I watch through the window as Ben ducks out into the hall-way, away from the youth room. "What, Riley?" His tone is annoyed as he talks into his phone.

"The baby's coming." Asha grips the armrest of the pas-senger seat with all her might. "Asha and I are in my car in the parking lot. We need you."

We walk into the main entrance, and I thank God for small towns and tiny hospitals. When we take Michael to his appointments in the city, you have to read these complicated hospital maps to figure out what floor, what wing, where on earth you are—and we don't have that kind of time.

"Hi, checking in." I steady Asha with one hand and grab a clipboard with the other. "She's having a baby." The recep-tionist flashes me a fake smile. Okay, maybe that was obvi-ous. The form on the clipboard wants me to detail exactly what kind of injury I have, so I start frantically looking for a different clipboard. Next to me Ben is staring at the brightly colored bulletin board with a blank face.

"Are you the..." The receptionist's tone is efficient and a little cold. "Related?" She picks up a red clipboard and hands it to me, then motions at a bored-looking teenager. He pushes a wheelchair over to us at a snail's pace.

"I'm a friend of the family." I nudge Ben forward, but he just blinks a few times. Asha winces, and I help her into the chair. "Ben?" He stares at me as if he doesn't know what the word *Ben* means. Obviously I'm on my own here. "This is her brother. He's the next of kin right now. Her parents will be here in a minute."

The receptionist comes around the counter and begins to talk to Asha about how far apart her contractions are and what her health insurance is.

"Didn't she already tour the hospital and get set up in the system or something?" I hiss to Ben. I watch Asha nervously. Shouldn't they wheel her back to a bed, get her into a gown, and then deal with the paperwork?

"I don't know." He stares at her, his eyes wide, and I get the distinct feeling that he might run if I turn my back on him.

"Okay, okay." I nudge the nurse aside and grab the handles of the wheelchair. "Let's wheel her on back, and then we'll work out the rest of the details." I feel a few people in the waiting room staring at me.

Asha reaches back, grabs my hand, and smiles at me, her eyes filled with fear. And even though her belly looks huge on her once-small frame, she suddenly seems so young and vulnerable, almost like a kindergartner on her first day of school.

"We only need a few more details. . . ." The nurse's voice drifts as she grabs Asha's tiny wrist and studies her stopwatch.

It hits me all at once how alone Asha is. You always picture this moment unfolding so differently. You think of yourself being much older and mentally prepared. Your husband will be there, and maybe some family members too. In your dreams it will be calm and orderly, and you'll have a painted nursery waiting for your little one back home. This isn't the way it's supposed to happen.

"No." I stare the nurse down, doing my best to appear uncompromising. "Now. I want to wheel her back *now*." Maybe I'm being bossy, and maybe I'm overreacting, but someone needs to fight for Asha.

The nurse rolls her eyes, and we finally begin to wheel Asha to the back of the hospital. We stop at the end of a long hall, and the three of us help her into bed. Where are her parents?

Just as I'm raising up the back of the bed so Asha can sit up, someone walks in. Thank goodness. They made it. I turn around and gasp. It's not the Nayars. It's Pastor Jandel, awkwardly holding a tiny white teddy bear. It's the kind of thing you bring a five-year-old, and it looks so incongruous in his big hands.

"Your mom called the prayer chain," he says to Ben by way of explanation. "I..." He looks at Asha with something like fear, but he takes a step closer to her and lays the plush bear on top of the sheet. "I live close, so I rushed right over." His thinning brown hair is sticking up in the back, and he's wearing a faded T-shirt from a mission trip, rumpled khaki pants, and off-brand flip-flops. "I wanted to say...I wanted you to know that we love you, we're here for you, and we're praying for you."

Asha stares at him for a moment, looking straight into his eyes. She bites her lip, then slowly picks up the teddy bear. "Thank you," she says, her voice hoarse.

I stare at him. Somehow when you strip away his suit and his self-confidence, he seems ordinary and vulnerable, just another concerned dad bumbling his way through the awkward moments of life, trying to do the right thing.

"Well..." Pastor Jandel nods and clears his throat. He doesn't seem to know what to do with his hands now. "I'll be out in the waiting room," he says, stepping back toward the door. "In case you need anything. Your parents are on their way."

I glance at Ben as soon as he's gone, but he's staring at the floor. Asha is still clutching the bear, and suddenly I wish I had something to give her too. Holding it seems to give her so much comfort.

I wipe her forehead with a towel as the nurses start running tests. Asha clutches the bear to her chest, and soon the Nayars rush in. Mrs. Nayar covers Asha's body in a big hug. Mr. Nayar stops in his tracks.

"Asha." Ben's dad looks like he's seen a ghost, his jaw clenched. He takes a deep breath, then steps toward the bed. Slowly, he reaches out and puts his hand on Asha's arm. Asha smiles at him, tears in her eyes.

"Thank you for calling us," Mr. Nayar says to me and Ben. "And for…" He glances back at Asha and presses his lips together. "For handling everything. You guys saved the day."

Ben turns to me and smiles. "Riley saved the day."

The Nayars turn as a nurse starts asking them questions. And there, behind the commotion of a new life hasty to make its debut into this crazy mixed-up world, Ben takes my hand, and it feels like heaven.

"Glad to have you back, Supergirl."

45

M s. Moore has her hands wrapped around the mug I made for Father's Day in sixth grade. It's weird to see her here, in my kitchen, drinking peppermint tea, but I'm glad she came. I couldn't have done this without her.

"Thank you all for coming." I'm not sure what else to say. I clear my throat. This is so awkward. "As you know, I asked you here to talk about Michael."

My brother sits in his regular chair, but his eyes are glazed over, and he stares straight ahead like he can't see or hear any of us.

"Riley," Mom says, clasping her hands together. "I'm not sure this is the best—"

"I know we're all concerned about what's best for Michael," I say, cutting her off. "And I know how hard you guys have worked to make sure he gets the best possible care." Maybe this isn't entirely true, but they did try, and Mom's shoulders relax a bit. I glance at Ms. Moore, and she nods. "But over the past few months, some things have changed, and I wanted to readdress the situation. Things have been difficult this year for all of us. Mom, you've been making yourself crazy homeschooling Michael." Mom bobs her head. There are dark circles under her eyes. "And, Dad." His arms are crossed over his chest. "You've been working to keep this family afloat. But I didn't really realize how hard this has all been on Michael until I talked with Dr. Matt last week."

Mom sucks in her breath, and Dad presses his palms against the surface of the table.

"You talked to Dr. Nguyen?"

I cast a pleading glance at Ms. Moore. She lifts her chin but doesn't say anything.

"I got in contact with him after I realized that no matter how much we want Michael to get better, we simply aren't able to give him the help he needs. I saw that he was regressing. I saw that I couldn't protect him even when I tried. I started reading this book about how autistic kids learn, and I realized we've been doing a lot of things wrong. And"—I glance at Michael, who is still pretending he can't hear a word of our conversation—"I talked to Michael about what *he* wanted."

I tap my brother's arm. "Michael." He doesn't acknowledge me, so I tap him again. "*Michael.*" He shrinks away, but finally turns toward me. "Would you please tell Mom and Dad what you said to me?"

Michael doesn't say anything for a moment. As he sits there, rocking back and forth silently in his chair, I start to panic. If Michael flakes out on me now, this is never going to work.

"Michael?"

He's flailing his arms a little in his chair. *Please, God.* He can't have a tantrum now. Not when everything is on the line.

I can hear the clock tick above the kitchen sink. Ms. Moore clears her throat.

"Well, Michael and I talked about it," I start, "and he wanted to tell you—"

"I can speak for myself," Michael blurts out. I freeze. He is glaring at me. "I just needed some time to think so the words wouldn't come out wrong." His voice is angry, and I smile at him, trying to encourage him. "You're always in such a hurry. Sometimes I just need more time."

I start. Does he think I rush all the time? I think back on the past year. Well, sure, I didn't always have time to wait around for him after practice or whatever, but what sister could honestly have done better?

"Michael, I—"

"Riley—" Dad starts.

"I didn't like Marina Vista." Michael's voice is flat and emotionless, but it doesn't hide his pain. "The kids were mean to me, and the teachers were too hard. They treated me like I was stupid," Michael says, glancing at me. "I'm not stupid."

Mom sniffs, and I see tears glistening in her eyes.

"How do you like being homeschooled, Michael?" I ask.

"Mom doesn't know how to teach like Dr. Matt."

Mom sniffs again, and I can see that the words sting, even though we all know Michael doesn't mean things like they sound.

"I miss Dr. Matt. He helped me not feel so bad."

Ms. Moore reaches for a box of tissues on the counter and

pushes it toward Mom. Mom pulls one out and dabs at her eyes.

"Michael," Dad starts, then stops. "We know Dr. Matt helped you, but you couldn't stay at the program forever. We're your family, and we want you here because we love you. We want to help you too."

"I know you do, Dad," I say quickly. "I was with you guys on bringing him home, and I really thought we could do as good a job as the clinic, but what I've started to discover is that we can't. We can't help Michael like the doctors in the program can. I know you didn't want him there, but I think he needs to go back and work with Dr. Matt again."

Dad reaches out and lays his hand on Mom's arm. Tears are streaming down her cheeks.

I bury my head in my hands. What am I doing? This was a terrible idea. Is there any feeling in the world worse than knowing you've made your mom cry? My legs twitch, and all I want to do is run upstairs and hide in my room, like I did when I was a little girl.

"Riley." Slowly I look up and meet Ms. Moore's eyes across the table. She's trying to stay out of the way, I know that, but she's also encouraging me. Knowing that she thinks this is the right thing, that I'm doing something good—for some reason, that means more than I can say right now.

"We need to do this for Michael," I say as calmly as I can. "The best way we can help him is by letting him go."

Dad pushes his chair back and stands up. "We'll talk about it." He shoves his chair in and steps away from the table. "Your mother and I will talk about it." He puts his hand on my mom's shoulder and helps pull her up, and together, without a word, they disappear down the hall.

No one else moves. Michael's staring off into space again. Ms. Moore sits still, her chin up. I wait, trying to figure out what to do. I feel horrible—selfish, mean, awkward. But also, if I'm honest, a little bit proud.

46

The nylon is thin and hot, and it feels like I'm wearing a plastic bag. I smooth the maroon gown down, trying to imagine what it will be like to march out of that stadium and leave Marina Vista forever. I place the thin cardboard hat on my head and start to hum that stupid song they always play at graduations.

I shake my head. I can't picture it. It's like trying to imagine your own execution.

The vague echo of the doorbell rings out through the house. Mom's busy washing the dishes after a silent dinner, but I hear footsteps and know Michael has it under control. I turn back to my reflection in the mirror. The gold tassel falls over my eye, and I brush it back. The minute everyone throws their caps into the air, it's all over; we'll all be scattered across the globe. And I'll—well, I don't know what I'll be doing exactly, but I have an idea. I pull the cap off and toss it onto the bed.

"Riley?"

I turn toward the sound. Zoe. I take a step back and grab at the billowy fabric of my graduation gown, my cheeks flushing. "I was making sure it fit." I unzip the gown, pull it off, and toss it onto the bed.

"I tried mine on too. It's way too short." She lets out a breath and leans against the door frame.

I narrow my eyes. Something isn't right. "What's wrong?" I gesture for her to come into my room. She follows me across the room and sits on the edge of my bed. "Spill it."

Zoe looks down at her feet, her long, thin legs making an awkward triangle against the bed. When you see someone every day, you don't really notice the subtle ways they change, but I think Zoe's transformed the most of all of us. When we first met her in detention, she was this shy, overweight band geek who only wanted everyone to get along. Somehow, in the past few years, she's blossomed, and now she's not afraid to speak her mind or go out and get what she wants. It's weird how things shift, a little bit at a time, until one day you look up and realize your best friend has grown up.

"Zoe?"

"Nick bought me a horse."

I grab her knee. "She's so adorable. I was there when he did it." I search her face, wondering why she isn't smiling. "He told you that, right?"

"Yes, but..." She threads her fingers together. "Well, any-way, I was out in the barn with Ophelia." Her voice is flat, and her eyes show that she's far away. "Cleaning out her stall, put-ting hay down and stuff, and I heard voices. It was Dreamy and Ed. They were fighting again."

"Oh no. I'm sorry." I edge closer to her on the bed, but she doesn't seem to notice. Zoe's parents went through a really rough time last year. If they split up again, it will kill her.

"They obviously came down to the barn because they didn't want me to hear, and I didn't want them to know I was there, so I ducked down low and tried to stay out of sight." She leans back and crosses her legs. "They were fighting about how to pay my tuition. Ed got a little more money out of the financial aid office, but not enough, so he wanted to take out another mortgage on the house—" Zoe shakes her head. "But Dreamy said there was no way they could make the payments on a second mortgage, and they'd probably end up losing everything. She thought the only way to make it work was to sell the stable—the land, the horses, everything. Give up on the whole dream."

"But I thought—"

She holds up her hand and keeps talking. "I can take out student loans, but they only cover so much, and I'll be paying them off until I'm forty. So I realized what I have to do." She takes a deep breath. "I have to say no to USC."

I lean in close to her, but she doesn't react. It's like she doesn't notice. I watch her stoic profile, silhouetted against my bright-white closet doors. She's eerily calm. "Are you sure?"

"I can't do that to Dreamy and Ed. I know they'd find the money if I asked them to. They'd give up everything for me. But I can't let them." Zoe pulls her legs up under her.

"I'm so sorry." I feel so dumb in situations like this. I know I should be able to say something that sounds less stupid, but I have no idea what that is. "I know how much you wanted to go to USC."

Zoe doesn't say anything for a moment. "Ana wasn't going to go anyway, not after she got into Princeton, but I don't know how to tell Christine. I made her apply, talked it up so much, and because of me she didn't apply to New York schools, and now..."

"Christine will understand," I say, but as the words leave

my mouth, I'm not really sure I believe them. "She has to, when you explain the situation."

"Eventually she will." Zoe leans back, resting her elbows on the mattress. "I know she won't be mad forever, but...I don't know. I pushed the whole thing on her, and now she's stuck with it. I should have known it was never going to work." She leans back all the way and stares up at my ceiling. "I just wanted to find some way to keep us all together."

I touch her shoulder, and she sits up again. I put my arms around her. "So what's Plan B?"

"I guess community college," she says into my shoulder. "Living at home. Gus was saying something about being an assistant manager at El Bueno Burrito."

My heart aches. I'm not going to college next year because I screwed up. I freaked out, made some bad decisions, and chose a different path. If I had wanted it, college was mine for the taking. But Zoe worked so hard for this. For her to come so close and still find her dreams out of reach is gut-wrenching. I pull her in closer. I think about all she's been through these past few years—how hard she tried to save her parents' marriage, how she fought to bring Ms. Moore back, how she made her future a priority and turned her schoolwork around. How she finally, after so many fits and starts, fell in love.

I pull back and study her face. "Is Dean still going to go to USC?"

Zoe takes a deep breath. She closes her eyes for a moment, then opens them again. "I broke up with Dean."

"What?" I shriek. "When?" My heart pounds in my ears. "Why?"

"It wasn't going to work," she says simply. I wait for a

moment, then nudge her. She sighs. "I don't know, Riley. Things have been weird for a while. You guys have seen that. Maybe I wanted USC partly because I thought if we stayed in the same place we could make it work. But once that was out of the question, it seemed obvious."

She wraps her arms around her legs. "When I think about you guys being so far away next year, I hate it, but I don't worry. I know we'll be okay. What the four of us have is stronger than anything on this earth. It's enough to keep us together when we're apart. But with Dean, I don't know."

I can hear the pain in her voice, even though she seems perfectly calm and controlled. I'm struck once again by how different she is from the overly emotional, sentimental girl I knew freshman year.

"When I think about him being there, and me being here, I can't see it. Ultimately we don't have enough in common to stay together when we're apart. I had to let him go."

47

'm delighted, obviously," Dr. Matt says, nodding at my parents across his desk. "I really do think bringing Michael back for another summer is best for him. But I will admit, I am surprised. Are you sure about this?"

Mom's fingers curl around the arm of her chair. "Yes," she says quietly. She presses her lips together, her face pale. Dad places his hand on top of hers.

Dr. Matt watches them for a second, then reaches into his desk and hands Dad a folder. "I'm sure we have a lot of this on file, but we'll need his information updated for him to be readmitted. Now, after the three-month program is over, we'll want to see Michael twice a week for therapy." He goes on to explain the costs and logistics of the program, and my parents listen politely, even though Mom looks like she's about to cry. Dad flips through a couple sheets and nods as Dr. Matt explains liability coverage and insurance forms. I'm only half-listening. The other part of my brain is busy trying to figure out how to make sure Dr. Matt says yes to my idea. I don't know what I'm going to do if he says no.

"Melanie can help you if you have any questions about the forms," he says, picking up a thin gold pen. He rolls it around in his palm and clears his throat. "And I'll say again that I am so glad you've decided to do this. I'm anxious to see improvement with Michael, and I know you are too." He smiles at my parents.

Mom sighs and pushes herself out of the chair. "Thank you," she says simply. She turns toward the door. "We'll let your office know if we have any questions." She lifts her purse onto her shoulder, and my parents disappear into the hallway without another word.

I stand like I'm going to follow them, but I stop and wait until they're gone and turn back to Dr. Matt. "Hey, can I ask you something?"

"Of course, though if it has to do with Michael's—"

I shake my head and hoist up my bag. "I read this." I reach into my bag and pull out the thick, heavy book he gave me about teaching autistic kids.

Dr. Matt looks at me over the tops of his glasses. "This isn't light reading." He reaches out and takes the book from me. "What did you think?"

"I loved it. I wish I'd known to give this to Mom six months ago." I shove my hands into my pockets and try to steady my voice. "There's a lot of good information in there." Dr. Matt nods and waits for me to go on. "I wish I knew more about this kind of thing—how to help kids like Michael learn, I mean. So I was thinking." I gulp. "Do you know of any kind of internship or anything like that? In this field, I mean?" I realize I'm speaking really fast. "I kind of a have a year off, and I didn't really know what I was going to do, but now I think I do if I can find a way to make it work."

Dr. Matt lays the pen down on his desk and leans forward. He cocks his head and chuckles. "You're looking for an internship? At the program?"

I nod.

"We don't have any official internship program, but like most facilities, we're understaffed." Dr. Matt smiles kindly. "I'm sure if I ask around I can probably find something for you to do at the clinic if you're willing. I don't know if we can pay you anything, but—"

"That's okay," I say quickly. "I'll get a job or something too. I'm just looking for a way to learn more about this stuff. I don't know for sure, but I devoured that book, and I really want to help kids like Michael. I think this could be something I'd like to do, you know, as a career or whatever."

"Riley?" Dad pops his head back into Dr. Matt's office. "We've got Michael. We're waiting on you." He glances from me to Dr. Matt and back to me, his eyebrows raised.

"I'll ask around, Riley, and be in touch soon," Dr. Matt says. "I'm confident we can figure something out for you."

Dad waits for me to explain, but I smile and brush past him into the hallway. I don't quite know how to tell them they're going to be moving two kids up to San Francisco this summer.

48

The youth room is buzzing tonight. It's the youth group's graduation party, and, unbeknownst to us, Fritz asked our parents to bring in baby pictures and plastered them around the room. Everyone is walking around looking at the photos and guessing which cherubic toddler turned into which teen. Some of them are obvious: the pale, chubby girl with the wild shock of red hair is Zoe; the adorable Asian baby scowling at the camera is Christine. Dave, Ana's ex, is posing with a guitar, his two-year-old smile proud, and baby Ben basically looks like a miniature version of himself.

Mine is pretty easy to pick out as well. It was taken behind our old house, the one we lived in before the whole dot-com thing. I'm bent over, my diapered bottom stuck out, pointing at a flower. I'm trying to show the flower to baby Michael, but Michael is staring off toward the right, not really looking at anything.

"Nice outfit," Ben says, elbowing me out of the way to get a closer look at my picture.

"Hey. I've always believed that less is more." I shrug, even though I feel my face burn. The least my parents could have done was pick a photo in which I was fully clothed. I glance around the room. "Asha didn't make it tonight?"

Ben shakes his head. "She's pretty wiped. She's hardly gotten any sleep, and Ravi cries, like, all the time." He rolls his eyes, but I see pride in his smile. "She'll be really excited to hear what you're doing tonight though. I know she'll appreciate it."

"I still can't believe she wants to set foot in this place again."

Ben shrugs. "She's a forgiving soul. Besides, she wants Ravi to grow up knowing about God, and for whatever reason, she thinks he'll get that here."

I think about all that she's been through—everything the people at this church have put her through. She's either completely crazy or she has a deeper faith than I can begin to imagine.

"Riley?" I turn to see Fritz standing behind me, holding out a clipboard. "I'm about to gather everyone, so get ready to make your announcement." He hands me the clipboard and hesitates for a second. "Thanks for doing this," he says quickly, then turns and walks toward the front of the room.

Fritz puts his fingers in his mouth and whistles, then asks us to take a seat in the rows of chairs in the middle of the room. When everyone is settled, he turns the mic over to me. I climb up on the small plywood stage and face the rows of students in front of me.

"Hi." My voice echoes out over the youth room. The mic squeaks, and I see Michael frantically adjusting knobs in the back of the room. "Is this better?" My voice comes out normal this time, and a few people nod, so I continue. "I know this is supposed to be a party, so I won't take a lot of time, but I wanted to say how cool it is to see all of these baby pictures here tonight."

I look out over the youth group. Ben is smiling, waiting expectantly.

"It seems like just yesterday we were running around

the nursery wreaking havoc." A few people laugh, including Tommy Chu, who really was a terror in Sunday school. "It's amazing to see how these tiny kids grew up with the love and care of this church and ended up turning into such awesome people. And I'm up here tonight because I want to make sure that every baby in this church gets that opportunity."

Zoe is nodding, but most of the people look at me, confused.

"I wanted to announce that I'm starting a babysitting ministry for Asha Nayar. I want to make sure she feels completely welcome and able to come to youth group. She can bring Ravi to the nursery on Sunday mornings, but we're looking for people to sign up to take care of him during youth group and other special events."

The room is completely quiet. Cecily and Maddie look at each other, eyebrows raised.

"We're not asking you to give up much time at all, just once a month or so." I lift up the clipboard. "I'm going to put this sign-up sheet in the back. I hope you can all try to help."

Everyone is watching me as I make my way off the stage. They're quiet. I really hope they go for this. If they don't step up and support her now, I don't know if I can take it. I walk to the back of the room and lay the clipboard down on a folding table while Fritz makes an announcement about a pool party at Tommy Chu's house next weekend. There's a short break while the guys from Three Car Garage get set up to start worship, and I slip out the back door.

The courtyard is empty, and my footsteps echo on the pavement. This used to be all grass, but now the smooth concrete leads right up to the side door of the new wing. I step inside and make my way down a series of carpeted hallways—past the sanctuary, beyond the bridal parlor, behind the gym— toward the church office. I push open the heavy wooden door and look around. There's the church secretary's desk, and I think the pastors have their offices right over there. I walk down the open corridor and see a light on in one of the offices. That has to be it. I hurry toward it, but when I get there, I stand awkwardly in front of the open door, trying to figure out what exactly I came here to say. Jesus said that if you have an issue with someone, forget about everything else and go reconcile with them. Well, here goes.

Pastor Jandel is absorbed in something on his screen and doesn't seem to notice me standing in the doorway. I tap on the door, and he turns toward me, his eyes wide.

"Is youth group over already?" He peeks at the corner of his screen, then looks back at me in confusion.

"No." I step inside the office and cross my arms over my chest. "But I wanted to talk to you."

"The budget reforecast is due this week," he says, gesturing toward his computer on his right. On his screen is what looks like a spreadsheet. "But if you'd like to call the church secretary tomorrow and make an appointment—"

"No." I plop myself down in one of the padded chairs in front of his desk. "I'd like to talk now."

He looks like he's about to argue, but then he sighs. "What is it I can help you with?" He taps a few keys and a cursor moves down his spreadsheet. "It's always good to hear from the youth of the church—"

"Youth." I roll my lips in and try to breathe normally. "Yeah, that's kind of what I wanted to talk about."

He waits, his eyebrows raised. There's a framed picture of his two little daughters on his desk.

"I have been part of this church my whole life," I say evenly. "You've been here, what, a couple years?"

He nods and scratches at something invisible on his pant leg.

"I appreciate what you've been trying to do for this church," I say, trying to get my voice under control. "I know you've been working hard to get new programs off the ground to reach people. I understand the importance of that. But in the meantime, you've been trampling on the people who have made this church what it is."

"I have?" The quaver in his voice makes him seem younger somehow.

"I'm talking about Asha Nayar." He nods as recognition dawns. "This year she made a mistake. It was a serious mistake, for which she needed serious help. But at the moment she needed help the most, this church turned its back on her."

"Riley." Pastor Jandel sits up straight. "That's just not true. Is that how you see it?"

"Yes, I do." My stupid eyes water like I'm a baby. "You tried to have Asha removed from the youth group."

Pastor Jandel leans forward and rests his elbows on his desk. "Suggesting that Asha might benefit from the young parents small group was not intended to be a punishment." He shakes his head. "Asha is facing decisions and pressures that the youth group cannot begin to touch on. She's had to grow up fast, and we..." He falters for a moment and seems to consider something. "I honestly thought she could learn from other people who are going through the same thing."

"But what about your e-mail to the prayer chain?" I take a deep breath and promise myself I will not cry. "You said you were going to 'deal with the girl.'"

"Obviously you didn't see my actual e-mail. I said nothing like that." He takes a deep breath and lets it out slowly. "I pray I will never be so careless with my words. My heart has really gone out to the Nayars and Asha this year."

"I don't know." I hold my head, thinking back through all the events of the year. "After all your talk about following the rules and how everything is black-and-white..."

"I do believe the truth is very clearly laid out in Scripture, Riley, and—"

"But there's a lot of room for gray too," I say. "I mean, the Bible was written like two thousand years ago, and it really doesn't cover everything we deal with today. And the more I look at it, the more I see that a lot of the stuff I've been told is true isn't really in there anyway."

Pastor Jandel leans back in his chair. "I don't have all the answers." He lets out a breath. "But I do know that God promised that the grass withers and the flowers fall, but his Word stands forever." I wait for him to go on, but he seems to be gathering his thoughts. "More than anything, I want this church to be a body that meets people's needs—spiritual and physical. That's what we were trying to do with Asha."

I sigh deeply. "I can see that your intentions were good. You wanted to help her and stuff." Jandel's shoulders relax a little. "But in doing so, you were judging her, making her feel like she was being punished. I mean, sure, she messed up, but if all sin is the same to God, then we're all just as guilty."

Pastor Jandel looks like he's trying to work out something to say but can't find the words.

"This is the kind of stuff that drives people away from God forever. It made me question a lot of things, and I know I'm not the only one."

Pastor Jandel still doesn't say anything. I push myself up slowly, and for a moment, I tower over him.

"I'm sorry, Riley," he finally says. "I appreciate your speaking up. I guess we old-timers didn't consider how our actions might be interpreted." He gives me his salesman's smile, but behind it I see something new, a kindness in his eyes. "I'll see what can be done to repair things."

We stare at each other, and the stillness echoes in my ears. Maybe Pastor Jandel and I will never see eye to eye, but I guess this is what the body of Christ is really like. It's made up of thousands of individuals with different notions and views on the world.

"Thank you," I say quietly and let myself out of his office, wandering back toward the youth room in confusion.

Three Car Garage is still playing when I make it back out into the courtyard. I hurry my steps. Maybe I can catch the end of worship time. I crack the back door to the youth room and slip inside as quietly as I can. Michael waves at me from the sound booth, and I laugh, then walk quietly toward the table in the back. I squint down at the clipboard and gasp.

Every line on the sign-up sheet I made has been filled in, and several people scrawled their names on the back of the sheet once the front was used up. I scan the names. Cecily and Maddie are there, right near the top. In fact, from the looks of it, most of the people in this room volunteered to help Asha. Even Michael put his name on a line, which should make for a heck of a nursery experience for everyone. Fritz walks over to me quietly and takes a seat on the folding table.

"You did it," Fritz whispers.

I look out at the people gathered here tonight. They're not perfect, to be sure, but if this sign-up sheet is any indication, they're trying. I push myself up onto the table too and swing my feet below me.

I guess I've always known that just because someone goes to church that doesn't mean they'll always do the right thing. No one ever said that having faith means you won't mess up. Maybe authentic faith, not just following-the-rules faith, makes it harder to know what's right in the first place. The more I see of real, true, deep faith, the more I understand that there usually are no easy answers. All we can do—all any of us can do—is take one faltering step after another, praying that God will lead us in the right direction. As I sit here in the back of the room, listening to voices of my church family, I can't help but think we took a step down the right path tonight.

49

When Ana and I are called to the office in the middle of English, I don't worry too much about it. We graduate next week. There's not a whole lot they can do to us anymore, so I try to enjoy the sunshine and the unexpected break. Ana doesn't say anything as we walk across the courtyard, and she blots her forehead and whispers something in Spanish as we pull open the office door.

"What's going on?" I whisper, but she shakes her head.

"Whatever happens, it's going to be okay, right?" she says quietly. Her skin is kind of green.

"Do you know what this is—"

"Welcome, girls," Mrs. Benassi calls out as we step inside the cool office. "Right inside." She gestures at the doorway to Ms. Lovchuck's office. "They're waiting for you."

I turn to Ana, but she won't meet my eye. She bites her lip, puts her head down, and walks toward the door. What in the world?

"Oh." Ana stops short in Ms. Lovchuck's doorway, and I have to jump to avoid running into her. "Ms. Moore. Hi."

I peek around her and see Ms. Moore leaning back in a chair next to Ms. Lovchuck's desk. What is she doing here?

"Riley. Ana." Ms. Lovchuck smiles, like she's genuinely glad to see us, and my stomach drops. She's never been glad to see us in the four years we've been at this school. Something is horribly wrong. "Please sit down," Ms. Lovchuck says, gesturing toward the two empty chairs in front of her desk.

Ana sits obediently, perching on the edge of her chair. I settle in next to her and remind myself to breathe.

"First of all, I hope you'll join me in congratulating Ms. Moore. She's just been appointed vice principal of Marina Vista. It will be announced later today." She nods, and Ms. Moore's cheeks turn pink.

"Congrats," I say, holding up my hand for a high five. Ms. Moore meets my hand. Ana squeaks.

Ms. Lovchuck clears her throat. "Now, as you both know, each year the top two students in each class are given the opportunity to speak at graduation."

I suck in my breath. They can't mean—

We took our finals this week and don't know yet how we did, but the results of those tests probably determine who's at the top of the class. Ana tenses up, so I reach out and grab her hand. She squeezes mine in return.

Ana has always wanted this. Being valedictorian is her dream. She should get this. But now that I'm sitting here, I can't deny there's a small part of me that would like the honor too. In spite of—or maybe because of—the whole college thing, something in me still kind of hopes to be recognized for the things I did right.

Ms. Lovchuck lifts her glasses off her nose and lets them dangle down on their chain in front of her. "Ana"—she turns and narrows her eyes at Ana—"you are quite possibly the most driven student Marina Vista has ever seen." Ana's cheeks flush. "You're smart, you're engaged, you've shown

tremendous empathy and leadership, and we couldn't be more
proud of all that you've accomplished."

"And, Riley." Ms. Lovchuck turns to me. "No one can say
that you've always exercised the best judgment." She coughs.
"Nor have you demonstrated the most effective use of your
abilities."

I let my eyes rest on the fish tank in the corner of the room
and watch the tiny silver dots dashing around the dark water.

"But no one," Ms. Lovchuck continues, "can deny that your
talents are formidable. Your test scores are off the charts,
your GPA is near-perfect, and all your teachers know that you
barely have to try to do well. I hope someday you appreciate the magnitude of the gifts you've been given." She leans
forward in her office chair. "But you've also demonstrated tremendous leadership skills, a deep and abiding sense of duty to
those you love, and, ah...*unique* problem-solving skills." She
meets Ms. Moore's eyes, and they share a laugh.

"We know you've chosen an unorthodox path. We know
it won't be easy, but we applaud the courage it took not to
conform to others' expectations of who you're supposed to
be. Many students in your place would have gone ahead and
done what everyone was telling them was right, but you listened to that voice inside of you and made the choice that was
right for you. That alone takes more faith than many of us will
ever have."

I feel like I should interrupt, explain that's not exactly how
it happened, that I freaked out; but when I open my mouth,
I'm not so sure. In the end, I chose not to apply to Harvard by
not getting my application in on time. By not deciding what
I wanted to do, I made a decision. With the world wide open

before me, I could have done anything—but I chose this. To be here. To stay close to the people I couldn't leave behind. Sure, maybe I could have picked a better way to get there, but in the end, it was my decision.

Ana's palm gets a little sweaty, but I don't let go.

"Ms. Lovchuck and I tallied up the final results of your tests this morning," Ms. Moore says quietly. I think I see her wink.

"And we're pleased to announce that Riley McGee will be this year's valedictorian. Ana, congratulations on being salutatorian."

Ana drops my hand and sucks in her breath.

"The difference between your GPAs was only two-hundredths of a percentage point. That's the closest margin in Marina Vista's history. Now, you'll only have five minutes to speak...." Ms. Lovchuck launches in with information about graduation that my brain cannot process right now. "So carefully think through what it is you want to say to sum up the lessons these four years have taught you. Maybe you could talk about your hopes for the future. You'll be seated on the stage during the ceremony, but go ahead and gather with the other students beforehand. I'll need you both—"

In the middle of Ms. Lovchuck's monologue, Ana yanks me to my feet and throws her arms around me. Neither of us say anything; the only noise is the gurgling of the water in Ms. Lovchuck's fish tank. As we stand here together, trying to make sense of what this news means, all I can think about is that first day in Mr. Mackey's class when Ana accused me of cheating, and even though I hated her for getting it wrong, I kind of admired her for standing up to me. I don't know if

I've ever told her that. Back in those days, I thought I was this invincible force—the indomitable Riley McGee—but she never let me get away with it. Ana was always challenging me, fighting me, pushing me to work harder. I knew even then that she would make me better than I ever could be on my own. I know she's always seen it as this big miracle that we ended up overcoming our differences and becoming friends, but the truth is, that was a choice too.

Slowly, Ana pulls back. "Congratulations," she says, the glimmer of tears in her eyes. "You deserve this."

And though I'm not sure I agree, I can see that she means it, and for some reason that means the world to me.

50

The big events in my life always seem to take place on a beach. It was here, just off this beach, where I first learned to surf, and, many years later, where I washed up onshore; I woke up with a whole new understanding of the fine line between heaven and earth. Freshman year I fell off those cliffs, just a little ways south of here, and began to understand that I'm fallible, and that my friends will be there for me anyway. Sophomore year I met Tom in the parking lot at State Beach. And then there was the whole Mavericks thing with Ben. For better or for worse, this is the scenery of my life—the steep, high cliffs, the rough sand, the crushing power of the waves, the vast expanse of silver sky stretching out toward the horizon. It feels right to be here now, celebrating the end of twelve long years.

It's Senior Skip Day. Every year the graduating students at Marina Vista gather on the Friday of the last full week of class and hang out on the sand, then have a big bonfire once the sun goes down. There's no official notice, but somehow everyone seems to know the plan. The sun is shining, and everyone is joking, laughing, enjoying the last few weeks of childhood.

Well, almost everyone. Ben isn't here. He's helping out with Ravi today. He never did have much patience for anything that reeks of school spirit.

I'm chatting with some of the girls on the squad, reminiscing about a colossal screwup at homecoming freshman year, when I catch sight of a familiar face picking her way down the path toward the beach. She's wearing sunglasses, clutching a big white beach bag, and her long dark wavy hair is flowing out behind her.

"Be right back, guys," I say. Ashley squeezes my shoulder, and I smile before I pull away from the tight cluster. I jog toward the approaching figure as Zoe catches up to her on the other side, her face incredulous.

"Ana?" I squint to make sure I'm seeing things right. It can't be her. Ana has never cut a class in her life. The girl lifts up her head and smiles, pulling her sunglasses up, and I laugh out loud at the guilty look on her face. "You do know this is Senior Skip Day, right?"

"As in, we're technically supposed to be in school?" Zoe skips down the beach, leading Ana down to the patch of sand where we've stowed our things.

Ana laughs and inhales deeply. "So this is what it's like," she says. "The sweet scent of rebellion."

She drops her bag onto the sand next to Christine, who's sprawled out on a beach blanket sketching in the front cover of someone's yearbook.

"Watch it," Christine calls without looking up, but I can see she's smiling as I drop down on the blanket beside her.

"So what you're saying is your parents have no idea you're not at school," Zoe says. She meets my eyes above Ana's head and stifles a laugh.

"Three months from now I'll be on my own." She lowers herself down onto the blanket and starts to pull things out:

sunblock, a floppy hat, a copy of *Crime and Punishment*. "They can't possibly ground me beyond August. Besides, this is kind of fun. Who knew?"

Christine snorts. "And the award for Most Improved goes to"—she raps her pen on the edge of the page in a makeshift drumroll—"God Girl!"

Ana smacks Christine's arm and laughs. "Hey now. I know I used to be kind of uptight—"

I snort.

"Okay, fine. I was insane." Ana pulls the sunglasses off her head, folds them carefully, and puts them on the blanket. I pick them up and slip them onto my face. The world suddenly goes three shades darker. "But I'm here now."

"I'm glad," Zoe says, pulling Ana into a side hug. "You've changed. We all have."

"You guys won't forget me when I'm three thousand miles away, right? You'll come visit?"

"Actually…" Christine closes the cover of the yearbook, puts it down on the blanket, and stretches her legs out in front of her. "I kind of have to tell you guys something." She mumbles this last part, and I see Ana's eyes widen. Christine always clams up when she has something important to say.

"What's up?" I try to make my voice light. Zoe leans in closer.

"I didn't tell you guys because I thought you were all set on USC, but I kind of secretly applied to NYU." She pulls her knees up and wraps her arms around them. "I mean, it wasn't supposed to be a secret, but then I didn't want to break up the SoCal party, and then I was wait-listed, so I thought, oh whatever, I won't say anything. But yesterday I found out I got in." Christine intertwines her fingers around her knees.

"Christine!" Zoe throws her arms around her. "Oh my gosh! New York!"

"New York is only an hour away from Princeton," Ana says, clapping her hands.

"Wow." I blink a few times. "Christine, that's fantastic." I try to imagine Christine on the streets of Greenwich Village. "You're..." I cough. New York. That's so far away. "You're really going to go?"

I accepted that Ana is moving across the country, but I had kind of gotten used to the idea of going down to see Christine in LA on weekends. I didn't think I would lose her too.

"Yeah." She bobs her head. "I am. I realized...I don't know. I've always known I'm artistic. But recently I started thinking that my art skills are a gift, you know? Something my mom passed down to me."

I smile at her, hoping she'll go on. She used to never talk about her mom, but she's getting better about it as time goes by.

"My mom always thought of art as a way of giving back to God," Christine says slowly. "I don't know that I see it exactly like that, but she's been in my dreams a lot recently. I don't know what she'd say about New York, but I do know she wouldn't have wanted me to waste my talent."

"But what about Ellis? I thought you didn't want to leave him." I'm growing more panicked by the second. I hold my breath, and somewhere in the back of my brain it registers that I'm not really asking about her brother. "And what about Tyler?"

"Tyler's moving to New York too."

"What?!" Zoe claps her hands, and Ana's eye widen.

"For real?" I let my mouth hang open.

She nods. "I know. It's crazy, right? But it was his decision. He's going to get a job and a cheap apartment somewhere, and...I don't know. We'll see." She smiles, and if you didn't know her, you might miss it, but I can see it in her eyes. She's excited; she's optimistic; she's in love. But she's also scared out of her mind.

I pull her into a hug and lean my head against her shoulder. It's strange to think that after all this time, all the guys that have come in and out of our lives in the past four years, Christine and Tyler are the ones who made it.

Soon Ana's leaning against Christine's other side, and Zoe slowly puts her arms around all of us. We stay like that, intertwined, listening to the sounds of the waves and the voices of our classmates behind us. The surf pounds, slowly wearing away at the mighty cliffs, grinding the solid rock into smaller and smaller pieces, spreading it out, bit by bit, across the shore.

51

stand at the edge of the track and look down the field. The long rows of bleachers edging up the sides of the stadium make the walls seem higher than I remember, and the giant scoreboard is kind of haunting. The stadium, built to contain thousands of screaming fans, is desolate when it's empty.

I walk around the bottom curve of the track. The spongy rubber feels good under my feet, and I follow it around for a while to the middle of the bleachers. I stop in front of the band section, right where we always stood to cheer. How many hours have I spent in this place? How many Friday nights did I stand here, soaking in the noise and the action and the excitement, thrilled to be part of it all?

Tomorrow I'm supposed to walk out there in my cap and gown, in the middle of that enormous field, and say something the rest of my classmates will remember for the rest of their lives. I shake my head. It's impossible. What could I say to explain what these four years have meant to me? How in the world am I supposed to bestow wisdom and insight when I have no idea what I'm doing?

I reach for the railing at the bottom of the row of bleachers and pull myself up, carefully threading through the bars. I sit down on a bench in the first row and smooth my skirt down.

It doesn't look any different from up here. I turn and lay

back on the bench, feeling the warm metal press against my back, and stare up at the vast blue sky.

I could really use some help here, God.

I should probably go back to Ms. Lovchuck and tell her she made a mistake. Ana didn't have any trouble coming up with her salutatorian speech. She should give the speech and I'll sit with the rest of the class and toss around a giant beach ball until it's time to collect my diploma.

But then I remember the look on Ms. Moore's face when they told me. Something about it—pride? satisfaction?— makes me feel like I have to do this. She's always had this weird way of understanding things no one else picks up on, and I can't let her down now. But that doesn't make it any easier to come up with—

"So this is what it looks like." My eyes fly open, and I sit up quickly. Ben is standing on the track below me, looking around the stadium. I brush my hand over my hair to smooth it down. "Weird."

"Don't tell me you've never been into the stadium before," I say.

"Okay," Ben says, pulling himself through the bars to the bottom step of the bleachers. He sits down without another word.

"Seriously? You've *never* bothered to walk twenty feet out of your way and poke your head in here?"

"Nope." He shrugs, then turns and looks out over the field. His thin blue shirt looks nice against his golden skin. My stomach warms. "It is pretty impressive."

"What are you doing here now?"

"Looking for you. It figures you'd be in the very last place

I check." He slings his bag around and pulls a decal out of the front pocket, then rests his bag on the ground. He inches closer to me so our knees are just barely touching and holds out the sticker. "I brought you a good-luck charm."

The decal shows a blond girl wearing a graduation cap, but the gown is strapped around her shoulders like a cape.

"Also, I wanted to say thanks. For everything with Asha, and, I don't know, everything."

"I only wish I had done something sooner."

"You did more than anyone else would have done. She hasn't stopped talking about how you knew exactly what to do in the bathroom that day. And then the whole babysitting thing. She doesn't really understand how awesome that is yet," he says, grinning. He watches me for a minute, his dark eyes dancing. He lets his arms rest on his leg, a few inches from mine. "So have you figured out what you're going to say tomorrow?"

"Not really." I let out a long breath. "I mean, I guess not at all. I don't really have any idea where to start."

"I know what you should say." Ben grins and inches his hand closer, brushing his fingertips against my leg. Goose bumps rise on my flesh, even though it's got to be close to eighty degrees out here today.

"What's that?" I'm careful not to move, afraid he'll pull his hand away.

"You should finally admit that you like me."

I freeze, but Ben slides his hand across my leg and plants his palm on my knee.

"I don't know if that's what the crowd really wants to hear," I say, trying to keep my voice as even and normal as possible.

"It's what I want to hear, and right now I'm the crowd." He rubs his thumb across the top of my knee. "I'll help you practice. All you have to say is, 'I, Riley McGee, finally accept and acknowledge that I find Ben Nayar to be the sexiest man alive.'"

I laugh and smack him.

"It's all very standard. Basic contract stuff." He pulls his hand off my knee and leans in a little closer. "I know you've been hurt in the past. But I'm not that guy. I'm not going to use you or cheat on you or lie to you. All I want is to be with you, be good for you."

Before I know what he's doing, Ben takes my hand and interlaces his fingers with mine. I don't pull away. He rubs his thumb over the back of my hand.

"Ben, this is never going to work."

"Maybe it won't," he says. "I can't really promise you it will. But I can promise you I'm willing to try."

"You'll be off at school—"

"Berkeley is fifteen minutes from the city. I think somehow I can manage the commute."

"You'll have classes and activities and friends I won't be a part of."

"I plan on hanging out with Asha and Ravi mostly. You know them."

"There will be college girls all over the place."

"I won't even notice them."

"Ben, be serious—"

"I *am* being serious, Riley." He pulls my hand close to him and lays his other palm on top. "I couldn't be more serious. I've been in love with you since I first saw you. I know you like me too, and I'm not going to sit here and pretend it's not true because you're afraid of what may happen in the future." He moves closer so his leg is pressed against mine.

I shake my head. "Next year—"

"Will you stop worrying about the future?" He pulls his hand away. "This moment. This is all that matters. Just you and me, sitting in the sunshine on a beautiful afternoon."

He waits and I nod, keeping my eyes on the empty bleachers on the other side of the stadium.

"I have no way of knowing if we'll stay together forever or if this will all fizzle out next week."

I turn my head; Ben is closer than I realized. His face is only a few inches from mine, waiting, watching me.

"All I know is that I can't imagine what my life is going to be like if you're not in it."

I take a breath and smell his soap, and sweet cologne, and the faintest hint of freshly mown grass.

I don't know what's going to happen tomorrow, or the day after, but I know that I like sitting with him, watching him, feeling his hand on my skin. I tilt my face up, just a little, and he moves a fraction of an inch closer. He rubs his hand across my legs, brushes his fingers against the inside of my knee. I reach my arm up and rest my hand on the back of his head, twisting my fingers through his silky hair, and then, slowly, I pull his head down, and just like that, his lips are on mine. He sighs and pulls me close, pressing against me, daring me to pull away. Soon I've forgotten all about tomorrow, about the days to come, and all I want is for this moment to go on forever.

52

The band is playing "Pomp and Circumstance" as my classmates walk two at a time up the narrow green aisle between the rows of folding chairs. Ashley Anderson is already seated in the first row. I check my pocket under my gown for the hundredth time. Good, I still have it.

Mrs. Lewis, the gym teacher, nods at Zoe and Jordan, and they start to march.

I was up all night trying to write this stupid speech. How am I supposed to say something meaningful and inspiring under this kind of pressure?

Mrs. Lewis nods at Christine and a swimmer named Emily. Christine turns around and flashes me a thumbs-up before she starts to march up the aisle.

I think I looked up every online graduation speech in the history of graduation speeches for inspiration, and around four a.m. I scrawled out something about holding onto your dreams. It won't be brilliant, especially next to Ana, who has been practicing her speech in the mirror all week, but at least I probably won't get booed off the stage.

I'm next in line. Mrs. Lewis nods at Dean and me. He holds out his fist, and I bump it; then together, we walk out onto the grass.

As we start the long march up the field, I keep my eyes

on the grass in front of me. If I look up, I'll see how huge the crowd really is and how many people are going to hear that I have nothing important to say. I try to block out the noise and rack my brain. Surely there's some wisdom buried in there somewhere that didn't make it onto my paper.

Dean branches off and turns left to file into his row, but I keep going toward the front. Ashley cheers for me, and I give her a weak smile as I walk past her to the stage.

The steps that lead up to the stage are thin and rickety, but Mrs. Canning, the school counselor, holds out her hand to help me up. I take a few shaky steps and drop gratefully into the empty chair in front of Ms. Moore, next to Ana.

"I had no idea there were this many kids in our class," Ana whispers. "Who *are* all these people?"

It is kind of amazing, seeing it from this perspective, watching as the last few students walk up the aisle. Before us, in this huge sea of garnet, are the people who have made up my life for the past four years. The people I've cheered with and for, the people I've seen in class every day, the people I've passed around campus but never bothered to get to know.

I scoot my chair closer to Ana, and it scrapes across the plywood stage. The last few students take their seats, and Marcus Farcus, the band's drum major, signals for the music to fade out. After a few squeaks and groans, they stop, and the stadium goes silent.

I hold my breath and touch my pocket again. It's still there. "You ready for this?" I whisper. Ana bites her lip and shakes her head. "Me neither."

Ms. Lovchuck steps up to the microphone and welcomes everyone to this momentous occasion. I snort, but Ana elbows me. As our principal goes on about how proud our teachers are of what we've accomplished, I let my eyes drift up to the stands.

Oh wow. I drop my head. There are *a lot* of people here. The whole stadium is full, and there are still people coming in through the gates.

"Breathe," Ana orders. I nod and try to obey. "You can do this."

I peek up at the stands again, and suddenly I'm not sure I can. It's not the thousands of people sitting there watching every move we make. I've never been shy, and it's not like me to freak out at the sight of a crowd. It's the fact that I feel like a fraud sitting up here. How can this school possibly let Riley McGee, class screwup, address her peers?

Ms. Lovchuck introduces the members of the school board and the district superintendent. I reach for Ana's hand. She's shaking too. And then, just like we practiced, Ms. Lovchuck introduces Ana and calls her up to the microphone. I squeeze her hand, and she stands up and walks to the front of the stage while the crowd cheers for her. The noise quiets down as she adjusts the microphone, but there are still a few people cheering and clapping in the stands. I scan the bleachers and see it's Ana's family—her entire extended family who came up from Mexico. Ana's mom is standing up and clapping, and even from here, I can see the pride in her face.

"Friends, classmates, family," Ana says, her voice strong and steady. Another round of cheering starts, and she waits for it to die down before she continues. "Thank you for the opportunity to be here today." Ana begins to tell her story—about her heart defect at birth, her family's flight to the United States for treatment, her miraculous survival. She shares about the guilt she feels for taking the heart of a baby who didn't make it, and her fear that she won't live well enough to justify both lives. Her voice is lyrical, and her words have the whole stadium riveted. As I listen, it occurs to me that I don't have to be afraid for Ana. I don't know how it took us so long to see it, but writing is what she was made for.

I look around and am a little surprised to see my family sitting right behind Ana's clan. Gammy flew in last night, and she's sitting next to Michael. Mom leans against Dad's shoulder, and next to them are Dreamy and Ed and Nick. Apparently Mom has forgiven Dreamy, or at least gotten over it for the day. And Christine's family is right behind them. Her dad looks like he's checking his BlackBerry while Emma is bouncing Ellis on her knee.

Somehow it seems right to see all our families sitting together like that. It's not like they're good friends; their only real point of contact is us. But whether we like it or not, they're a part of this miraculous circle simply because they are the people we love most. As long as they're a part of us, they're a part of this.

I don't realize Ana has stopped speaking until I hear the crowd breaking into applause. People are standing up and cheering.

Wonderful. I get to follow the first graduation speech in history that anyone actually listened to. I feel my shoulders tense up, and Ana drinks in the applause. I don't think I can do this.

"This is not a mistake," someone says in my ear. I turn. Ms. Moore is leaning forward in her chair, whispering. "This is your moment."

I watch her, waiting for more, but she smiles and leans back in her chair.

I know the woman cannot read minds. It's physically impossible.

But then, she's always known. Ms. Moore was the one who saw the truth about who we were from day one. She's the one who recognized that each of us—Zoe, Christine, Ana, and me—was special. She saw that each of us was living out our second chance at life, and that we were all confused about why we were saved, what it meant, what was expected from us.

Through the years, we've wondered if Ms. Moore was one of us too—whether she ever had her own miracle. I don't know for sure, but I do know that she's helped us see how much we need each other. She's helped us realize that together we can do things none of us could have done on our own. She's taught us that even if we don't understand why things happen, that doesn't mean there isn't a reason. And now, as I scan the crowd, I'm beginning to see something else I think she knew all along: that the Miracle Girls were brought together for a time so that we could go out into the world and touch the lives of others, just like she touched ours.

Ana lowers herself down into the chair beside me, and I can see she's shaking. I put my arms around her and pull her into a hug, and our huge mortarboards bang against each other.

"You did great," I say, trying to fight the tears that sting my eyes.

Ms. Lovchuck walks back to the microphone, and I can

hear her telling the crowd about all the things I've been involved in through the years. I try to pull myself together.

"You'll do great too," she says and pulls me in tighter. I can feel my eyes filling with water. I run my sleeve under my nose and take a deep breath.

"Riley?" Ana says as I start to pull away. Her eyes are rimmed in red, and her cheeks are wet. "I don't know what I'm going to do without you," she whispers.

Maybe it's because it's so unexpected, or so honest, but tears are streaming down my cheeks when Ms. Lovchuck calls my name.

I pull my speech out of my pocket and push myself to my feet. My classmates clap, and I have a few seconds to pull myself together as I stumble my way to the front of the stage.

"I am thrilled to be up here tonight, Marina Vista," I say, recalling the first lines of my speech without looking at the paper. I take a deep breath and look out over the faces that have made up my life.

In the front row of bleachers, I see Fritz and his wife, Judy, waving at me, a whole crew from church gathered around them. There's Dave, Ana's first love, and Tyler, Christine's great love. Cecily and Maddie are here, next to Asha, holding Ravi. Even Pastor Jandel has shown up tonight.

I turn back to my classmates and squint out over the crowd. I can make out the faces of Tommy Chu, Kayleen, a soccer player named Jake. People I never really got to know well, but who were a part of my world anyway.

I keep scanning. *Aha. Zo.* She's smiling at me, waving. I feel my shoulders relax a little. Zoe might have the purest heart of anyone I know, and perhaps the strongest faith. She's our peacemaker. I don't know how I would have made it through high school without her.

And then...I look over toward the other side of the aisle. Christine. She's laughing, swatting at a giant beach ball that's bouncing around the class. It's hard to believe she's the same person as the angry, hurting freshman I once knew. If I ever doubted the power of forgiveness and reconciliation to change a life, I never will again.

At the back, behind the rows of students, stand the faithful teachers of Marina Vista. There's Mr. Dumas, the wry art teacher; Ms. Sanchez, the Shakespeare-loving AP English fiend; Mrs. Narveson, the wackiest history teacher in, well, history. And there's Mr. Mackey, the math teacher who assigned me to detention that first day. Even if I forget everything they ever taught, I will never forget their thirst for knowledge and their love of learning.

And then...I bite my lip, trying to locate Ben among the sea of faces. Where are the Ns? I scan the crowd, but I don't see him until he suddenly stands up on his chair and starts waving his arms at me. My stomach flips. I laugh, and the sound echoes out across the stadium.

I look back down at my paper, but my eyes are watering again, and the letters are blurry. I try the next part from memory too. "I'd like to thank the faculty and staff of Marina Vista for the great honor of standing here before you, and I'd like to thank you, my classmates, as well."

My voice echoes around the silent crowd. The back row is starting to do the wave. *Oh goodness.* This is not going well. I lift the paper up closer to my face and squint at the words. I can almost make the letters out, but the more I can read, the more embarrassed I am by what I've written.

"The past four years have been better, and stranger, than I could ever have imagined."

Several people in the front row stare back at me with blank faces. Ashley is texting.

"And I wanted to share with you a little bit of what I've learned in my time at Marina Vista."

The beach ball flies closer to the front of the class, and someone in the stands yells, "Get on with it!"

I brush my hair back behind my ear and look down at my paper again, and then, before I know what I'm doing, I lower the paper.

And suddenly I know what my problem is. This speech is fine. It's a little funny, a little insightful, a little searching. It's nostalgic about the past and optimistic about the future. It's exactly what they all expect from a graduation speech. And that's precisely the problem.

I think back to what Ms. Lovchuck said that day in her office. Something about having the courage not to conform to other people's expectations of what I should do. I remember what Ms. Moore said to me about this being my moment. I crumple my speech up and drop it on the stage. A few people cheer.

"I don't really have any wisdom to share with you," I say, and I can tell that my voice sounds louder and more assured than it did just a moment ago. "I made a lot of mistakes the past few years. I did things I'm not proud of, and I hurt people I care about. I made poor choices. I disappointed the people who have sacrificed all their lives to give me the best of everything."

I gaze out at the crowd to see how they're reacting to this change in plans. People seem to be paying more attention.

"I'm simply here trying to figure things out, just like all of you. But I guess there are a few things I've learned too." I search for Zoe. She gives me a thumbs-up. I take a deep breath.

"When I started out at Marina Vista, I was kind of going through something. You all might remember that," I say, and a bunch of people cheer. "I thought I was invincible, that I could tackle anything. But I was wrong, and I fell, hard. But the things I learned, the one thing that kept me going, was the people that were there by me as I tried to pull myself back together."

I cringe. That didn't make any sense. "I mean, I guess what I really want to say is that it's the people in our lives that really matter, right? It's not where we go to school, or whether we go to school"—someone whistles, and I laugh—"or what we someday end up being. It's the people around us that matter. It's you guys—friends, family, classmates—who matter. It's—"

I break off as tears sting my eyes again.

I cast a quick glance at my family. They're leaning forward, waiting, watching. I don't want to let them down this time.

"I can't imagine what it's going to be like to walk out of here tonight and say good-bye to you all. We'll probably never all be in the same place like this ever again." I quickly glance over my shoulder at Ana. Tears are streaming down her face.

I bite my lip and try to keep going, but I have to take a deep breath.

"But what I'm learning is, I think that's okay. I mean, I could stand up here all night and keep talking to put off saying good-bye, but somehow, it all has to end."

I glance at Christine. She's watching me now, waiting.

"I—" I try to speak, but my breath catches. I close my eyes for a moment, trying to block out the faces staring back at me. My legs feel weak. I don't know if I can do this. "I—"

That's when I feel a hand on my shoulder.

"It's okay," Ana says, murmuring quietly so the microphone doesn't pick up her voice. "You're doing great." I close my eyes and nod and wait. I feel like I'm going to collapse, but with Ana's help, maybe I can do this.

"I—" I open my eyes just in time to see two red blurs dash toward the steps. They're not really going to storm the stage. They can't.

But then I hear footsteps echoing across the platform, and suddenly Zoe is at my right hand, and Christine at my left, holding me up. Ms. Lovchuck moves to shoo them off, but out of the corner of my eye, I see Ms. Moore shake her head, and for some reason, Ms. Lovchuck obeys.

"We're here for you," Zoe says quietly. I nod and try to remember what I was trying to say.

"I guess what I mean is, I don't really understand why God lets some things, like sickness and disease, happen to some people"—I won't let myself look up at Michael—"and good things, like second chances, happen to others. But the one thing I do know is that God is good," I say, sniffing a little. "I see God's goodness in the miracle of friendship, and I feel it in the unshakeable affection I feel for my family. I know that God loves me, because they do. And I know that when we're far apart, this is love that never lets go."

I blink back tears and look out over the bewildered faces of my classmates. No one moves for a moment. And then, slowly, someone behind me begins to clap.

It's Ms. Moore. It has to be. I'm not sure I'm really done, or that I've said what I really wanted to say, but I know that what I've said is enough. It wasn't expected or traditional or in any way logical, but it was me, speaking from the heart, doing it my own way.

A few other people begin to clap along with Ms. Moore, and then a few more, and suddenly, all of Marina Vista is on its feet. Maybe they kind of liked what I managed to say. Maybe they're cheering because my crazy speech is over, or they're excited that finally they're about to receive the diplomas they've been working toward for so long.

All I know is that as I stand there on the stage with my best friends supporting me, it doesn't seem to matter too much. I know the four of us will be friends forever. Even when we're not in the same place, what holds us together is bigger than time or distance. God bound us together, and we're not going to fall apart. But we're never going to be like this again—all four of us, rooted together in this place, staring out at the possibilities before us. We'll grow up, split off, move on. Soon this moment will be gone, and there will be so many things pulling us in different directions. In the end, only love will be able to keep us together.

Ms. Lovchuck gestures for us to move out of the way so

she can hand out the diplomas. I pull away, but I feel Zoe start to shake and I know she understands what I'm thinking. Ana sniffs, and Christine sucks in a deep breath, and I smile, because even though I'm pretty sure we all feel ridiculous standing up here on stage holding up the entire graduation, I realize they're dreading letting go as much as I am.

And in that moment, I feel nothing but peace, because I know that love is enough.

about the authors

Anne Dayton graduated from Princeton and has an MA in literature from New York University. She lives in New York City.

May Vanderbilt graduated from Baylor University and has an MA in fiction from Johns Hopkins University. She lives in San Francisco. Together they are the authors of *Emily Ever After, Consider Lily,* and *The Book of Jane,* and the four-book Miracle Girls series.

Learn more at www.anneandmay.com.